Resolve OF A Duchesse

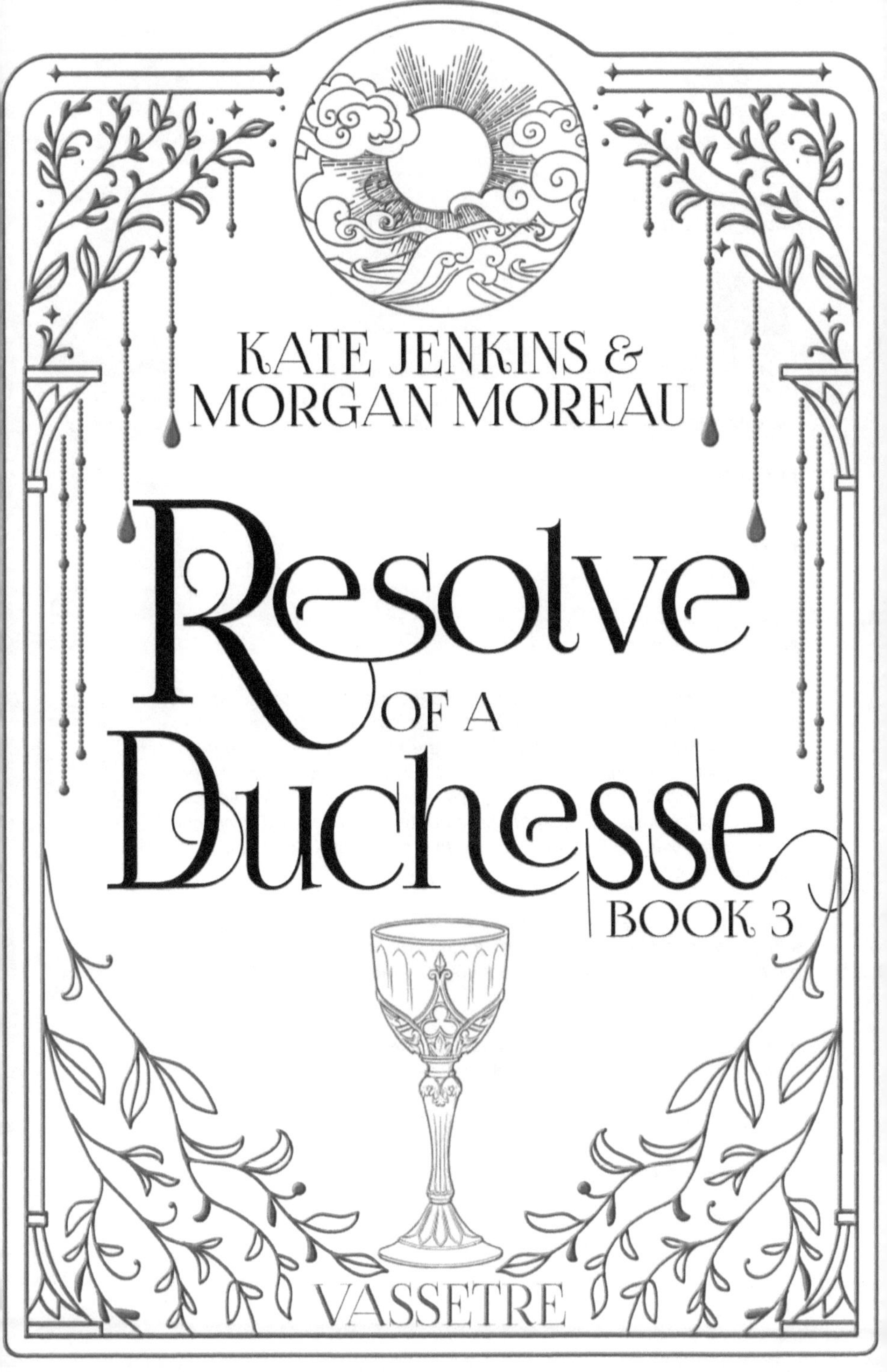

KATE JENKINS &
MORGAN MOREAU

Resolve OF A Duchesse

BOOK 3

VASSETRE

To Morgan, who had to edit my awkwardly written smut and put up with my "Ohh, we should do this" moments.

To Everyone in the Silver Star, Red Dragon chat who answered all my random smut related questions with patience, grace, and a ton of helpful suggestions.

To Nom and Kala, for being so supportive as we wrote this.

To the person who reviewed *The Fractured City* asking if Arian and Collette would get together. Thank you for the inspiration.

~~ Katie

To Kate. We were insane when we agreed to this.
To Robbie, 'cause that Insta chat keeps me going, "Huh?"
To Grey, who enables my television obsessions.
Also... to spite outlines.

To the cast of *Interview With the Vampire*. This is why: "My daughter was my sister was my throw pillow. When he wouldn't look at me kindly. Lestat Lestat Lestat Lestat Lestat Lestat Lestat Lestat Lestat Lestat Lestat Lestat Lestat Lestat Lestat..."

~~ Morgan

Table of Contents

Azmarin Empire

Other Locations

Azmarin Empire: A country to the north.
Dathria: A country to the east.
Myrefall: County in Coralia.
Quenall: The capitol of Coralia.

Fythias

VASSETRE CHATEAU
VILLA DU CIEL
E DE LA FORÊT
FORÊT D'AMBRE
ÎLE AUX SIRÈNES
MAISON DU PARADIS
ONIE
LIRAC

Cast of Characters

Alain: Human. Deceased king of Fythias.

Alaoin: Human. Child of Eloise and Louis.

Phineas "Finn" Allard: Human. Steward of Vassetre Chateau.

Anaise: Half-Human, Half-Sirene. Member of Sabine's guard.

Tristian Anouilh: Human. Comte du Ciel.

Aphros: Nereid. King of the Nereid People.

Eloise Aresenault: Human. Princess Consort. Wife of Prince Louis.

Grégoire Arsenault: Human. Prince. Middle Child of King Rodolphe

Louis Alaoin Arsenault: Human. Prince. Youngest Child of King Rodolphe.

Avana: Elf and Dwarf Hybrid. Failed Assassin.

Brielle: Human. Guard Captain of Prince Louis.

Claudine: Human. Caretaker at an Orphanage.

Baron Cyrille: Human. A Minor lord sent by Prince Grégoire to ask for Sabine's suit.

Dion: Human. A Fythian Comte.

Lisbeth Dubois: Human with magic. Personal companion of Duchesse Sabine.

Meri Dubois: Human with magic. Former guard captain, current head cook.

Elodie: Human. Head over the Weavers Guild

Faron Istro: Elf. Personal Guard to Sabine.

Glaucus: Sirene. Local Merperson.

Henri: Human. Baron and suitor for Sabine

Jacqueline: Human. Caretaker at an Orphanage.

Marcelle: Sirene. A Vassetre Chateau Guard.

Hugo Onfroi: Dwarf. Retired Guard Captain

Peronelle: Human. Steward of Prince Louis.

Phindel: Elf. Friend of Faron from Coralia.

Raidne: Sirene. Local Merperson.

Thaumas: Sirene. Local Merperson. Former lover of Sabine.

Sabine Vassetre: Human. Duchesse Vassetre.

Chapter One

"It is lovely," Sabine said to Faron as they neared their destination. The Duchesse Vassetre pushed a delicately curled strand of light caramel hair from her face as she observed Prince Louis's home from the carriage window then placed her hand back in her lap. Faron's large hand immediately settled on top, bringing a smile to her lips.

"It is," Faron, her bodyguard turned fiancé, noted in his deep voice. "You seem a little disappointed though." His long black wavy hair was pulled back into a ponytail, though he usually wore the long strands around his face. The style showed off his prominent pointed elf ears, though Sabine doubted anyone would see anything beyond his sizable height when first meeting him.

Sabine shrugged. "I believe our future king was too generous with his interpretation of a coastal location." By Sabine's estimation, another half day's ride would take them to the nearest ocean access, though the humidity coupled with the warmer weather in southern Fythias was welcome. She doubted she'd have had much time to visit the shore had she been in walking distance, so the matter was of little consequence either way.

Louis's estate, a moderately sized chateau, gleamed in the sunlight as their carriage pulled up the long winding road that bottlenecked before opening into a grand court-yard. Made from a vibrant white brick and topped with a reddish-brown roof, the chateau felt welcoming, even from a distance. At its center sat a dome-shaped entrance, deco-rated by a cherrywood set of double doors with large win-dows, surrounded by a bricked arch. A line of three windows sat directly above the arch, with a final, larger window a story above, built into the fine, reddish roof.

A watch tower situated to the left of the entrance had been long ago topped with a steepled roof, this one more tanned than red. Sabine guessed it was the oldest part of Louis's estate, though it looked in good repair, blending with the newer parts well enough. The rest of the chateau, composed of squared buildings with numerous windows, looked to be newly constructed based on the red shutters she saw a handful of workers attaching to a window near the front.

A small garden flanked a cobblestone walkway, leaving Sabine eager to explore more of the grounds. Louis, she knew, enjoyed nature, and she couldn't believe his dwelling would be so limited in greenery. She could already imagine Lisbeth, tucked away in her own carriage with the head members of the Vassetre estate, complaining about the lack of nature. No doubt, the others would have to talk her down from remedying her complaint without permission.

"It's pretty. Less like a prison than the last estate we visited. Though out of the three estates I've now seen in Fythias, I find I like our home best," Faron said as he looked out the window.

"I agree," Sabine replied.

After the carriage circled the path, it came to a stop in front of the ornate cherry doors. The carriage gave a gentle jerk as the driver dismounted, and soon, the doors were opened, and a footman offered a hand to Sabine to help her down. Thankfully, her feet landed on surprisingly clean cobblestone rather than dirt.

Faron stepped down after Sabine, and he took up space just behind her as he normally did when he worked as a bodyguard. His gaze darted around, seeming to both take in the scenery and look for threats. She smiled to herself as the waiting staff stared at the giant elf, doubtless noticing nothing about his tanned skin and dark, intelligent eyes. No, they'd hear comments and jabs about his size for the duration of the stay.

Sabine couldn't blame her fiancé's studious actions, and not just because he paid no attention to his new fans. Although they were arguably safer—at least for now—within a royal household, one never knew when a potential threat would arise. Even a prince could not guarantee anything. "You've gained some admirers, my love."

Several carriages back, the heads of Sabine's estate— Finn, Meri, and Lisbeth—dismounted, with Finn immediately stepping up to guide Louis's staff in unpacking the carriage. One by one, he indicated Sabine's items which were removed first. He pointed out every single trunk and pack belonging to Sabine and Faron, though occasionally, Lisbeth, with her dark tan and bouncy ginger hair, would interrupt to correct what she deemed poor handling of Sabine's things. As always, Finn's attention to decorum and detail would ensure everything ran as smoothly as possible by affirming the rank of those within Louis's household while also clearly establishing Sabine's own.

She looked back to Faron, whose shoulders had visibly relaxed. He must have deemed them safe. He leaned closer to her, and Sabine thought he was going to say something important about the grounds or their situation. Instead, Faron surprised her by saying, "Lisbeth thinks you brought Marcelle because you wanted to play matchmaker. I told her you didn't have time."

Sabine rolled her eyes, finding herself surprisingly irritated by the mere suggestion. Lisbeth needed more to do if she thought making those kinds of suggestions were appropriate in the midst of working to avoid war. "I have never in my life played matchmaker, and I don't intend on starting now," she replied, looking up at him. "I brought Marcelle because he's a capable soldier and my acting guard captain."

"Lisbeth thinks it's because you agree Avana and he would make a cute couple." Faron shook his head, almost apologetic for having brought it up.

Sabine just raised an eyebrow, thoroughly unimpressed. If they were home, Lisbeth would have shared the theory directly as she dressed Sabine for the day. She simply didn't have the patience for her lady's maid's fanciful wishes. "Do you know how little I care about whether or not they'd make a cute couple?" she asked. "Besides, Avana is barely grown."

"I assume with everything else going on, it's not even the last item on your list of things to care about." Faron shrugged. "At most, if they got together, you'd tell them congratulations and move on. Though, personally, I agree with your assessment. Avana is practically a child in elf years, and I've no idea how to convert Sirene ages when it comes to Marcelle."

Sirene maturity, from what Sabine had learned, occurred at a similar rate to humans, though they lived longer by a handful of decades. Not that it truly mattered. "I would be happy for them if they wanted to be together and figured out a way to do so," she added with a shake of her head. "I just don't find the musing of my decisions being made for sillier reasons all that helpful." The only romantic pairing she found herself concerned for was her own with Faron, and even then, his position in their current venture to stop a Coralian invasion extended beyond their engagement.

"Neither did Meri, but I think Lisbeth was trying to take her mind off things. She's been incredibly worried since she found out about the army and the ships, and she doesn't lead your staff as Finn does or have former guard experience like Meri."

"Which is understandable," Sabine said, her irritation waning. "If it helps her to cope with what's to come, then she should focus on it. She just needs to know when it is appropriate to voice her thoughts and when she should keep those things to herself."

They came to a stop near the entrance as they waited for other carriages to stop and occupants to exit. Faron leaned down so he could whisper in Sabine's ear. "If I decide my coping method is to spend hours feasting on you, then I should be able to focus on that as well. Right?"

Sabine raised a playful eyebrow. This sort of distraction appealed much more to her. "I will make sure you have time to devote to the task, my love," Sabine replied.

"I'll need a decent amount of time—six hours, at least—to truly enjoy you. Do you think Louis will let you take a day from your duties?" Faron's eyes gleamed playfully, though his tone suggested he was completely serious. In truth, Faron never seemed satisfied with the allotted time they had for chasing their desires, no matter how many hours passed.

"I'm quite certain we can find sufficient time," she replied, though approaching steps pulled her attention away from Faron.

"Your Grace," a tall, reed-thin woman with bright red cheeks and deep chocolate eyes said, bowing to the couple. Her hair, an ashy shade of blonde streaked with white, had been pulled back into a severe bun. "I am Peronelle, the steward of His Highness's estate. Let me be the first to welcome you." She extended a hand toward the chateau as though Sabine somehow did not realize what Peronelle was talking about. "I have our people delivering your things to your rooms and those rooms assigned to your staff. Your own steward has been quite helpful in the matter."

"I am glad to hear it," Sabine replied. She gestured to Faron. "This is Faron Istro, my personal guard and fiancé."

Peronelle nodded. "It is a pleasure," she said.

Faron gave the woman a nod in greeting.

"I was informed he will be sharing a suite with you," Peronelle said. "By your steward."

"He will be, yes," Sabine confirmed.

In the distance, she watched Lisbeth and Meri assisting Finn with oversight of their belongings, with Lisbeth in particular making sure that Sabine's finer items were well looked after. Sabine's earlier annoyance not forgotten, she looked around for the others. Avana hovered near Marcelle, possibly confirming Lisbeth's observations. They looked well together, with matching blond hair and ethereal faces, though Avana's short stature contrasted with Marcelle's height.

"I believe the suite will suit his stature well," Peronelle said, drawing her attention again.

"I thank you," Sabine replied. "His Highness is a gracious host."

Peronelle nodded. "Indeed. If you follow me, I will show you to your rooms, and I will make sure your people know where to find you. His Highness is resting now, or he would have shown you himself."

Sabine waved toward the rest of their party, so they would know she and Faron were going inside, before following after Louis's steward.

"Is this how it was supposed to be at Tristian's?" Faron asked in a near whisper.

Sabine nodded. "I am of a higher rank, so it should have been grander."

"So Tristian being late to greet you could have been considered a grave insult. Enough of one that you could have left without a word to him," Faron mused.

"Exactly," Sabine replied. They knew why he hadn't, of course. He'd viewed Sabine as lesser and unimportant because she was a woman. Had they not set forth to Tristian's with a purpose, she could have left to show her dissatisfaction with his treatment. He was dead now, thanks to Avana and Faron intervening in his attack against Sabine. She felt death was far more retaliatory than snubbing. "I rank only below the prince himself. Tristan should have been falling all over himself to make sure I was pleased with my findings."

Upon entering the chateau, Sabine took in the surroundings, though her gaze mostly remained on Peronelle, who walked with a natural elegance and efficiency most could only hope to possess. They passed several grand portraits, great bouquets of flowers on every flat surface, and lush carpets with vibrant reds, golds, and blues. Louis's home spoke of wealth and taste, though the styling was, without question, much more traditional than that found within the Vassetre estate.

From beside her, Faron seemed torn between taking in the beauty of the estate and, if the way his eyes darted about, memorizing the layout of the chateau itself. Sabine assumed he made the effort in case a quick escape was needed. She would have to talk with him about how often he worked, even when he was not there in the capacity as guard. She could already guess as to how well he would listen.

They arrived at a set of double doors which Peronelle opened without ceremony. "Your suite, Your Grace," she said, welcoming them in with a wave of her arm. Sabine stepped inside, seeing the same colors and lushness follow into the room. The floor beneath them, composed of polished stone, had been covered by thick, soft rugs. The layout of the space reminded Sabine of her rooms back home, with a sitting area closest to the door, an area to work further into the space, and the bed and washroom in the back.

"This is lovely," she said. "And I think it will suit our needs."

"Thank you, Your Grace. His Highness will be pleased to hear of your enjoyment. I shall excuse myself so I can escort your staff to their own spaces if it pleases you."

"Yes," Sabine said, turning to look at Peronelle. "They will need some rest after the trip, and I'm certain they'll enjoy an hour or two of quiet."

Peronelle nodded. "I will make sure they have it."

"Thank you," Faron said.

Once they were alone, Faron began stalking around the room, checking the windows and ensuring the room was secure. He finally stopped in the middle of the suite and just took in their surroundings. "It's a much nicer room than the one you were given at Tristian's. I rather hated all the lace, bows, and other frills." Faron grimaced.

"It is," Sabine agreed with a nod. "I take it you approve of the security as well as the luxury?"

"Security could be better, but it passes."

"And tell me, what about the security isn't to your liking?" Sabine asked with a teasing grin. Louis's home would certainly be secure, given his ranking and sensible nature.

"The guards here are not our men, and this is not our home," he said as he gathered Sabine to himself, though she looked up at him with raised brows. "The security is fine. There're even men outside the windows," he finally admitted.

She put her arms around him in return. "You are my guard as well as my fiancé. And I feel quite secure when you are near."

"And yet, I seem to have done a terrible job the last three times you were attacked. Do you think if I tied myself to you, the number of attacks on your person would decrease?"

"I think any tying you did would have very different motivations," Sabine replied. She drew him down for a kiss. "But I'd still feel very, very secure."

Faron kissed her again, his lips lingering close to hers. "And that is all that matters."

Sabine might have taken their moment alone in another direction, but a knock sounded at the door before their trunks were brought in by members of Louis's staff. As they had not known how long they would reside in Louis's home, numerous items accompanied her party west, so it took a bit of time before everything had been delivered.

"Would you like us to unpack for you, Your Grace?" one of the maids asked.

Sabine shook her head. "No. My staff will attend to it once they are rested. Thank you."

After affirming nods were given, the staff filed out, leaving Sabine and Faron alone again. Sabine adored their willingness to allow her time and peace. So many households had the habit of pestering guests.

"I think you better enjoy this time. I doubt we're getting much more to ourselves," Sabine warned.

"I am enjoying this time. Being able to hold you like this is its own reward," Faron replied.

"Come, let us rest and enjoy ourselves. We were on the road for far too long this morning."

"As you command, my love."

Chapter Two

Faron stood against a dark blue southern wall of Louis's grand office. Positioned as close to the door as he could get without blocking its path, he could not be ignored as he towered over the other occupants. The office, well-furnished in rich colors, had several bookcases running along three of the walls. Small tables sat around the room, littered with rolls of fresh parchment and letters creased from deliveries and rereads. Louis clearly used the space with great frequency and didn't let his staff clean up as often as Sabine did. Upon first entering, Sabine had given the disorganized chaos a quizzical look.

"Oh, don't mind the mess," Louis had responded. "I trust my staff with my life, but my brother managed to sneak in a spy over the years. I have to be cautious with who I allow access."

Currently, he and Sabine stood at his desk, a map of Fythias laid upon it, as the two discussed the Coralian army and ships. Faron would sadly admit that, while he had been paying attention to their discussions of tactics and troop movements, his mind began wandering once they started talking geography, a subject he was rather terrible at. His attention now rested on the figures he could see out the window past Louis and Sabine. Meri was giving Avana a lesson on patience using her sword while Lisbeth, Finn, and Marcelle looked on. It was a better use of her time than practicing her poison mixing, which the small half-elf had declared as her morning plans over breakfast.

"If I had to guess, he will make port in L'Orilan," Sabine said, tapping the spot on the map and drawing Faron out of his silent ponderings. "It's got the most reliable western docks and a guaranteed ability to replenish supplies easily."

"You're right," Louis said with a nod, his golden hair bouncing with the effort. He tilted his head and studied the map. "It's also the closest place to safely dock a ship near these lands, though theoretically, he could remain at sea anywhere, as long as he had sufficient boats to get soldiers to shore."

Physically turning his attention back to the ongoing conversation, Faron considered what he had heard about Sargarus over the years, both rumors and facts, before something else occurred to him. "If I may? At the chateau, Grégoire received a letter with the Coralian seal. One we couldn't find when his room was searched. If Sargarus was expecting to meet Grégoire, then he may not have sufficient supplies. That said, everything I know of the man says he is cunning and often plans for many possibilities."

"Assuming he planned to restock upon reaching Grégoire's home, he would still have enough to keep them going well after crossing the border," Louis replied, rubbing his chin in thought. "That could account for the ground troops. The sailors, however, would still be limited in where they stop."

"How are you planning to deal with the troops approaching the border?" Faron asked curiously and sheepishly, as he was sure they had already talked about this and he hadn't been paying attention.

"The troops stationed there have been there for some time, we think, because of an attempted invasion of Azmarin. Even if they wanted to come into Fythias, they'd have to cross the mountain range. Then the estates along the northern border would defend the country should they initiate an attack," Sabine replied. "Although we don't think they will go as far east as our home, the possibility of it was why so many of our guards remained behind."

Faron thought that through. "Do the estates along that side have a large enough standing army?" He knew how many soldiers Sabine had, but was the combined might enough to hold off or defeat the Coralian army?

"Army to army, I think we're pretty comparable," Louis said then shrugged. "The men under Sargarus's command will be divided, at least by two, given the movements by land and sea. I also assume he will have others stationed in Azmarin and perhaps elsewhere." He walked to his desk and sorted through some letters before holding one up. "The last report from my scouts sent an estimate of who will approach the border. I think we'll be able to hold our own there."

Faron nodded, relieved to hear that they would have the manpower to handle the Coralian threat. He also acknowledged the fact he was going to need to become much more familiar with political topics and conditions in Fythias since he planned on marrying Sabine. It would not reflect well on her if her husband was uninformed about the state of her lands or the kingdom and its people. "What is the plan for Sargarus's ships if they come into port?" He had heard a few ideas tossed around, but it hadn't sounded as if they had come to a decision yet.

"I don't know if L'Orilan could drive them from the land," Louis decided. "It's a vulnerable city, both because of the port and the distances from noble estates. They do have some defenses." Louis tossed his letter back on the table and rejoined Sabine. "Assuming they land there."

Faron nodded as he considered this. The Fythian capital would be a major loss if occupied by Sargarus and the Coralian troops. "Are you considering moving more troops or evacuating the city if possible?"

"It's one of our largest trading ports," Sabine replied, shaking her head. "There would be major problems resulting from an evacuation, and not just in L'Orilan."

Faron had been hoping for a different answer. He understood, however, why it would be problematic. He wondered if it would be worth asking if they could send a message to the city advising those with magic to hide or flee. Same with elves. The Sirene would have a quick exit, but magic users and elves were in great danger. Sabine would already know, and Faron told himself to trust her to have a plan. He settled back against the wall. "What is the plan if he takes the city?" he asked instead.

"The leaders within the city will receive advanced warning, though they will spot approaching ships a day or so before the ships arrive. The delay will allow those who cannot fight to hide or flee while others prepare for conflict," Louis explained.

The prince crossed to his liquor decanters situated on a black cabinet close to the window. He poured himself a drink, motioned for the others to help themselves, then fell into a dark green chair in front of his desk. Even with his golden hair, bright smile, and boyish good looks, he couldn't quite conceal his worry. "It is possible Sargarus and a select group of soldiers will arrive and reside within the city without causing conflict while the majority of the fighters remain on ships. In which case, we do not need to strike first."

"It's also possible he will try to take over the city," Sabine replied. "In which case, swift action will be needed."

Faron had to admit to himself that, once again, he was lost to their reasoning. He assumed the capital would be one of the few cities they didn't want Sargarus to take, but Louis and Sabine had been born into this life and he had not. Therefore, he would bow to their expertise, especially Sabine's, as he knew, beyond a shadow of a doubt, she would do everything she could to save the people of Fythias. "I admit I do not know about warfare of this scale, and politics eludes me completely." He gave Sabine a wry smile. "Maybe you and I can fix that if we have time."

"Of course, my love," Sabine easily agreed. "I'm happy to answer any questions you have."

"I just wish to have a better understanding of everything," he said easily as he settled in to watch and actually listen.

"You will," Louis assured him after he finished his glass. "We've both spent our lives learning the intricacies of diplomacy and politics. It takes time to put it all together. To understand and predict movements."

"Thank you," he told Louis honestly. "I just worry I don't have a lot of time with everything going on. If that proves true, I will default to the quiet, intimidating personal guard."

"Trust your future wife to taunt another into considering war to soothe their ego," Louis joked. He sighed, contemplating his empty liquor glass. "For now, you never know what sort of expertise you might need. All we can do is act with the information we have for now."

Faron had to consider the fact Sabine would do such a thing. Not because she was hot-tempered, but for the sole reason that Sargarus was close to Grégoire and possibly Tristian. Both had considered his fiancée an afterthought at best and a brainless supporter and patron of the least noble of the princes at worst. Faron knew that when they met Sargarus, he would insult or patronize her, and it would go downhill from there. "That is very true. I will still try my hardest to learn what I can to be as helpful as possible."

Sabine opened her mouth to reply when a knock sounded at the office door before it swung open to reveal Peronelle. "My apologies for interrupting, Your Highness. Her Highness insisted you needed time with your son this afternoon."

"Of course," Louis said, cheerfully waving her further in.

Looking down, Faron spotted a very blond little toddler clutching Peronelle's hand. He beamed upon spotting Louis and, after releasing the steward's hand, ran as fast as he could across the office. Peronelle nodded without acknowledgment and exited the room.

The child stumbled a time or two as he made his way to Louis. Faron found he couldn't keep his eyes from drifting to Sabine. Now was the worst time to be thinking about children, but Faron still found himself wondering if she would glow like he'd heard pregnant women did or if he would have to flee from her anger as his father had to do from his mother when she was pregnant with him, at least based on the stories he'd heard. He also wondered what their children would look like, and he decided right away, boy or girl, he wanted them to look like Sabine. To share her vivid green eyes, playful smile, and caramel hair. He looked away blushing when he saw Sabine staring at him with a raised eyebrow.

"Did you miss me?" Louis asked his son when the little boy threw himself into his father's arms. "I missed you terribly," he added when the little boy seemed to ponder an answer. He kissed the top of the boy's golden hair. He looked up at Sabine and Faron. "I'd love to introduce my son, Prince Alaoin."

"He looks just like you," Sabine replied, smiling at the little prince as he waved at her.

"He does," Louis confirmed. "Mostly. He takes after Eloise's father with the way he's built, though." He made a gentle gesture to Sabine. "This is my friend Sabine and her fiancé Faron. Can you say hello?"

"Hi!" Alaoin replied.

Faron gave the little boy a wave as he tried to remember how old he was. He recalled the subject had come up at the dinner with Grégoire, but he thought Louis had said Alaoin was a year old. "Should we go, to give you time with your son?" he asked, giving the boy a soft smile.

"I think I'm about to be told where I need to go," Louis confessed. He rose from his chair, balancing his son on his hip. "We'll resume our discussions later, Sabine?"

"Of course," Sabine replied, walking over to Faron. "Let's leave them to it."

"Enjoy the rest of the day, Your Highnesses," Faron said with a bow before offering his arm to Sabine to escort her out.

They'd made it only halfway down the hall before Louis and Alaoin emerged from the office, Louis sprinting quickly with a laughing Alaoin in his arms. The prince and his son disappeared around a corner, giggles echoing in the distance.

"I guess we can safely assume Prince Alaoin is really in charge," Sabine observed.

"I think that's true when it comes to any child. Well, any child with loving parents," he amended as he thought of the orphaned children in Coralia and Tristian's village, as well as Avana. Yes, some of them are on the streets because their parents were no longer among the living, but others were there because their parents just did not care.

"Do you plan on letting our future children rule the estate?" she asked, amusement shining through her perceptive eyes.

Faron considered his answer, once more picturing in his head how any children he had with Sabine may look. "Yes, unless they disrespected you. Then I'd toss them in the ocean."

Sabine laughed and patted his arm. "I'd prefer it if you didn't toss any of our theoretical children in the ocean."

Faron opened his mouth with the intent to say something else ridiculous. He loved her laugh, and he fully recognized she didn't get nearly enough fun moments to enjoy. "Well, they'll have rooms with locks. If I secure the windows…" He trailed off, pretending to think over awful punishments.

"Oh, they'd have to have done something terrible to be locked in a room," Sabine replied, still smiling.

"Disrespecting you is terrible," he answered simply.

"True," Sabine agreed. "But what if they did something slightly less offensive?"

"Depends on how slight. At what age can I put them to work in the gardens?"

"I suppose when we determined they have the mental and physical capability of doing so and the offense warranted the discipline."

"So any time after the age of five, then?" He gave her a grin.

"I somehow think you will find it difficult to even be very stern with small children," Sabine countered with a similar grin.

Faron's lips twisted even as a part of him warmed watching her smile. "They do cry a lot, don't they?"

"So I hear."

Faron stopped in front of their temporary bedroom door. "We could get several small dogs instead. It's the same thing, right?"

She laughed again and shook her head. "Though I am tempted to say yes just to see you tending to a small dog."

"That's not a no." Faron opened the door and motioned for Sabine to enter first. "I am willing to bet we could find some with short, stubby legs."

"You do that," Sabine replied, passing him into the room.

Chapter
Three

Faron slumped down on the sofa in his and Sabine's temporary receiving room, his legs stretching out before him and the back of his head resting on the top of the sofa. He stifled a yawn as he let the voices of Meri, Lisbeth, and Finn wash over him. Marcelle and Avana were absent, Marcelle having volunteered for guard rotation and Avana not about to miss out on a chance to explore a new city. Sabine was with Louis and had asked him to check in with those who were not occupied, something he was more than happy to do.

"Not sleeping much?" Meri asked as she sat beside him, her tone both amused and concerned.

"Not really, and not for the reason you're thinking," Faron said. Then he revised, "Some nights." He smiled to himself, thinking over how some of those nights went. Sabine always proved to be quite inspirational, and Faron often longed for another opportunity to be closer to her.

"Just make sure Her Grace is getting enough sleep," Finn advised from his seat. He'd taken the desk since he was spending this social gathering both reviewing and responding to news from back home. His curly red-brown hair hung loosely about his shoulders, something Faron only observed when he wasn't occupied with running the estate. Seeing Finn relaxed only served to keep Faron content in his current state.

"I've been doing my best to ensure she has several hours of solid sleep a night," Faron insisted. "Admittedly, I've been having trouble sleeping since the second attack. It'll be fine."

"We have a few people with us who make a good sleeping tonic," Finn pointed out. "If you need one, I'm sure Meri would be happy to oversee. I'd suggest Avana, but she likes playing with poisons a little too much."

"I'll consider it," Faron said. He knew that sooner rather than later, his body would force him to get more sleep. Still, the sleep potion was a valid option. "How has everyone's day gone?" he asked, changing topics.

Lisbeth gave a delicate shrug. "When not preparing things for Her Grace, I've been getting to know the gardeners and the gardens, at least today."

The look Meri shot her wife told Faron there was more to the story, but Lisbeth had been behaving, and he was hopeful he wouldn't have to talk to her about overstepping as she had been.

"I've been either with the guard or in the kitchens. Both are good places to catch gossip, but it's all been the normal type of gossip so far," Meri volunteered, sweeping back her short bangs from her face. The gold from her enchanted bracelet, which silenced her ice powers, briefly glinted before her sleeve covered it again.

Faron looked over at Finn even though he knew what the other man would say already.

"You see what I've been doing," Finn replied, tapping a quill against parchment in emphasis.

"So you haven't been out being social and trying to make friends?" Meri said, her tone joking. They all knew how busy the steward was.

Faron chuckled. "I've been with Sabine almost the entire time. She and our soon-to-be king have been discussing politics and how to handle Sargarus. Both of those conversations went over my head quite a bit."

"Is Her Grace still infinitely more practical than the prince?" Finn asked, sitting his quill down. "My understanding is that she would rather prepare for an appearance from Sargarus over hoping none occurs."

"I believe she is more practical than the majority of people I've encountered. I may not be a good judge," Faron replied, shrugging. Meri nodded and Lisbeth laughed.

"She tends to be," Finn acknowledged. "Louis was quite idealistic when he was younger. When possible, he wants to see the best in others. He's got a good heart, though."

"He seems to, and he appears to know what he's doing. Of course, he could be wearing a great façade that could fall apart once he's face-to-face with Sargarus, but we won't know until we get to that point," Faron conceded. He wondered if Sabine would finish up with Louis soon. He missed her and was hoping to spend some time going over what had been discussed today that he may not have fully understood. Hopefully, they could indulge in some other activities as well. "Anything of note Sabine should be informed of?"

Finn shook his head. "Nothing I know of."

Meri shook her head, evidently having nothing to share. Lisbeth, however, looked thoughtful for a moment before a mischievous look crossed her face. "I'm going to see if I can

talk Sabine into putting Marcelle and Avana together more. They'd be such a cute couple."

Finn's gaze rose from his work, landing on Faron for a brief moment before going to Lisbeth. "'Her Grace,'" he corrected. "Faron can refer to her more informally, given their relationship. To the rest of us, she is 'Her Grace.'"

Faron could tell by the look in her eyes Lisbeth knew she'd slipped up the moment she said it, and he was grateful to Finn for speaking up. It wasn't the biggest deal, the slip, not when it was just the four of them, though he'd noted many members of staff used formal titles when speaking of their employers, even in private. Lisbeth had committed a faux pas without question. However, Faron knew that wasn't the only reason why Finn had corrected Lisbeth, and as much as he didn't want to have this conversation, Faron knew they had to.

With a sigh, Faron straightened up from the more relaxed position he was in. Clasping his hands together, he looked first at Meri, whose grim expression confirmed she was unsurprised, then to Lisbeth, whose eyes were slightly narrowed now that all the attention seemed to be on her.

"This seems to be about more than just my slip with Her Grace's name," Lisbeth said. Surprisingly, her voice was free of the expected justification. "What's going on?" she asked, confused.

Finn, thankfully, responded first. "Her Grace hasn't said anything directly to me, though I have some suspicions," Finn replied. He relinquished the items he'd been reviewing and leaned back in his chair. "Faron looks guilty, though, so he'd probably have better answers for you."

Fuck. Faron closed his eyes and gave a deep sigh, not wanting to see what he was sure would be a hurt look on Lisbeth's face. She'd have wanted him to immediately come to her if there was a problem. Counting to five, he opened his eyes, feeling more prepared for what he hoped wasn't a major confrontation.

"Yes, Sabine and I have had a conversation about some of your antics as of late." Faron shook his head, noting the look Meri shot Lisbeth when she opened her mouth to respond. "I know the last—how long has it been?—month," Faron mused before pulling himself back to the conversation, "has been very stressful for you, and I know that, while you're normally good at keeping your head when you hit a certain level of stress, you move away from cleaning everything in sight to trying to remove things that could possibly upset you or the people around you. And sometimes, you even try controlling everything around you. I remember how you were after your house burned down before your parents thought it best to send you here." Lisbeth blushed, showing she remembered as well.

He continued, deciding to focus on specifics. "That sort of behavior has resurfaced, and it hasn't gone unnoticed."

"What have I done?" Lisbeth demanded.

"Well," Faron said, hating that he apparently had to make a list. "You wanted to sell what we still assume were Tristian's mother's dresses just because they took up space in the room allotted to Sabine. An act that, when discovered, would have had consequences for Sabine, and you as well, given how we responded to his men destroying your gardens." No doubt Tristian would have demanded punishment and repayment, neither of which would have looked good for Sabine.

He paused and licked his lips, trying to remain calm and rational, and he moved onto the second topic. "After she was injured, you cleared her schedule without talking to Finn, me, or even her first, which is something you frequently try to do whenever you think she needs a break. While I supported Sabine having time to recover from her attack given her physical state after we returned from Tristian's, you should have discussed the idea with at least Finn before acting. We won't get into the fact that you had planned to burn her letters that same day, letters that you know she'd have had to answer for, regardless of a burning."

Faron felt his heart go out to Lisbeth as she grew more dejected with each word, even if he knew he needed to speak the truth about her behavior, how it had been perceived, and what the possible repercussions might have been. Thankfully, Meri placed a comforting hand on Lisbeth's knee, though she did nothing to interrupt the conversation. Lisbeth gave her wife a brief smile before looking back at Faron.

"Now, you want Sabine to throw Marcelle and Avana together in hopes they will decide to form a romantic partnership because they would look cute. Have you talked to them about if they even like each other?" He gave Lisbeth time to shake her head, though she did so slowly and reluctantly. "There you go. Avana doesn't like to speak about her time with Grégoire, but for all we know, awful things could have been done to turn her off the idea of a romantic relationship. She could also just be looking for a friend, and he's been nice to her since she arrived. Marcelle could also be of the same mindset. I've not asked either, but nothing about their behavior rings as romantic to me. Either way, they're both adults, and you can't force your ideal situation on them. They will get together, or they won't."

Faron paused in speaking his thoughts, feeling as though he should add something a little kinder to the conversation. "Sabine knows you're not acting out of malice or ill-intent but from a place of love. Still, it's important you stop before you accidentally take it too far. It will kill Sabine to have you disciplined or otherwise let you go."

Lisbeth looked at a loss for words as Faron finished, and he looked at Finn to see if he had missed anything or if more needed to be said. He didn't think he'd been too harsh, but he'd been as honest as he could be given the situation. Doing otherwise would have been unfair to Lisbeth.

Finn, it seemed, did have more to add. "In addition to Faron's concerns, it should be noted that Her Grace should not have to talk you into reason. She should never have been made to remind you not to sell or discard of property that did not belong to you. She shouldn't have to worry about other people deciding how her time is spent. She also shouldn't worry about her correspondence getting burned."

Finn managed to convey each point professionally but not harshly. His relaxed shoulders and near serene expression emphasized the warning rather than any punishment. "She already shoulders a greater burden than any of us have experienced in these last weeks. Trying to rope her into a matchmaking scheme only serves to cause her strife."

"This is what I've been trying to talk to you about," Meri said, turning to face Lisbeth. She took Lisbeth's tanned hands into her darker ones, rubbing her thumbs across the tops. "I know you don't mean any harm, but you could still cause harm if we don't find a way to better help you manage your stress."

Lisbeth turned her head away from them, gazing off into the distance as she gathered her thoughts. Faron wondered if she felt attacked or if she wanted to justify her actions to the rest of them. When he'd almost gotten himself fired, a part of him had felt secure, even justified, in the actions he'd taken to maintain Sabine's safety. Those feelings had soon dissipated once he'd understood the perceptions around his actions and the alternatives he'd not considered.

After a little while, Lisbeth turned back to them, her green eyes full of steely determination. "You're all correct. I've been acting without thought for Her Grace and how my actions could be seen by others. It is never my intent to cause her harm or frustration. I will do better."

Faron couldn't help but sigh in relief, even though Lisbeth usually didn't respond stubbornly or defiantly. While she did tend to act without thinking, Lisbeth had always been one to admit to her mistakes and try to improve.

"Thank you. I know confronting me with this probably wasn't easy," Lisbeth said.

"Better you hear it now from one of us rather than Her Grace when she loses her temper," Finn said. He straightened in his seat and picked up his quill. "She's never unfair, but she has far too much to contend with. I doubt she'd be pleasant if she had to issue reprimands."

Lisbeth nodded. "I'll apologize for my actions at a later time. I think, right now, I'd like to spend some time in the gardens." Lisbeth stood and brushed away imaginary wrinkles in her skirt.

"May I join you?" Meri asked, to which Lisbeth nodded. "We'll talk more, later," Meri said to the group. Lisbeth gave Faron and Finn a small smile before they left.

"That went over well," Faron said to Finn.

"It did," Finn agreed. "I don't think she'd considered her behavior before, but she seems to recognize where she had fallen short. It's something."

"Lisbeth has always taken criticism and correction well. Her parents used to say they were lucky." He hadn't understood why her parents had felt that way at the time, but he'd eventually realized a child with plant magic could cause a lot of damage, even accidentally, if they were too upset. Just because she couldn't cause harm on purpose didn't mean she couldn't accidentally take down a small building.

Faron stood. "I should go see if Sabine is finished with Louis." He hoped she was. He wanted some time alone with her. He always wanted time alone with her.

"I hope she is. He keeps her in his office all day long, and she's never been one to sit and do nothing."

"Too bad we can't tell the prince to stop," he said with a chuckle, imagining how well that would go over.

"I think Sabine would address the intrusion before he did," Finn said with a light laugh.

"True." Faron headed for the door. "Make sure you take a break as well. You work just as hard as Sabine does."

Chapter Four

After entering his and Sabine's shared suite, Faron stared at the piles of books sitting on his nightstand. They'd appeared since he'd left their rooms that morning, and a turn of his head showed more waiting on a nearby table. His ear homed in on running water from the bathroom, where a naked Sabine currently prepared for her bath. He considered joining her, though he had promised her a break from their more amorous activities. They'd had, admittedly, a rather late evening.

Before his thoughts could go further down that particular path, he caught sight of even more books on a bureau deeper in their suite. Now that he thought about it, Faron was sure he had seen books stacked on the table in the receiving room. Tilting his head to the right, he read the titles of the ones on his nightstand. Three or four he identified as history books, both for Fythias and Coralia based on the names. Another, he surmised, covered military tactics, and one with the word "Azmarin" embossed on the spine had been decorated with tiny swords. Its contents remained a mystery for now.

Faron realized Sabine must have put in a request for these books at some point today when they were not together. He wondered if she'd asked for these specifically or just requested a selection of books on the various subjects Faron had expressed interest in learning. Hearing the water turn off, followed by a gentle splash, Faron found himself turning toward the bathing chambers. "Sabine, love, did you ask for all these books?" he called out.

"You have better hearing than I do," Sabine called back. "You should really come in here."

Faron strode over to the bathroom and leaned against the doorframe, smart enough to know if he walked in any farther, keeping his hands to himself would become difficult to say the least. Sabine lounged in the large tub, the water a dark lilac color thanks to the addition of oils, salts, or fragrances. The color clouded his view of her exquisite body, but he'd have to do very little to see more. "I was asking about all the books that have suddenly appeared in our rooms," he said as he looked her over.

Sabine nodded. "You said you wanted to learn. I have gathered a few books to help you, my love."

"And I am grateful, but there are more than a few," he said with a laugh. "Am I to read them all in their entirety, or are there only certain chapters I need to study?"

"I imagine you'd benefit more from a thorough exploration of all the pages," Sabine replied. "Fythias alone has centuries of information which are relevant, and then you'd have to bring in the connections to our allies and enemies of the past."

Faron glanced back at the bedroom. He wasn't the fastest reader, unless it was a particularly enjoyable work of fiction, and even those were few and far between. For a moment, he regretted saying anything about wanting to learn, though he quickly pushed that regret aside. Faron was not undertaking some great burden for himself. He was improving his experience and knowledge so he might stand next to Sabine and aid her in effective leadership. Taking the time to study, when time permitted, was a small task. He would need to ask for more parchment and ink so he could take notes on anything he didn't understand or would further question. "Then I shall read all of the books," he said simply, turning back to look at her.

"I'm glad to hear it. I think you will find them interesting enough. The formation of estate guards features heavily in a few of the texts, as does some military history you might like." She paused and swept her hair from her shoulders so it hung over the edge of the tub. "Some of the more recent history you might already be aware of. There was a temporary peace between Fythias and Coralia under King Zephraim the Wise. He seemed more aware of how Coralia needed to function."

"It's possible. Of course, I have spent a good amount of time listening to you talk about the situation in Fythias, both past and present, these last few months. With any luck, some of it would have sunk in."

"You mean listening to me go on about the country has left an impression?" she asked with a teasing grin. "You do like to focus on me, don't you?"

"I would have thought that to be entirely obvious at this point." He returned her smile.

"Fair point, I suppose. And now, since you're standing there maintaining such strict discipline to keep distance from me, I think you should entertain me."

"Well, I did promise you a proper night's rest, and we both know what will happen should I take a single step farther into this room." Faron raised an eyebrow before asking, "How would Her Grace like to be entertained?"

"Oh, I think you might come up with something," Sabine replied. "But you may not leave that spot."

Faron studied Sabine from where he relaxed against the doorframe as he considered her words. He wouldn't dare deny her anything she asked. "There are several things I can think of that would entertain you. If you have any requests, however, I'm all ears," he said playfully, his voice taking on a deeper tone.

"I believe I am in the middle of relaxing," Sabine reminded him. "I am not up to issuing direction just now."

"I can understand that. You have been tasked with so much decision-making given the political state of our country." Faron's hands rose to the laces at the top of his shirt and began to untie them. The opening the lacing covered only allowed Sabine to see some of the upper portion of his chest, covered in a light patch of dark hair. He thought it made for a nice start. Adopting a thoughtful look, Faron ran the fingers of his right hand along the opening, barely touching his skin but close enough for the moment. "I need another moment for consideration."

"Oh, take your time," Sabine encouraged. "I am quite at my leisure."

Faron chuckled and brought his hands to the waist of his pants and slowly started to untuck his shirt before slowly pulling it over his head and tossing it aside, revealing his tanned chest. He rested his hand on the belt of his pants, letting his thumb drag across the space leading up to his navel. The other dropped casually to his side. He said nothing, only suppressed a smile as he noted Sabine's eyes darkening with lust as they raked up and down his bare torso.

His gaze locked on her as the hand resting on his pants started undoing the lacing, stopping right before he could have freed his cock. He waited though, knowing Sabine could see his hardness outlined by the fabric. As usual, the fit of his trousers left little to the imagination. He ran his knuckles up and down the hardened outline, breathing deeply through his nose to keep himself relatively calm. He kept it slow and teasing for both of them. "This is entertaining, correct?"

"Oh, indeed," Sabine confirmed. "Do you like touching yourself in front of me?"

Faron pretended to think over her question for a moment before answering. "Yes." He continued with his slow pace, which wasn't nearly enough to alleviate any part of his desire. He wasn't ready to expose himself yet, preferring to draw out every possible moment of the experience.

"Do you deserve to?"

Faron did consider her question this time. "It depends on your perspective. Yes, because I handled the situation with Lisbeth. No, because I have yet to read any of the books you so thoughtfully had delivered."

"True," Sabine replied. She brushed a loose strand of hair from her face then ran her damp hand down her neck and to her chest. "You should finish stripping."

Faron didn't argue or play around this time, and since he'd removed his boots upon entering the room, all he had to do was finish unlacing his pants, which he did before kicking them aside. He did this with minimal movement in order to stay where Sabine had commanded him to. Now fully nude, his erection on full display, Faron adopted his more relaxed pose once more. "What would you have me do now?"

"Oh, I think you should continue teasing yourself, my love. You seemed to enjoy it."

Faron couldn't help his grin as he reached for the oil they'd used the night before, which sat on the vanity just inside the door frame. He reached for it without having to move his feet and poured some onto his palm before taking himself in hand. Making eye contact with Sabine, he slowly began to stroke himself

"Oh no, my love," Sabine said, watching him intently. "Show as much vigor as when you were dressed."

Faron obeyed, pumping his cock faster, his thumb swiping over his head as he reached the tip before sliding back down to the base, over and over again. He bit back a moan as well as the urge to let his head fall against the door-frame. He knew he could come just from the way Sabine was watching him, but he was enjoying this. Eventually, he was forced to slow his strokes or else this exchange would end too quickly, but he noticed her eyebrow raise in response.

"Did you ask permission to slow down, my love?" Sabine grinned wickedly, as they both knew he had not. Faron was left to contemplate obedience.

"I did not, Your Grace," he replied, his words growing more breathless.

"I think you should keep up the old pace," she decided. "Of course, you do not have permission to come yet."

Faron let out a low growl at her words as his strokes once again sped up. He didn't know how long he could last, but he would not disappoint Sabine by not following her directions.

"Tell me, Faron. What are you thinking of over there?" she teased.

He watched as her fingers slipped down her firm, round breast, making him yearn to touch her all the more. "You. And how you tasted on my tongue as I devoured you. How you felt around me as I bent you over and fucked you on your desk." His hand sped up and his breathing grew ragged. "How your lips looked wrapped around my cock, gagging on it."

"Tell me about your cock and my mouth," she demanded. "And don't you dare come until I am satisfied by the answer."

"What do you wish to hear? How beautiful you look with your mouth wrapped around me? The noises you make as I fuck your throat? The way you greedily lap up my cum?" he growled out, his motions becoming frantic, but he held himself back as she commanded.

"Did you like me swallowing your cum, Faron?"

"Yes. Spirits, yes," he moaned.

"What do you want now, Faron?"

"I want to come," he said through gritted teeth. "And then I want to spend the rest of the night with you, taking you again and again."

"Beg me."

Begging did not come naturally to Faron. A man of his size, strength, and experience had no need for it. By the Spirits, though, there was nothing Sabine could ask or demand of him that he would not obey. He would crawl on his belly, worship at her feet, and even murder for her. Begging, by comparison, was such a small ask.

"Please, Sabine," he tried, growling in frustration as she shook her head.

"You can do better than that," she chided.

"Please, Sabine, by the Spirits, let me come. Please."

"Do you deserve it?" she demanded.

"No," he said. "I deserve only what you decide I deserve, but please."

She must have been satisfied because Sabine nodded once. "You may come."

Faron shouted her name as he gave in to his needs, spilling over his hand and onto the floor. When his body calmed, he rested his weight against the doorframe as he caught his breath.

"You wicked woman," he gently teased.

She smiled, triumphant. She placed her forearms on the edge of the tub and rested her chin on top of them. "Did you enjoy yourself?"

"Not as much as when I'm buried inside of you, but yes."

"Good," she replied. "I rather enjoyed getting to watch your expressions as you came for me."

"As I enjoy yours," Faron responded. He had to admit he did feel better, more relaxed. Giving up his control, as foreign as it felt, left him feeling tranquil. He understood why she so enthusiastically submitted to him with such frequency during those moments: the only thing Sabine had to worry about was listening. All of the choices, all of the responsibilities, rested with him.

"Good," Sabine replied. "You should clean up your mess then join me."

Faron nodded and moved to the wash basin and quickly cleaned himself before moving to the tub. Stopping in front, he held his arms out and presented himself to Sabine. "Am I clean enough, Your Grace?"

"You are," Sabine replied. "But we will see how long that lasts."

Chapter
Five

Hi Bine,

Just a quick note to let you know things are well near the estate. Rumors of an approaching Coralian army near the northwest border have reached us, but none of our friends have confirmed sightings. Naturally, you know I will notify you of anything of importance I see or hear. We've contacted the Nereid since they are closer to you, but your future king may have already done so. They are closer to both Coralia and West Pythias, and they are in more danger than the Sirene. At least, considering their scales.

Tremors of fear are radiating throughout the Mers, though I know you know that. I also know how hard you will fight for us, Bine. Just let us know if you need backing because you have whatever you want from me, as much as I can give you. You always have.

In lighter news, Raidne enjoyed playing with your elf. She said he seemed terrified of her, which was probably wise on his part. We won't tell him he is safe with the Sirene so long as you are happy with him, right?

Yours,
Thaumas

The village outside of Prince Louis's estate, larger than the one back home, buzzed with life under the bright morning sky. Louis's wife Eloise had insisted on a leisurely morning, allowing Sabine to have some free time. She'd slept later than normal, though this had been interrupted by a couple of rounds of gratifying sex. Eventually, after rising, more sex, and washing and dressing, she convinced Faron they needed to explore in the time they were allotted.

The cobbled path from the estate down to the village made for an easy walk, with firs and spruces spaced along the path providing a woody fragrance and ample shade. Sabine smiled to herself, remembering Louis's insistence on a coastal life.

An archway met them at the end of the path, separating the chateau from the small town. The market area began less than a dozen yards into the town, which meant they'd be able to do some shopping or browsing while they were there. Colorful pastel shops organized into a neat little square surrounded a large fountain. Adults and children, accompanied by dogs and other domesticated animals, sat and stood near, the younger splashing each other and laughing. Carts and stalls sat in spaces between shops and the fountain, each displaying goods.

"The village is beautiful," Faron said from her right as he glanced around. As always, Faron used the opportunity to take in the people and look for possible threats, though Sabine suspected they were safe in the village surrounding Maison de L'Harmonie. Faron smirked and leaned down to softly whisper in Sabine's ear. "Maybe venturing out wasn't a terrible idea. Though, I still like my suggestion for how we could have spent the day best."

"I imagine if I were to leave all the planning up to you, I'd never need any of my fine clothing," Sabine countered.

"That is not true," Faron disagreed. "If only because you have duties that, sadly, must be seen to. However, anytime you were not forced to entertain others, let's just say clothes would be optional and more than likely torn to shreds."

"You could always ask which clothes I would allow you to tear from my body," Sabine offered as a compromise. "I do like quite a few of my things."

"I am happy to do so." Faron flashed Sabine a smile, the teasing look in his eyes leaving her feeling delightful. "You would lose far too many dresses otherwise."

Sabine laughed, knowing she'd lost some dresses already. She didn't mind. As much as she joked with Faron about his endless appetite for her, she couldn't deny feeling the same way about him. "I think Lisbeth, and the maids who report to her, would put up quite the protest. They are the ones who get tasked with thinking up repair possibilities, and they hate saying there is no hope for a formerly lovely gown."

"I'm hardly surprised some of those dresses were irreparable," Faron replied evenly, but his smile was one of pure satisfaction. "But you could always wear things you wouldn't mind losing as the day wears on."

"Such a suggestion only works when the timing involves a particular part of the day, my love," Sabine said as they reached the market area. She received smiles and nods of welcome, though she didn't miss the brief faltering of those welcoming expressions as Faron's size initially registered with them. The smiles returned soon enough, though, and he received similar greetings.

"Do you think if I slouched, it would make a difference?" he asked.

"Perhaps," Sabine replied. "Of course, it's also possible you would be seen as even more menacing," she added. "I would think you'd be used to second glances."

"It could look as if I'm trying to hide something if I slouched," he admitted. "Still, it's often interesting to note I am viewed as some oddity because I am tall. I'm not unnaturally so."

"No, you are not," she agreed as she looked around. The scent of leather grew stronger as they entered the market area. A glance to her left confirmed a leatherworker shop, and next to it, a cobbler. The window between them displayed a series of fine belts and boots.

He tilted his head as he considered that. "Has anything caught your eye?"

"So far, the very strong scent of new leather," Sabine replied. She indicated the shops they passed. "Probably nothing I need, though."

Faron nodded. "Is there anything you *are* in need of?" Faron's eyes darted from her eyes to her wrist, where his braided hair rested. He took her hand in his, lifted it to his lips, and kissed her wrist. "Other than the obvious."

She smiled, enjoying the softer moment. Despite his stature and fondness for roughness during sex, he generally showered her with gentle affection, which contrasted with his size and strength. Those softer moments often inspired something more carnal. "I believe I require a proper fucking," Sabine replied. "At least, my fiancé's behavior indicates as much."

Faron's grin grew sharp as he glanced around quickly. "There is a dark alley with decent coverage to your left. If that is what you wish, I am more than willing to grant it."

"How interesting you've so quickly scouted a spot."

"It's important one always be prepared." He glanced in the direction of the alley. "Are you interested, love?"

"Perhaps later," Sabine decided. "Besides, building your anticipation always brings me great pleasure."

"Yes it does," he replied, his voice having gone deeper. "I look forward to burying my face between your thighs later. Making you squirm and want to cry out, unable to in case you draw attention to us. It's going to be enjoyable."

Sabine had no doubt, and part of her considered going off with him now. She just knew if she made that choice, they'd never do anything else in the village, and they might never have another opportunity to visit. "Until then, direct your thoughts elsewhere, my love."

"I shall endeavor to do so, but you should be aware of one crucial thing. The idea of ravishing you never leaves my mind." He chuckled and glanced around once more. "We should find a jeweler."

"Then let's find one," Sabine suggested. As they'd never explored the village before, the process involved investigating each business, booth, and cart they passed, but the discoveries of the different foods and goods intrigued Sabine more than anything else. The market in her village bore the distinct goods of a coastal town with fish, shrimp, and shells. Louis's market held a smaller selection, but the vast options for grapes, spices, wine, and cheeses more than made up for the deficits.

"I would say we should ask about a jeweler, but I find myself enjoying browsing the shops," Faron admitted after examining a small pot of freshly ground cinnamon. The scent, so warm and inviting, had been strong enough for Sabine to detect without ever holding it, so she purchased some for Meri.

The food selections gave way to luxury items like silks, perfumes, and body oils. Sabine stopped at one booth where a red jacquard coat with a black silk lining sat on display. A row of elegant black buttons ran down one side of the front, and cuffs on each arm had been accented by black lining and complementary black cufflinks. Long and wide at the shoulders, she thought the jacket might fit Faron without much tailoring. Sabine pointed to it. "You should try it," she said to him. "I think it would suit you quite well."

Faron looked at the coat for a moment before nodding and asking the booth owner to try it on. He slid it on with ease, letting the coat fall on him without making any initial adjustments.

Sabine nodded seeing that the coat fit him well across the shoulders and down the arms, just as she had expected they might. "What do you think?" she asked.

"It's comfortable," he commented as he moved his arms around and rotated his shoulders. The fabric gently shifted with each movement, but the whole coat continued to sit on Faron quite nicely.

"It also fits, which is rare. I often must have my clothes tailored to fit. What do you think?" he asked her as he continued to flex and observe himself.

"I think you look quite handsome," Sabine replied, smiling to herself. He so rarely did anything nice for himself, and seeing his obvious pleasure in the coat told her they would be buying it. "We may need the cuffs hemmed a little, unless you like wearing them longer. But it does suit you."

Faron considered the cuffs after lifting his arm to see where the edge landed with some movement. "You're right. We should have them hemmed." He shrugged off the jacket, moving to talk to the stall owner along with Sabine.

After negotiations, Sabine exchanged coins for the jacket. Lisbeth could easily adjust the cuffs in less than an hour, so she didn't see a need to find a local tailor to do the work. Faron, meanwhile, got directions to a jeweler, so when the transaction was over and Faron had the jacket in hand, they began their walk in that direction.

"Thank you for the coat," he said softly as they walked.

She glanced up and noted the pleasure in his eyes. He had a fine selection of personal items, but Sabine acknowledged the jacket would be one of the nicest articles of clothing he owned. She would need to make sure to not only bestow him with gifts of affection, but also make sure he had access to her financial resources once they were married. "You're welcome," she replied, smiling.

A comfortable silence descended on them as they walked the short distance to the jeweler, who had a beautiful brick-front store. "Supposedly, they're the best jeweler in the kingdom," Faron shared.

"So they may just be the best in the area," Sabine surmised. "Or they could actually be quite skilled." Looking at the pristine state of the shop, and the size, she suspected they were likely very good at what they did.

"Only one way to find out." Faron opened the door and waited for Sabine to enter first.

The shop consisted of a large main room with a door leading to the back. Because the door was closed, she couldn't judge as to whether it led to additional work or living spaces, though she imagined there would be an upstairs area based on the height of the building from outside. A single counter stood in the middle, and the shopkeeper, a short tan man with a sparse sheet of black hair clinging to his head stood stooped over, carefully examining a heavy gold bracelet inlaid with pearls. She could just see the tips of his pointed ears.

"Would you like to look around, or should we ask for assistance?" Faron asked just before the shopkeeper spoke up.

"Hello there. Just a moment, and I'll be right with you." He picked up a silver tool and began manipulating one of the inlaid pearls on the bracelet as he went silent again.

"We might as well look," Sabine suggested. The small space didn't have much on display, though the careful presentation of each piece suggested the jeweler was precise, skilled, and kept busy. Only a few finished rings sat within a case, many thick and set in bright yellow gold. She wondered if he had any settings or loose stones.

"Do you think you'd like gold or silver for the band?" Faron asked.

"Silver, I think," she decided. "Silver looks better with my complexion." Sabine also felt that some gold tended to look too gawdy, especially if one wore a lot of it at one time.

"Silver would look lovely on you," the shopkeeper said, approaching the two from behind. She hadn't heard him finish up his work on the bracelet. "Sorry to have kept you waiting, but the owner of that bracelet swears every jewel is in danger of falling off." He shook his head as though ridding his mind of the frustration. "I see you two are interested in rings."

"It's not a problem," Faron said, giving the man a friendly smile. "We are looking for an engagement ring, with a silver band as you heard."

"Congratulations, young man," the jewelry said with a beaming smile. "Your bride is lovely." He took Sabine in with a similar kindness and bowed his head respectfully. "You're a petite woman. I would recommend a delicate band, and the silver would suit you best. What were you thinking for a stone?"

Faron looked to Sabine. "I was thinking of something that would match your eyes, but I'm happy with whatever you wish."

Sabine nodded. "A green stone, then," she said.

"Perfect. I have a selection of emeralds and garnets you might like," the man shared. He excused himself into the back room and returned shortly, two black boxes in hand. Placing each on the counter, he motioned the couple forward. "Oh!" he exclaimed then pointed to Sabine's wrist. "You've followed the elven tradition as well. Most couples don't think to follow more than one."

"It seemed appropriate given I'd not bought a ring when I proposed," Faron responded with a playful glance at Sabine.

Sabine returned the smile as the jeweler chuckled. "Let's make sure you get her a nice one, then," he said. He opened the first box containing emeralds. "I have garnets, as well, as I said," he added, indicating the other box. "But with your fiancée's distinct eye color, I thought these were more appropriate. Take a look."

Faron looked down at the jewels, and to Sabine, it appeared as if he was studying them. It was obvious he was looking for the right color, but it seemed he was examining the cut of the gems as well. "Get closer. Tell me if you see any you like."

Sabine did step closer to examine the options. All of them were finely cut and polished; she didn't imagine any choice would be a bad one. She also didn't have any particular preference. Some shades were lighter than others, but all of them beautiful, and she knew she'd be happy with whatever Faron picked. "I think I would like you to choose."

Faron spent about fifteen minutes looking through the gems. Every once in a while, he held one up so it hit the light, studied it for a moment, glanced at Sabine, and then put it back. Finally, he held up one, put it in the light, glanced at Sabine, and declared, "This one."

The emerald, a green much darker than her eyes, twinkled before her. She motioned for him to hold it higher, so she might see it in the light. When he complied, she smiled, understanding why he'd picked it. The dark green gave way to brilliant varieties of sparkling jades, teals, and seafoam. Sabine doubted any matched her eyes, but it was a beautiful stone. "I love it."

"Good. None matched the beauty of your eyes, but this was beautiful in a different way," he said as he lowered it.

"Look at you being romantic," Sabine replied, smiling happily.

"It is a beautiful stone," the jeweler confirmed. "And it would look lovely on you. Would you care to pick out a band, or would you like me to make one for you? As I said, I think something delicate for your fingers."

Sabine looked to Faron. "You're choice."

"Go ahead and make something in silver for her if you would," Faron said, his cheeks growing pink from Sabine's teasing, though he made no recognition of it.

The jeweler chuckled and went through the process of measuring Sabine's fingers, suggesting designs, and arranging payment terms for the item with Faron. "I think I can have this done by the end of the week," he said once the details had been settled. "Sooner if you need."

"The end of the week would be fine," Sabine replied. "I do not know how long we will be here, but certainly at least that."

"If something happens and we have to leave before the week is over, we will come back afterward," Faron assured Sabine. "As long as you can hold onto the ring for the amount of time we have to be away?" he asked the jeweler.

"Of course, though there is a small fee depending on the length of time. After six months, I am allowed to sell it to someone else if I don't hear from you."

"Then we shall make sure to have it by week's end," Sabine replied.

"I'll start work on this right away and see you soon," the jeweler said as he grabbed a small bag and placed the gem inside. Faron paid the man half of the cost with the promise of the rest once they saw the finished product. Their business completed, the man said, "Again, congratulations on your engagement."

"Thank you," Faron said and offered the arm not holding onto his new coat to Sabine. "Would you like to look around more?"

"You can decide," Sabine said as she rested her hand on his arm. "I am feeling quite pleased with our outing so far."

Faron led her from the shop and headed away from Louis's residence. "How about we find a place to eat then see where the day finds us?" He leaned closer and whispered to her, "If that happens to be that alleyway, I wouldn't be disappointed."

Sabine playfully swatted his arm. "Food first, and then I shall consider it."

Faron laughed. "I assume you want me to pick lunch? Or is there something you're in the mood for?"

"Let's just see what we find, and we can decide from there?"

Faron nodded, and they left the shop together in search of a meal.

Chapter Six

Dearest Sabine, Duchesse Vassetre,

I hope my letter finds you well. I would be delighted if you could join me for breakfast. My husband is quite fond of you and relies so heavily on your wisdom, experience, and support. I know we have you to thank for his certain position as the future king of Fythias. I cannot fully express how thankful I am for your presence, not only in our lives but in the lives of our fellow citizens.

I confess I am jealous for not knowing you so well, though we have met before. I believe I am doing myself a disservice for not befriending you earlier. So, let us begin the process come morning. If tomorrow is not convenient for you, please let me know a better time.

Yours,
Eloise Aresenault, Princess Consort

Sabine accepted Princess Eloise's invitation for break-fast, so she'd risen the coming morning to meet with the future queen consort. From what she understood of Eloise, the woman was a striking figure, opinionated, and quite doting on her small family. Of course, the view had been shaped by comments and discussions from others. Grégoire had remarked on Eloise's poor health, but his opinion had never been backed by anyone else as far as Sabine knew.

Lisbeth bustled around the opposite side of the room, laying out the clothes Sabine would wear for the day, as well as matching accessories. Lisbeth had been quiet the night before as well as this morning, as if something weighed on her mind. As Faron had confirmed speaking with her, Sabine supposed the two were connected. Thankfully, Lisbeth remained her usual cheerful self, and even with worries over a possible upcoming war and an official correction over her recent behaviors, Sabine felt certain her friend would speak up when she was ready.

"I have everything laid out, Your Grace," Lisbeth called out, holding up one of Sabine's prettier but less decorative dresses. Fabrics of blues, greens, and silver composed the design, and its elegance came from the quality of materials and stitching rather than any additional ornamentation.

"Very nice selection," Sabine replied, taking it in. "It's customary to be less finely adorned than someone who out-ranks you. I think it will do nicely."

Lisbeth smiled brightly. "I'm glad you approve." She carried the dress over to Sabine to help her dress. The dress may have been less decorative, but it was still hard to get into without help. "The staff here are all very nice and profes-sional. When they gossip, it seems to be about Prince Alaoin and his mischief, and they adore the prince and princess," Lisbeth said.

Sabine knew it to be nervous babbling more than anything, which meant Lisbeth was working up to an important, but not comfortable, conversation. "Prince Alaoin is quite a handful," Sabine agreed. "And with the way Faron looks at him, I suspect he'll want children sooner rather than later."

"Is that something you want as well?" Lisbeth asked.

"I do want children," Sabine replied as Lisbeth straightened her top. "I'd prefer we not be on the verge of war when I have them, though."

"Maybe tell him that?" Lisbeth suggested. "I'm sure the two of you have spoken about children, but maybe a conversation about the timing is needed?"

"We have had that conversation, but it may not be a terrible idea to remind him all the same," Sabine replied. "Supposedly, they should all resemble me as well, which means I'll have to enlist Meri to help discipline them." Sabine laughed at the thought. She did not doubt that big, "scary" Faron would easily be swayed by small children.

"If they look like you, we are all in trouble. They will get away with everything. We will have to hope they also have your disposition. I don't think the kingdom would survive small children who look like you but act like Faron," Lisbeth said.

"Faron barely handles behaving like Faron," Sabine acknowledged.

"True," Lisbeth said, amusement in her voice. Silence settled as she finished helping Sabine dress. "I wanted to apologize for my behavior as of late," Lisbeth said suddenly. "I will work on thinking things over more before I act."

Sabine nodded and smiled to herself. "I appreciate it, Lisbeth. I know you never mean any harm."

"Thank you. I truly didn't, but that's still no excuse."

It wasn't, but Sabine was willing to move past it now that her behavior had been addressed and she was trying to do better. "Much more offensive things than being overeager have happened as of late."

"Also true, but you didn't need the added stress of me acting the way I did." Lisbeth put a small silver necklace around Sabine's throat. It was simple and lightweight. "Are you looking forward to breakfast?"

"I think so," Sabine replied. She examined herself in the mirror and felt she looked nice enough for the meal. "I've met Princess Eloise formally, but we haven't spent much time together."

Lisbeth nodded. "I hope you have an enjoyable time with her." She stepped back and looked over Sabine one more time, smiling at a job well done. "Enjoy breakfast. I'll make sure everything's clear here."

Sabine thanked her and left her suite, strolling along the corridor in the direction of the dining room. Although Louis's home looked so much different than her own, it felt warm and open. The walk to the informal dining room was a short one, thankfully, despite the numerous possible distractions along the way.

As Sabine drew closer, she could hear a woman's voice and childish laughter.

"You two have a wonderful afternoon. Make sure your Papa takes a break, alright, my little love?"

Sabine turned down the hallway and was greeted with the sight of Louis, a squirming toddler in his hands, and a beautiful young woman standing close to them, bidding them farewell.

Louis smiled upon seeing Sabine but quickly made his apologies as Alaoin demanded they be on their way. So

Sabine turned her attention to the princess and inclined her head in a respectful nod. "Good morning, Your Highness."

"It is a very good morning," Eloise responded as she watched her husband and child walk away. Her voice held a soft, comforting quality. Eloise's slender form, medium height, pale complexion, and thick near-black hair rendered the softness of her tone a little surprising, though Sabine found her to be quite striking. She could also see why Grégoire had tried to tell everyone she was sickly.

Eloise turned her attention back to Sabine as her family disappeared from view. "I hope your morning has been as good as mine."

"Indeed it has," Sabine replied. "I enjoy slow beginnings with my fiancé."

Eloise gave her a knowing smile. "Slow mornings are some of the best. Though they become few and far between when you add a toddler to your life." She laughed a little as she motioned Sabine into the room.

Sabine followed along. Although she'd noticed quite a bit of interaction between Louis and his son, Eloise's words made it clear that they were active parents rather than letting wetnurses, nannies, and governesses raise the child. "Alaoin is adorable. He looks just like his father."

At the mention of Alaoin, Eloise's smile grew radiant. Sabine saw the same sort of affection in the way Faron gazed at her. "Yes, and it seems like he's taking after him as well, but only time will tell."

"There are worse people to take after," Sabine pointed out. "When Faron and I have children, I've been told everyone hopes they look like and take after me. I suspect the prospect of managing more than one giant elf would be intimidating for some."

"I bet he was the tiniest baby. It seems like the largest ones always are. They are tricky like that." She led Sabine to a table that was filled with covered trays of various sizes. The table as well as the room were decorated in beautiful earthy tones with a lot of natural lighting. "I think, in the end, as long as they are healthy, your Faron will be happy regardless of who they take after."

"I think so, too. I would not mind having a child who resembled him, of course. I think my fiancé is quite magnificent."

"I should hope so." Eloise sat at the head of the table and motioned for Sabine to sit at her left with one hand, while motioning to a servant with the other. Sabine took a seat, feeling at ease in a way she never had with any of the princess's in-laws. The feeling left her certain of her political alignment.

There was a moment of silence as the servants uncovered the food and the two women picked out what they wanted to eat. After Eloise took a few bites of her eggs, she asked Sabine, "Are you enjoying your time here? I've heard your last trip out was quite eventful and not in a good way."

"My time here has been lovely. Your home is comfortable, and Faron and I got to enjoy some time in the village a couple of days ago. We found a jeweler to make a ring for me."

"I am so happy to hear that. Things have been so stressful, and I know my husband monopolizes your time. I'm glad you were able to get some time away." Eloise's tone was wistful as she spoke. "I can talk to him and make sure Louis gives you more time with your Faron if you wish."

"I don't think you'd ever truly be able to grant us enough time with one another," Sabine said, smiling. Even now, she felt the strong pull to her soon-to-be husband, though she'd left him only less than half an hour before. "We do need to find time to marry before long, of course."

"I know it's unorthodox, but you could elope, even today. Unless the rite is that important." Her eyes dropped to the branded bracelet wrapped around Sabine's wrist and back up. "Have a party later to celebrate and appease the nobles once everything is done. Or don't, and forget the nobility and what they expect from your marriage, and do what makes you happy, at least in this instance."

"I think we know it would be an elopement if we married anytime soon," Sabine replied, piercing a piece of melon with her fork as she spoke. "And I'm not particularly worried about impressing anyone with a lavish celebration. I know who I want to spend my life with, and for me, it's really that simple."

"I wish Louis and I could have had a more intimate wedding," Eloise admitted. "But that's what comes with being a prince. Everything is a spectacle."

"You could always do something intimate for yourself," Sabine suggested. "I find that, even with all the responsibilities and duties I shoulder, when I can do something for myself, I feel much more at peace, much more like an actual person." She sometimes felt guilty for taking selfish moments, but mostly, Sabine felt entitled to them.

"I try. We both do, but it feels like Louis especially has very little time for anything outside his duties. He makes sure to take time every day to spend time with Alaoin and me, but some nobles act as if they own him and his time."

Sabine nodded. "There are those who do not respond well to boundaries, but they must be put up and held, or whatever time he finds for himself will slowly get chipped away." She smiled at Eloise. "I am happy to exert my power

and influence to help our future king find more time for you, Alaoin, and himself."

"That might be necessary. Louis is horrible at setting boundaries with anyone who's not Grégoire. Sometimes, I think he feels it necessary to be available for his subjects whenever they need him, especially since Grégoire only made time for his followers. He would have made such a better impression had that not been true."

"I don't think Grégoire was much concerned with impressions," Sabine pointed out. She took another bite of fruit. "He was much more concerned with gaining power."

"Very true. But let us not talk about that awful man. I don't know what happened to him," she leaned forward as if to share a secret with Sabine, "but I hope it was horrible." She sat back once more. "Tell me what my husband has you doing all day that gives you no time for yourself, and then tell me how you met your fiancé, please."

Sabine laughed as she placed her fork down and picked up her glass. She found she liked Eloise quite a bit now that she'd had time to speak with her. "Oh, your husband has a variety of tasks to see to. Discussions of possible strategies and counterstrategies. Then, who we might trust to side with us should war become a reality. We're hopeful the Nereid might be interested. The Sirene have indicated they are. Then, of course, who within the country is trustworthy." Sabine mentioned a few they knew they could count on and additional others they thought were likely.

Sabine waved a dismissive hand. "Forgive me, but I'm worn out on politics so early in the morning, but I'm happy to talk about my fiancé." Sabine recounted the story, though she left out some of Faron's less fine moments, because what did they really matter now? "So he asked me to marry him, and naturally…" She ended the statement by holding up her hand so Eloise could see the bracelet.

Eloise gave a delighted smile at the bracelet, though the princess had laid eyes on it before during this very meal. "I'm surprised he didn't whisk you away right then and there to be wed."

"I think he might have had we not grown so busy soon after."

"Louis told me some of the details about what happened at Tristian's." She reached out and put a hand on Sabine's. "I always despised him. Though, Louis would tell you I dislike most of the nobility."

Sabine smiled in appreciation and nodded. "I think, for the most part, Fythias is filled with good people, but some of the nobility can be challenging. In Tristian's case, he was quite evil. I think Faron is still quite unhappy about how swiftly the comte was dealt with."

"Louis has made similar comments about the comte as well as his brother. I think he would have liked to fight it out with Grégoire instead of him up and running away the way he did." Eloise picked a few more items for her plate. "I'm … not the best when it comes to handling the nobility. Louis more than makes up for my faults, but being minor nobles, my parents always thought I would marry either a third son of another minor noble or a commoner from the village. They didn't think it important that I learn more than how not to embarrass myself when I was allowed to court. Imagine their surprise when I did, in fact, catch the attention of a third son who just happened to be the prince." She covered her laugh behind her hand.

Sabine laughed as well. "My mother was a commoner in the village, and I remember she used to get great joy in navigating the different expectations her marriage created for her."

"I have been told stories about your mother and how she handled herself. She was held up as an example I should strive to follow by several of the younger ladies when I first accepted Louis. Then the people who truly knew your mother got wind of that and made sure to tell us all about how she bodily threw the comte's father from your estate for being rude, as well as a few other stories. Suddenly, she stopped being the person I should emulate." She sighed. "Your mother sounds like she was an amazing woman."

"She was," Sabine replied, and she thought she would feel that way even if they had not been mother and daughter. "I think she had the sort of tenacity one needs to be in a powerful position."

Eloise was quiet for a moment, picking at her food before finally saying, "I love Louis with all my heart, but I often wish he was not the prince." She gave Sabine a wry look. "But he is, and soon he shall be king, and I queen, and we will do all we can for our people."

"It is a duty many would not wish for," Sabine acknowledged. She felt for Eloise, though the future queen didn't verbalize a wish to run away, Sabine knew it was there, deep down. She had the wish herself, but she usually loved her position. "But as someone who has a title beneath those, it has its rewards, and if you find people to support you, people who love you, it is infinitely more tolerable."

"Louis said the same." Eloise laughed as she leaned closer to Sabine again. "Last time several of the noblemen came to talk to Louis, I arranged for the ladies to join me in helping out some of the poor people in our city. Several were ecstatic to help. The others, well, to say it went badly for them is an understatement." Sabine could see she felt slightly conflicted about her enjoyment of the situation, but not enough to not share it. "I love working with the people so much, I forgot that it isn't shared by all the nobles."

"It is not," Sabine agreed. "Perhaps, make a point of staying in contact with those who do, and grow your circle organically from there."

Eloise nodded. "I've been trying to keep in touch with the ladies who enjoyed the outing." The small smile on her lips told her Eloise was very pleased with how those letters were being received, before she bit her lip in obvious nervousness. "Would you be interested in joining me for a trip to the orphanage? If you can spare the time."

"Of course," Sabine replied. "And naturally, if Louis is occupying my time when you wish to go, just tell him off."

"Oh, no need for that. If I ask, Louis will make sure you're free. I may have to gently remind him, but he generally grants me anything I wish. I have found I have to be careful with that."

"I know all about that," Sabine assured her. She knew there was nothing she could ask of Faron he would not give.

"I think we might be the luckiest ladies in the kingdom," Eloise said before taking a sip from her cup. "I'll try and arrange for a trip out for us later this week."

"I'll look forward to it," Sabine promised. "In the meantime, let's enjoy our lovely meal."

Chapter Seven

Faron leaned against the wooden railing that surrounded the training yard and watched as Meri and Avana trained together. Lisbeth had asked him to keep an eye on them, knowing that with the news of Sargarus's eminent arrival, Meri might push herself too far and need help getting back into the estate. He understood Lisbeth's worry. While Meri was happy with her role as head chef of the Vassetre estate, she'd been raised to fight, and she'd worked hard to become captain of the guard. In the face of such a grave threat to Sabine, as well as the rest of Fythias, Meri was feeling rather useless. He also assumed having nothing to do while at Louis's estate hadn't helped matters much.

She had decided to combat that by offering to help with Louis's guards training and sparring with Avana in her free time. While it was good to see her active and feeling like she was contributing, he, Lisbeth, Finn, and even a very occupied Sabine all noted her limp was getting worse day by day as she pushed herself. No one had the heart to tell her to stop, even if suggestions to take things easier had crept into conversations.

So far, Meri and Avana had been sparring for almost an hour. Meri had started off with more easy, smooth movements, and Avana made for a very teachable opponent. Even so, as the morning wore on, Meri's skill won out over her disability. Her stiff leg did nothing to detract from her simply being the more skilled fighter.

She stood in the middle of the sandy training circle, her sword held in front of her, angled away from her body. Her stance was relaxed, her movements controlled yet fluid, as if her sword was an extension of her arm. Avana, on the other hand, was almost nonstop motion. Her movements were smooth, but it was obvious she had been trained that quick, aggressive tactics would win any fight. Faron assumed it was because her trainers had thought that with an elf's agility and speed, she would dance circles around anyone she had to fight. It hadn't worked against Sabine, nor was it working against Meri, but it had taken him slightly off guard the first time he'd tested his skill against Avana.

Meri kept her eyes on Avana, turning her body only to make sure the other woman didn't have an open shot at her back. She waited patiently, almost serenely, with her eyes on trained Avana's face.

Avana continued to circle Meri, looking for an opening. The rigid set of her shoulders told Faron her patience was running low as she dug the back of her left foot into the sandy ground—a tell if there ever was one—and launched herself at Meri.

Meri, noting the same thing Faron had, was quick to block every blow. She easily knocked Avana's sword to the side after the fifth blow and moved forward to end the spar not with her sword but with her free hand, her fist stopping inches from Avana's surprised face. Her shock became even more pronounced when Meri used her bad leg to send Avana sprawling to the ground with Meri's sword pointed at her throat.

"Yield?" Meri asked.

"Yes," Avana said, and as with the other matches she'd lost, her voice was laced with excitement.

"Help me to the bench?" Meri asked Avana, who, after standing up, slotted herself under Meri's arm and helped her limp to the bench, only stopping long enough to hang up their practice swords.

Faron pushed off the fence and headed toward them in case Avana needed help, but the two made it to the bench with little issue. Faron and Avana both ignored Meri's sigh of relief when she sat down. She stretched her bad leg out in front of her and started to rub the muscles in her upper thigh, though it would do little to nothing for the pain. "You did good, but you need to be more patient," Meri said as she soothed her aches. "You have three tells for when you're going to attack."

"Three? I thought I only had one, maybe two," Avana mused, no less excited by the news.

"You have three. You dig your heel, you drop your shoulders, and your eyes dart to where you plan to attack first," Meri said, glancing at Faron to see if he caught anything else.

He shook his head. Those were the exact things he'd caught as well.

Avana made a thoughtful noise. "I'll work on those. Why haven't you pointed them out before?" she asked, confusion lacing her voice.

"Because I wanted to make sure they really were tells and not just something you did when comfortable with your sparring partner. We've sparred five times now, and they haven't changed. I might as well start to retrain you now instead of leaving you open to problems later down the line," Meri explained. "We also need to work more on your defense. I understand your trainers rarely thought you'd be in a true fight. You were supposed to be an assassin after all, but it's still an area that needs work."

Faron noted the tilt of Meri's head as she considered her words to Avana, as well as Avana's rapt attention on the other woman. "How many fights have you been in?" Meri asked, and that was a question Faron was interested in.

Avana made a thoughtful face. "Including my trainers and not counting Sabine? Maybe three or four."

"Your trainers?" Faron asked, concerned.

"When I got older, I decided a couple of them didn't get to beat me just because they wanted to." Avana gave a shrug and looked down at her hands, missing the horrified look Faron exchanged with Meri.

Faron grasped for something else to say as he watched Meri's eyes harden.

"How long did those fights last?" she asked.

Faron was surprised by both the question and her calm tone, something he wasn't sure he could have pulled off just then.

"Just a few minutes. They felt longer, though," Avana said.

"That's how real fights work, especially during a battle. Which is why you need a better defense and more patience. In a large-scale battle, each fight can last from forty seconds to five minutes, depending on the skill of your opponent and how tired you both are. Though, I've found most fights last about two minutes," Meri explained.

"How many battles have you been in?" Avana asked before Faron could.

"Several small-scale battles against bandit groups and such, and one that could be considered a large-scale battle. Though, not as large as a battle with Sargarus's forces would be." Meri's brows creased and her lips pressed together in thought.

"I don't want to fight in a battle that big," Avana said.

"No one does, but to be honest, I don't think it will come to that," Meri said.

Faron nodded when Avana looked to him for reassurance that Meri was right, though he truly didn't have the same confidence Meri had that it wouldn't come to such a thing.

"Even if there isn't a full-on fight with Sargarus, that doesn't put Sabine at any less risk," Faron couldn't help but add on.

Avana looked thoughtful, then she nodded as if their word was law and she would take it as such.

Faron looked across the training field, wishing he had Avana's ability to take things at face value like that. It was too easy to get lost in his worry over Sabine and what could happen if Sargarus's forces were able to cross the mountain. From the corner of his eye, he noted the way Avana eyed Meri's leg.

"Was the large battle where your injury happened, or was it one of the smaller battles?" she asked.

Faron couldn't help his interest. He knew it had happened when Sabine's estate had been attacked, but he had assumed it wasn't a large battle.

"It did. I don't know the exact number of assailants, but the battle felt like it went on and on." Meri got quiet for a moment, her eyes taking on a faraway quality. "It had been a night like any other: quiet, peaceful. I was taking the late watch because one of the other guards was ill. It was near midnight, and I was counting the minutes until I could get some sleep, when one of the blacksmith's boys ran up to the gate screaming about a large force approaching from the western side. Found out later he and some friends had snuck out with alcohol they had taken from his father's liquor cabinet. They'd been halfway through the first bottle when they'd spotted low light through the trees and gone to investigate. Afterward, Her Grace made sure the boys didn't get in trouble with their parents, because if they hadn't been out there and seen the soldiers coming…" Meri gave a shiver.

Faron couldn't help but concur.

"The warning only gave me a few minutes to rally the guard, but it was enough. They were expecting us to be in our beds, not out there ready to meet them. To this day, I believe that gave us the advantage in the fight, especially since I'm sure they had more people than us. The battle that followed, it was bloody and chaotic, more so than any other fight I'd been in. Both sides having magic users made it even worse. I can't say that any of the people I fought were especially talented with a sword or their magic, but it doesn't matter when you're tired, when your body wants to stop fighting after you've killed your tenth person. Mentally, I had to take the battle one fight at a time. Even with my magic able to take on larger groups at a time, I barely had time to make sure my guards were doing alright, but we held the line as best we could. It would have been a stunning victory with few casualties had it not been for the fucking assassin." Meri paused again to take a deep breath, a hand running down her face. "There are three things I've always wondered about that battle I'll never know the answer to. Were the soldiers a distraction for the assassin, or was the assassin a backup plan in case they couldn't butcher us while we slept? Either way, why didn't they use the Veinfire arrow earlier? Why did they wait until the fighting was over to use it on me? Had they shot me with it earlier, they wouldn't have lost so many people." She looked down at the gold bracelets she wore that controlled her magic.

"Maybe the archer couldn't get a clear shot at you until they were retreating," Avana suggested.

"Possible, but I think they waited until my back was turned from the gate. I think it was more of an afterthought than anything, just another way to try and demoralize us in case they decided to try again. Wouldn't have worked with the way Her Grace stepped into her new position right away, showing a strength and resolve that, to this day, is still unmatched. As that asshole Sargarus is going to find out when he finally makes port." Meri's grin was vicious, and Faron couldn't help but match it.

"Enough about all that, though. It's lunch time, and I don't know about either of you, but I'm starving," Meri said, moving to stand. Faron held out a hand, only for her to gently swat it away. "I've got this." She stood, only to end up sitting right back down on the bench. She let out a huff and held out her hand for Faron to help her up. "If you try and bride-carry me, I will make Her Grace a widow," she threatened when Faron moved to pick her up.

Faron laughed. "Okay. Okay." Instead, he wrapped an arm around her shoulder as best as he could, while Avana slipped under her other arm. "Let's go eat."

Chapter Eight

Faron ate dinner with Finn, Lisbeth, Meri, Avana, and Marcelle that evening, as Sabine had been occupied with Louis. Eloise had insisted Faron was welcome to join the two, but he opted to eat with their friends instead. He didn't know enough to contribute to discussions in any meaningful way, and he didn't want to interrupt them.

As he'd risen from his seat in the banquet hall, Peronelle stopped by to inform him that Sabine had returned to their suite half an hour earlier and had eaten dinner already. Eager to join her, Faron all but sprinted. Had he known what he'd find upon arrival, it was possible he would have learned to fly if it would have gotten him there any sooner.

Faron paused upon shutting their suite door, taking in the sight of his fiancée before stalking across the room, a hungry grin on his face. In the middle of the bed, reclined a wine-relaxed and very naked Sabine. It seemed while he was eating with their friends, enjoying a typical alcohol-free night, Sabine had decided to enjoy some libations with their hopefully soon-to-be king and his wife. How much she drank, he didn't know, and right now, he honestly didn't care. No, he was more interested in the pretty picture his fiancée made, especially with the blue rope they'd bought so many months back laying on the bed in front of her.

"Should I assume my fiancée has made plans for the night?" Faron asked.

"Indeed," Sabine replied, looking up at him, her bright green eyes full of promised mischief. "If you aren't too exhausted with all of your self-assigned duties."

Faron stopped at the end of the bed. "I find myself suddenly full of renewed energy. I wonder why?" he said, his tone dry as his eyes raked up and down Sabine's form.

"Good," Sabine replied. "I do have certain expectations."

He placed a knee on the mattress and leaned forward. "What would those be?"

"Those would be making use of the ropes you decided to buy when you first started working for me."

Faron's eyes trailed from Sabine to the rope and back again. "I can certainly make use of those, but I wonder... How do you feel about adding a blindfold as well?"

"Oh, you jumped to that idea quite quickly," she teased. "What must swirl through your mind?"

"So many things," he replied as he took her chin in his hand, tilting her face up so he could kiss her. She returned the kiss, her lips coaxing his into something deeper. Faron's tongue traced her bottom lip as he climbed all the way onto the bed. She responded in affirmation, pulling him closer. Faron let his tongue slip into her mouth, enjoying the taste of Sabine, sweeter than normal thanks to the wine she'd drunk. His body pressed closer to hers before he drew back and just drank her in.

A look of longing and regret crossed Faron's face as he pulled away completely, rising from the bed. "I need to collect a few things. I will be just a moment. Stay there," he said firmly and crossed the room into their bathing chamber.

It took only a matter of minutes for Faron to collect the long black strip of soft cloth he knew could be used as a blindfold and a small hand towel. He also discarded his clothes while there. He paused for a moment, thinking he should have waited until he was with Sabine again, but he truly did not have the patience.

Heading back into the bedroom, he couldn't help the blush that arose when Sabine looked at him, eyebrows raised, before saying, "Eager are we?"

He set the towel down and climbed back on the bed, this time behind Sabine. "For you, always and forever." He gently pulled her hair away from her face and then put the blindfold over her eyes, tying it securely while ensuring none of her hair was caught in his knot. "Can you see anything?" he asked.

"I cannot."

"Good," he purred before reaching around Sabine and picking up the rope. He had wanted to put this to use for quite some time, but the timing seemed to always be off. Even now, a part of him did wonder if the house of the soon-to-be king was the right place for this. The rest of Faron did not care.

Keeping the rope in his left hand, Faron used his right to place her arms behind her back. Starting just below her elbow, Faron wrapped the rope around and down to her wrist in an intricate pattern. As he tightened the rope, a thought occurred to him. This was the first time they had engaged in this form of play, and they had never discussed boundaries the way they should have, though Faron was certain he knew what activities to avoid.

"If at any time, you become uncomfortable or no longer enjoy what we are doing, tell me to stop," Faron said. "Say something like…" He cast his gaze around the room before looking down at the blue rope he was finishing tying securely around her wrists. "Red. Say red, and if you're alright with everything, say blue."

Sabine laughed softly, evidently aware of where the color idea came from, though she hadn't watched him look around thanks to the blindfold. Finishing the knot, Faron moved away from Sabine, rising from the bed to take in the picture Sabine made. Kneeling in the middle of the large bed, completely nude, blindfolded, her hands comfortably secured behind her, she looked practically edible.

After several minutes of him just watching her, Sabine called out, "Faron?"

He almost felt guilty, having left her to question his presence. "I'm here, my love. I was just admiring the picture you present."

"Oh?" she asked, her tone inquisitive and yet amused.

"If I had any artistic ability, I would paint you as you are right now. No one other than us would ever see it." Faron could picture it, the painting. How large he would make it. Where he would hang it. How often he'd want to replicate it.

He moved back to Sabine. Placing one knee on the bed, he began trailing his fingertips across her skin, his touch barely there. He started with her shoulders, working his way down her arm to her elbows and then back up. He did this several times, watching the goosebumps as they rose on her skin, listening to her breathing catch. He moved behind Sabine, bracketing her between his legs, allowing her to lean back against him. He brought his hands up to her collarbone, keeping his touch featherlight as he traced patterns into skin, between her breasts, down her stomach, and into the hair above her hot center before coming back up. He let his hands trace under her breasts, down to her hips, and up and down her legs, enjoying being able to freely touch her in a way he hadn't before.

"How are you?" he asked as her breath quickened, hitching every time he came close to her clit or her nipples before moving away from them.

"Good. I'm good," she breathed.

He lifted his hands from her, causing her to moan in disappointment. "Wrong answer," he whispered in her ear.

There was silence for a moment before Sabine breathed out, "Blue."

Faron placed his hands back on her hips. "Good girl," he whispered and began tracing her skin once again, losing himself to the sensation for several more minutes. Not nearly having his fill of just touching Sabine, but wanting her to enjoy herself as well, Faron slowly drug one hand down to the little bundle of nerves between her legs, gently flicking it with his index finger. He slid his other hand to her breast, enjoying the fullness of it in his hand before gently squeezing.

He played with Sabine like this for almost as long as he had spent tracing her skin before she whispered, "Faron, please."

He chuckled against her neck. "Is it not enough for you, my love?"

"You know it's not," she replied.

Faron laughed, biting down on her neck as he plunged two fingers inside of her without warning, the hand that was squeezing her breast moving to her taut nipple, rolling and pinching it between his middle and index fingers. Removing his teeth from her neck, Faron said, "You're going to come on my fingers and then my tongue several times before I fuck you." He grinned at the hungry moan that came from Sabine's lips as he increased the speed of his finger, his palm pressing against her center to add to the friction.

Faron kissed and nipped at Sabine's neck as her breathing became more frantic. He waited until her breathing turned to desperate panting before biting down, the sensations of pain and pleasure bringing her to climax immediately. He didn't remove his fingers, but he did stop, his index and middle finger buried deep within her. "One more this way, I think," he told her as the hand on her breast moved up to her collarbone. He wouldn't wrap his hand around her neck, not after what Tristian had done, but he could hold her like his, his hand splayed across the base of her neck. "Sabine?" he asked.

"Blue," she replied, and he began thrusting his fingers inside of her once more.

It wasn't long before Sabine climaxed a second time. Faron knew she would let him push her over the edge a third time, but instead, he removed his fingers and let her fall boneless against his chest while he licked his fingers clean. They sat together in contented silence, Faron listening to Sabine's breathing while she came down before asking, "Ready to continue?"

She nodded before saying, "Blue," softly. He pushed her into an upright position, giving her a moment to stretch her legs as he placed a few pillows behind himself. Laying back, Faron gently placed a hand on her hips and helped her turn around before guiding her to straddle him. He knew she thought he was going to have her ride him, could feel her anticipation in the way Sabine tried to move back, to place herself above his cock, but he had told her how the night was going to go. So, before his temptress could throw out his plans, he tightened his grip on her hips and dragged her up his body until her legs were bracketing his head. Without warning, he slipped his tongue inside her and began thrusting, one hand on her hip to help her stay upright, the other moving around her leg to play with her clit.

Faron watched as best as he could as Sabine's head fell back. Her lips issued moans that steadily grew louder as she began to ride his face.

Knowing Sabine was drawing close to her climax, Faron, feeling playful, removed his tongue and fingers, smiling when Sabine's head dropped forward. He swore he could feel her glare even through the blindfold.

"Faron," she said in a tone that was half annoyed, half needy.

With a chuckle, he licked from her entrance to her clit and back again before resuming his previous action. Sabine resumed grinding against his face, only for her to let loose a noise of deep frustration when he stopped again. "Faron!"

"Sorry, my love," he said. This time when his tongue entered her, he didn't stop until she came again. Even as she trembled, Faron's eyes remained focused on her to make sure he wasn't pushing too hard. Faron continued to fuck her with his tongue until her shaking stopped, giving Sabine a moment to come down from her high before tapping her leg once.

"Blue," she answered breathlessly.

With a nod he knew she couldn't see, Faron contemplated his options before firmly grasping her hips once more and dragging her down his body, stopping when she was positioned over his cock. Letting go of Sabine with one hand, he positioned himself and then slowly lowered her onto his straining member. "Think you can ride me?" he asked.

Sabine nodded and began slowly lifting herself up and down. Faron, his hands not leaving her hips, laid his head back against the pillows and just enjoyed the feeling of Sabine tight around him, basking in being connected in the most intimate way possible, as she slowly picked up her pace. He watched her, his eyes tracing every part of Sabine as she bounced on his cock, his name falling from her lips repeatedly.

"You're stunning," he breathed as one of his hands released Sabine's hip to trail up her stomach to her breast. Taking it in hand, he played with her nipple as he held himself back from pounding into Sabine, until he couldn't take it anymore. He needed more than Sabine was able to give with her hands behind her back, unable to leverage herself for more.

Sitting up, he used the hand on her breast to push Sabine onto her back, letting her get as comfortable as possible with her arms tied behind her, and waited for her to say, "Blue," before he threw both of her legs over his shoulders, nearly bending her in half, and set a brutal pace that had them both panting and moaning. Hands bracketing her head, Faron continued his pace, words of love and encouragement for how well she was taking him falling from his lips. As Sabine tightened around him, Faron considered holding off on his own climax, to see how many more times he could make her come, but decided she'd had enough for now and let go with a loud roar as he emptied himself inside her.

Faron slowed his thrusts until he was completely spent, looking down once to take in the beauty of being connected with Sabine in such a way before pulling out and gently helping her up. He removed the blindfold, careful of her hair, and set it aside. He then moved to sit behind her and quickly undid the knot and removed the rope. Gently, he took her right hand in his own and massaged upward. He repeated the actions with the left. The entire time, he spoke to Sabine, who seemed rather dazed, telling her how good she'd been, how well she'd taken him, how much he'd enjoyed himself and that he hoped she had as well.

Slowly, she came back to herself, though he could tell she was extremely close to falling asleep. "Oh no," he said, laying a kiss on her nose. "No sleeping yet. I have made a mess of you. Bath first, then sleep."

Sabine made a noise of discontent even as she raised her arms so Faron could more easily lift her off the bed.

"I love you," she whispered against his chest.

"And I you."

Chapter Nine

Louis, Prince of Fythias,

The invitation to visit you in Fythias comes when we need friendly tidings. The recent loss of our queen, coupled with the Coralian threat, leaves the Nereid in a tenuous position. Thankfully, your outreach leaves me feeling hopeful.

As we all know, decisive action is greatly needed and appreciated. Fythias has always been a friend to the Nereid, and we look forward to seeing you. Coralia has other targets for now, but I have no doubt we will soon see their attention turn to us. We'd like to avoid any future involving Coralia's interference.

I shall set off in the next few days and hopefully arrive within the week. Until then, stay safe and vigilant.

Aphros
Acting Nereid Ruler

Faron ignored the chatter going on around him as he finished his cooldown stretching. The quick training session with Louis's guards had turned into a much longer event than he'd anticipated. Though the activity had filled most of the afternoon, he thought Sabine might be happy for him to be a little worn out. She might get a full night's sleep if he was sufficiently exhausted. Assuming there wasn't a repeat of the night before when she'd enthusiastically initiated their fun. Perhaps they should make efforts to have solid nights of sleep now and then, but given their draw to one another, he just wasn't sure how possible it was.

He also thought Sabine might find it funny that, despite him keeping his shirt on, he had managed to draw a crowd of onlookers during his training. Faron had never doubted his appeal. He was well-built, conventionally handsome, and useful. His height, of course, always drew attention, as did the fact that he was an elf. Even in places where being an elf was safer, some humans looked upon elves with quite fantastical notions. Of course, Faron always tried to be fair in these matters. He knew his engagement to Sabine attracted some attention, but all the gawking was hard to ignore.

Stretching done, Faron used one of the supplied towels to wipe down his face and neck, then he untied his hair from the ponytail as he left the training yard. Damp with perspiration, he had yet another confirmation of his hard work. If he attracted more comments and stares, he didn't give any indication of noticing.

He waved to some of his sparring partners as he passed them and grimaced as he saw they looked a little worse off than he did. Training could, and often did, result in a few minor injuries like scrapes and pulled muscles, and it was not uncommon to be covered in grime and sweat if training grew a little intense. They would be okay when given a few hours and some rest, he was sure.

As he made it to the estate's entrance, he spotted Marcelle and Finn walking in the same direction, heads close together as they discussed something. "Good afternoon," he called out.

"Afternoon," Marcelle responded with a wave. His casual dress and long blond tresses hanging loosely about his face suggested he had some free time, and that free time being spent with Finn, who had a tendency to overwork, brought a smile to Faron's face. "You look like you've been quite busy today."

"Not really," Faron explained, though he knew he must look much less put together than he normally appeared. Sparring with different opponents all afternoon would leave him looking filthy. He just hoped they saw it as productive. "Sabine gave me some free time today since she's safely tucked away in Louis's office. I thought this was the best way to use it considering their expecting news of Sargarus making port in the next few days."

"From what she told me at lunch, his ship has been spotted in L'Orilan," Finn confirmed. "Some of Louis's contacts, and one of her friends who has a summer home in the city, both sent word this morning, so the inevitable will happen. Unless he immediately diverts, he will arrive in port within the coming days. What happens from there on is anyone's guess." Finn sighed, though gave no other indication of his mood.

"Do we know how many people he's brought with him?" Faron asked.

"A couple of ships," Marcelle replied. "That wouldn't be enough men to take the whole city, but he'll have more than enough protection while he's here."

Faron scowled. Sargarus didn't have a large force with him, but it didn't mean he couldn't do some damage. It also didn't mean more people wouldn't later join him. There could be more ships, and the people waiting on the other side of the mountain could cross at any time. "What about the army coming from the north?"

"They are still over the border in Azmarin," Finn replied. "Or they were as of two days ago. The mountain range may have slowed them, or they may be waiting. Either way, we don't have an update with that group."

"And when they do cross the border, we have no idea the direction they will travel or if they plan to meet up with Sargarus," Marcelle said with a shrug. "Logistically, the people at the mountain wouldn't be of use for weeks even if they crossed today."

"Great," Faron said. He rested his hands on his hips as he thought through the possibilities. In truth, Sargarus not having a full-blown army at his immediate disposal mattered very little if one could assemble within weeks. He'd have to consult Sabine. "Any other news?"

"We've also heard from the Nereid. Their king will be here in a few days' time. It ought to be an interesting meeting. Her Grace has never met with the Nereids before, nor have most of our travel party," Finn added. "But we knew they were coming. It was simply a matter of when."

Faron took a deep breath and pushed down the anxiety the news of Sargarus's pending arrival caused and decided to focus on the other news. "I've met one or two. They look different from the Sirene in characteristics, but I know Sabine will be happy to meet more Mers."

"We are more handsome," Marcelle added, causing Finn to laugh.

"Oh, good. We're more acquainted with the handsome Merpeople. No need to worry," Finn joked.

Faron laughed. "I can't say you're wrong. We all know the more handsome the person, the better the fighter." He shook his head in mirth but was glad Marcelle had made the joke either way. "Any other news?" he asked.

Marcelle shook his head. "Everything back home is fine according to every letter we've received. We get almost daily updates from Thaumas and others from the estate. Elodie, the head of the Weavers' Guild has been sending economic updates. Even Onfroi has come out of retirement to oversee the remaining estate guards while we are here."

"Prince Louis seems relatively calm. Her Grace was relaxing last we saw her," Finn said as he shrugged. "We're playing a waiting game."

Faron loathed waiting, especially when they were waiting on someone like King Sargarus, but there wasn't anything he could do. "I'm glad she's finding time to relax. The princess told Sabine she would ensure she had more time to herself, but with Sargarus so close..." Faron shrugged.

"Her Highness is quite skilled at diverting the prince's attention, which Her Grace will benefit from. She cannot be of use if she is overworked," Finn said. "Now, if you'll excuse us. We have some of our own downtime, and we would very much like to visit the tavern."

"Enjoy your time there," Faron said, giving them a nod of farewell as he went to find Sabine. He hoped she was in their suite, but if not, he would check the library and gardens, knowing she enjoyed both of those places. The walk to the room was quick, and Faron didn't run into anyone else he wanted to stop and speak with.

Reaching his destination, Faron reminded himself it was their room and he didn't have to knock. He laughed at himself, surprised that he had to continue to remind himself that they were together and shared spaces. Pushing open the door, he stepped inside and locked the door behind him before walking further into the room. "Sabine?" he called out.

"Yes, love?" Sabine called from the sitting area.

When Faron found her, he saw she'd taken up position on the long sofa. On the closest table sat a pot of tea and a tray of fruit, cheese, and some pastries. In her lap sat a book. She looked lovely and relaxed, and Faron couldn't help but remind himself of how lucky he'd been to find her.

"I wanted to see if you were here or if I needed to send out a search party," he joked, walking over to her then bending down for a kiss.

As she usually did, Sabine kissed him with an eagerness, though when the kiss broke, he saw her nose wrinkle, though she did not pull away from him. "You're covered in sweat," she observed. "Training either went very well or very poorly."

"It went well for me," Faron replied with a smile that was more of a grimace as he thought about the soldiers he'd trained with. "How was your afternoon?"

"Peaceful," Sabine replied. "Louis expects the arrival of the Nereid king in the next day or so based on the letter he received this morning. I believe he is looking forward to it."

"Finn mentioned that when I saw him and Marcelle on the way here," Faron said, straightening up. "I'm glad you had a peaceful afternoon. You deserve the rest." He looked down at himself, noting he looked disheveled and dirty. "I should bathe before my stench becomes unbearable."

"You should," Sabine agreed with a nod. "Though it's not too bad yet."

"Well, you're welcome to join me if you wish. Though I doubt that would help the smell."

Sabine laughed and shook her head. "Not in the state you're in. There's always later, though."

"I shall hold you to that," he said, leaning in for another kiss before striding to the washroom.

Faron soon had the water going and the large tub halfway full. While it was filling up, he gathered the items he'd need for a thorough wash before settling into the steaming water and allowing his body to relax. He wondered if adding some of Sabine's bath oils would aid in soothing his tired muscles. She insisted on the wonders of her various products, but he'd never experienced them for himself.

Faron gave himself ten minutes to rest in the water before he started washing up. He first scrubbed his long hair and then his body, sweat and grime falling away to reveal clean, tanned skin. Once done, he debated draining the water and refilling it, but he truly wanted to be with Sabine more than he wanted to relax in a bath. "Are you sure you don't want to join me?" he called out, already knowing the answer.

"Are you clean?" Sabine called back, though he heard her put her book aside, stand, and walk toward the back of their room. She soon appeared in the doorway, poised, beautiful, and absolutely everything he wanted.

"I just finished washing, so I would assume so. But you could check if you're unsure."

Sabine stepped further inside, though she remained just out of Faron's reach. "You should drain the tub if you wish me to join you."

Faron did as she instructed, unplugging the tub before standing as the water drained. He held his arms out a couple of inches from his middle, showing off his chest and torso as though presenting himself for inspection.

She stepped forward, still keeping her hands to herself, though Sabine took a long time to visually examine him. Still, vivid green eyes started at his collarbone and dipped lower. "I suppose you are acceptable."

"I'm glad to hear it. I would hate to displease you."

"You rarely do, my love," Sabine replied. "Now, if I am to join you, fill the tub. I need to undress."

"Do you need help undressing?" he asked as he turned the water back on. Faron studied the gown Sabine was in. He was almost sure this was one of the ones he wasn't allowed to rip up.

"I do not," she replied. She began working the fastenings on the front of the dress, though they'd been well concealed by the flourishes. When it was open, she shrugged out of the deep blue overdress, which, now that Faron saw her remove it, looked more like a jacket than a dress. She carefully removed the last few layers, leaving her stockings for last.

Faron watched Sabine closely, enjoying watching her strip down, so much so that he almost didn't turn off the water before it got too high. "You're stunning," he told her. Faron knew he'd told her as much more than once, but he would swear his mind somehow forgot until he had the opportunity to study her smooth, fair skin, the swell of her soft breasts accented by delicate pink nipples, the dip of her waist, and the perfect junction at her thighs.

"You are as well, you know," Sabine told him as her stockings were tossed aside. "So much so that you nearly take my breath away." She extended her hand to him, a silent request to be helped into the tub.

Faron took her smaller hand in his and helped her into the tub, only lowering himself once she had stepped inside.

She settled between his legs and leaned back against his chest, and Faron couldn't help but bury his nose in her hair.

"How are you feeling?" she asked. "Things are escalating, even if the escalation is slow and we're still not entirely sure how things will play out."

Faron laid his head back against the rim of the tub and stared at the ceiling as his arms wrapped about Sabine. "I know that you and Louis have several plans laid out for many different possible scenarios, but I hate the waiting and wish there were more hands-on things we could do. My mind keeps going through all the ways Sargarus being here could go badly, and a part of me wishes we were at the port with soldiers at our back to make it clear he isn't welcome here and make him leave these shores."

"Greeting him that way would be seen as a declaration of war, you know," Sabine replied. "But I know how worrying this is."

"I know. I just feel like this is going to end in a battle no matter what. Sargarus may be intelligent according to some, but he's also not known to be levelheaded or rational. He'll arrive expecting Grégoire and an alliance. What he's going to find will upset him greatly."

"No doubt," Sabine easily agreed. "And it is tempting to meet his arrival with force. We'd just be the instigator. He has to strike first. It's imperative."

"Doesn't mean I still don't like the idea," Faron joked, and it was a joke this time because Sabine was correct. Making Sargarus the aggressor in this was the right thing to do.

She turned her head to look up at him. "Try not to worry, my love. I know it is scary and frustrating, especially when you know what living under Sargarus is like. I promise I would not do anything to increase his chances here."

"I do not worry about you or Louis. I know you will both act with Fythias's best interest at heart. It's him I don't trust. I doubt there is anything you could do to make me question you."

"What about when I threaten to make you go live in the village?" she teased.

"Should you ever do so, I have to assume I would deserve it," Faron replied. He hoped to never give Sabine cause to do such a thing, but he knew he could be unbearable at times and wouldn't blame her for sending him away when need be.

"You would," Sabine agreed. "Now, try to quit worrying so much. Let's enjoy the water and maybe each other."

Faron nodded and closed his eyes. He would want her soon, no doubt. He spent very little time where some part of him wasn't focused on Sabine. For now, though, he was willing to relax and be in the moment with her.

Chapter Ten

The Nereid ruler, Aphros, along with a sizable travel party, arrived at Louis's estate, receiving the same fanfare Sabine and her party received when arriving weeks before. With his olive skin, brown wavy hair so dark it was almost black, and an intense pair of golden eyes, Aphros might have been mistaken as human if Sabine hadn't caught the red-and-blue luminescence on his skin marking where his scales would be were he not in his human form. Upon closer examination, she realized the golden eyes were not human-like at all. Instead, they reminded her of a cat.

Aphros appeared without any air of superiority or arrogance which sometimes colored the character of royalty. Sabine wouldn't have known he was even king had his fellow Nereid not addressed him as such. Still, his smile upon greeting them—framed in a dark beard matching his wavy locks—was one of sincerity and warmth. Despite his appreciation for the welcome, his exhaustion could not be hidden, and the ruler had requested rest and privacy until dinner. Louis, the ever-accommodating host, acquiesced, and Peronelle went about the task of seeing Aphros and his party to their allocated rooms.

When Sabine entered the dining room that evening holding onto Faron's arm as he escorted her to her seat, she noted the Nereid looked livelier and more energetic. The rest must have agreed with him. "Good evening, Your Grace," he greeted as Faron pulled out her chair, an intricately carved dark wood cushioned in a deep crimson velvety material. It matched the remaining furniture and the drapery around the great windows throughout the room. In the daylight, she thought the space might be quite stunning. "You're looking lovely this evening."

Sabine didn't think she looked exceptional. She'd dressed in dusky blue silk, paired with creamy lace and pearls, both on the bodice of her dress and dangling from her ears. Though her gown was undoubtedly fancier than what many dined in, given the company, she was suitably casual. "Thank you," she replied.

"And your escort looks well," Aphros added. Sabine agreed. Faron had dressed in the jacket she'd purchased for him in the market, and the red still looked quite nice on his tanned frame.

"Thank you," she replied. So far, only she, Aphros, and Faron had made it to the long dinner table, but Louis and Eloise often took their time in the evening, preferring to put Alaoin to bed together. She didn't mind playing hostess for the time. "Did you rest well this afternoon?" she asked him.

"I did," Aphros replied. "I'm afraid my time was already stretched thin before my departure. By the time I arrived, I craved a nap and some solitude. I'm sure you have experienced the same desires in your position."

"Indeed, I have," Sabine confirmed. "Thankfully, I am surrounded by wonderful support. They care for me so that I am better equipped to care for everything else."

Faron took the seat next to Sabine as she instructed him to do earlier when he had brought up his role for the night. He was, primarily, her fiancé and not her personal guard. Faron gave her a warm smile at her words and murmured, "We try. Sabine is not one to sit idly by when there is work to be done."

Aphros raised an eyebrow and the corners of his lips turned up in what would have been a smile with a little more effort. "I see," he said. "It is good to hear she has others to look after her, especially those who seem to so openly adore her."

Sabine smiled as Faron's cheeks darkened. It always amused her, knowing how obvious adoration would cause him to blush. "I don't think Faron and I have ever been particularly subtle about our mutual adoration. It's gotten worse since we got engaged."

"Engagements are good reasons to show more affection," Aphros insisted. "Tell me, when do you two plan on getting married?"

"Very soon. I'd like the ring first, though. The jeweler is set to be done in the next day or so," Faron answered.

"Then hopefully, we will have something to celebrate before Sargarus arrives," Aphros replied. He turned his gold eyes to a passing servant, thanking them for providing wine while they waited for Louis and Eloise to join.

Faron gave Aphros an approving glance for thanking the servant, even as he leaned over to Sabine and said, "So, should we marry as soon as we get your ring or wait a few hours?"

"I'd say we wait long enough to find an appropriate person to oversee the rites," Sabine whispered, grinning. "No longer, though. I am eager to make you my husband."

"I can work with that," Faron replied.

"Good," Sabine said, her heart swelling in anticipation. Although, as far as she was concerned, Faron was already serving as her husband. Making it official just felt all the more special, and it would provide Faron with the protection of her name, title, and estate.

The doors of the dining room opened, and in walked Louis and Eloise. In a show of respect, Sabine rose to her feet, as did her dinner companions. Eloise shot Sabine a warm smile as they reached the head of the table before turning to greet Aphros with Louis. Like Sabine, she'd dressed well, though casually. Her lilac gown, covered in a fine layer of intricate lace, served to emphasize her friendly warmth.

Louis's easy demeanor, relaxed shoulders, and affable expression showed a man who felt more confident in their immediate future. Sabine found she couldn't carry the same confidence, although she logically understood that they were in a much better strategic and political position than Sargarus was. Having the home advantage didn't always guarantee success, but logically, she knew they had the upper hand.

Louis motioned for the group to resume their seats, and as they did so, more staff joined the room, circling the table with more drinks and the first dinner course. With Aphros present, seating had changed from the days prior. The Nereid leader sat to Louis's right. Eloise, who sat on her husband's left, had a seat across from Sabine, which made discussion easier.

"Did you enjoy having time to yourself?" Eloise asked Sabine. Eloise's bright smile indicated the princess had very much enjoyed some downtime with her husband and son.

"Indeed, I did," Sabine replied. "It has been quite some time since I had a whole day of leisure."

Eloise beamed with pleasure. "We shall have to find ways for you to have more time before this escalates any further." She turned to Faron. "And you must be her Faron."

Faron laughed. "Yes, I am Sabine's Faron."

Sabine liked the way he and Eloise framed their relationship, though Sabine would have just as easily designated herself as belonging to Faron. "I think I will require you to exclusively refer to yourself in such a way from now on," she teased.

"I can do that," Faron said without hesitation. "It is not as though I think of myself in any other way."

"I have no doubt," Sabine replied, pleased.

"You two are adorable." Eloise turned to Aphros. "Aren't they just adorable?" she asked him before the smile fell from her lips and her eyes took on a soft sympathetic look that Sabine didn't understand.

Aphros smiled despite whatever faux pas Eloise committed and nodded. "Indeed. They are quite suited for one another. They should count themselves lucky. Many never find someone they pair with quite as well."

"I like to think we are as well," Faron agreed as his hand settled on her leg under the table. He gave it a gentle but absolutely possessive squeeze, which sent shivers all the way to her center. The small gesture was enough to distract her from whatever happened between Eloise and Aphros for now, though she briefly met Faron's gaze with a promise-filled expression. Faron's eyes darkened, and he leaned closer as if to whisper something in her ear. A servant accidentally interrupted them to inquire what Faron had been drinking. He quickly told them tea and turned back to Sabine, but the moment was gone. Sabine intended to capture it once again.

Food and drink arrived on the table, with each item looking more and more delicious. Sabine, who always appreciated good food, was pleased to find that not every item was seafood. Perhaps Eloise, or a cook, had been informed that Sabine preferred only the freshest of fish and crab for her meals.

"Meri visited the kitchens," Faron said quietly, earning a nod of understanding from Sabine.

Dinner passed leisurely, and Sabine listened as Aphros talked about his people and their lands. The Nereid kingdom sat on the eastern coast of Coralia, composed of a small series of islands and a larger kingdom below the water. Although they resemble the Sirene in terms of having separate land and water forms, Aphros made it seem as though Nereid consistently remained more humanoid no matter where they dwelled.

"It's so interesting both the Sirene and Nereid are considered Merpeople when you're both very different races," Louis remarked as plates were cleared from the table.

"I think so," Aphros said. "It would be like claiming elves, humans, and dwarves were all the same sort of being because they all dwell on land. The Nereid and Sirene are quite different from one another, and not only in appearance."

"I'm sure there is someone out there who does view elves, humans, and dwarves as all the same type of being. We just haven't met them yet," Faron said casually. "People can be tremendously stupid. Especially when it comes to anything deemed magical."

"Oh, no doubt," Aphros agreed, nodding deeply. "It's just humans who tend to lump everyone else together while separating themselves. At least, it's that way in much of Coralia."

"I lived there most of my life. Humans have reigned supreme there for quite some time, and of course, now humans with magic are getting ostracized. The othering never ceases to amaze me. Thankfully, I have not found that to be true here," Faron said. "A noble or two may wish it to be so, but they are in the minority, thank the Spirits."

"Indeed," Sabine agreed. "And we do not want such sentiments to spread any more than they have already."

"And we'll not let them," Louis added. He was leaning back in his chair now, Eloise's hand in his own. "I swear on my life. Fythias has always been safe for all, and it will continue to be as long as I breathe."

Eloise shot Louis a dark look at his words. The hard set of her eyes and her clenched jaw showed she agreed with him, but the heat of her stare equally demonstrated she didn't like him swearing on his life.

Aphros smiled. "Let us hope it does not come to that. Your son, I think, is a bit too young to be king."

"Much too young, and I do not wish to be a widow," Eloise added on.

Aphros gave another pained smile, and Sabine suddenly understood. It made her place her hand on top of Faron's and her fingers close around his. Faron turned his hand and laced their fingers together. He gave her hand a small squeeze. She glanced over and studied his expression, stoic and distant, and Sabine knew Faron also caught on.

"I do not recommend becoming widowed if one can help it," Aphros replied. "There is much to attend to beyond personal grieving, especially when one is so high ranking. There is scarcely time for grief, or so that has been my experience these last few months." He shrugged as though what he was personally dealing with didn't matter much, though the distance in his gaze contradicted his movements.

"I don't know anyone who wants to become widowed, but there are things we cannot help," Faron said softly.

"A great many things," Aphros agreed, nodding.

It looked as if Faron had a question, but before he could ask it, Eloise clapped her hands. "Let us find something happier to discuss. Anything?" She looked around, her eyes meeting Sabine's and growing round with silent pleading.

"I believe you are our charming hostess," Aphros said, sounding far more encouraging than his expression suggested. His graciousness prevented any of the telling signs of anger or offense from showing on his handsome face. Even the bright gold of his eyes, which could hint at coolness, showed an understanding. "What topic would please you?"

Eloise tried to hide her blush and her sudden awkwardness behind a napkin. "Well, my favorite topics as of late would include Alaoin," she said in an overly cheery voice. She dabbed at nonexistent spots on her face before finally lowering her napkin. "There is also my work with the children in town." She looked at Louis for help.

Louis nodded encouragingly, his golden curls bouncing boyishly. "You do marvelous work with the children, and I hear you've recruited our dear Sabine to assist while she is here."

"I have," Eloise confirmed, her smile growing less nervous now. "I was hoping we could go in a few days, so long as everything works out."

"I don't see why we couldn't spare her," Louis easily agreed. In all probability, Louis would have gone along with his wife in that instance had Sabine been needed or not. "You just tell me when you would like to go, and I'll make sure she's available. I will even keep Faron entertained while you're both gone if needed."

Faron's hand tightened on Sabine's, and she couldn't help but wonder why being alone with the soon-to-be king would cause such a reaction.

"I was thinking we could go the day after tomorrow. Maybe around midafternoon?" Eloise suggested.

"I think that would be a wonderful time," Sabine agreed, pulling her attention away from Faron.

Eloise's grin grew to twice its size at Sabine's agreement. "I'm glad you think so."

"I would not mind helping if more help was needed," Aphros offered. "I find I need distractions quite often."

The princess blinked as her smile faltered, but it soon returned, brighter than even before. "You are more than welcome to join us, and I know the children will love seeing you."

"Then I shall," Aphros replied.

"If you need a guard, I volunteer. Otherwise, I will be happy to give you three time together," Faron offered.

Sabine knew it took a lot for him to not just declare himself their escort. She squeezed his hand. "If you wish to come, I would not object," Sabine said.

"I would be happy to go with you, but if you want time with your new friends without my hovering, I support that as well," Faron replied.

Aphros chuckled then pushed his dark hair from his face. The flickering candlelight spread along the table highlighted the red-and-blue luminescence on his hand. "You're so obviously an engaged couple."

"Aren't they?" Eloise said, laughing.

Sabine caught Faron's blush before he hid it in his water glass. She couldn't help but smile in amusement. "I think it's rather a good thing to be so openly adored."

"You are easy to adore," Faron said after taking a drink.

"I would agree," Louis interjected. "It is one of the reasons I think we are quite lucky to have Her Grace on our side." With the meal ended and Louis's praise, it seemed he was ready to do something beyond sitting at a table. "Now that we are full to bursting, why don't we retreat to somewhere more comfortable and play a game or something."

"That's a wonderful idea," Eloise said as Louis stood to help her stand from her chair.

Aphros rose from his seat. "I am game," he decided.

Faron and Sabine stood, and Sabine took Faron's arm when it was offered, saying, "This ought to be fun."

Chapter Eleven

Night drew on, accented by the faint light of the moon shining through the curtain gaps at the window and the melodic chirping of crickets on the grounds below. Now and then, soft steps echoed from the corridor or whispered, indecipherable conversation penetrated the heavy doors. Courteous and attentive, the staff who worked at the Maison de L'Harmonie carefully avoided disruption so late in the evening.

Sabine sighed contentedly, tucked against Faron's side as they waited for sleep to settle over them. Even with the threat of war upon them and so much uncertainty about their futures, Sabine could push away everything but the two of them with little effort as they simply existed in the same space, naked and perfect.

Her fingers brushed through the light dusting of dark curly hair running the length of Faron's torso, feeling the way his chest rose and fell with each breath. She smiled to herself, picturing decades of these moments with him.

The sex they shared—hot, raw, and frequent—could never replace these moments.

Only weeks before had she thought she'd never again spend her time pressed against Faron, leisurely passing time between rounds of lovemaking. At the time, she had not realized the true depth of sorrow associated with the possibility, although she'd been keenly aware of the engulfing sadness she'd carried. Thank the spirits she'd never face such turmoil again, and they had the support of not only their household, but that of their future king, queen, and allied Nereid neighbors based on their earlier dinner.

Sabine opened her eyes and studied the braid of Faron's hair she wore around her wrist, representing their engagement. She'd be happy to marry as soon as they had the ring because waiting until things were more settled could take months, if not years. The idea of joining themselves together not only gave Sabine something to look forward to, but it created a familial tie she'd lost long ago. Though she loved Meri, Lisbeth, Finn, and the others, their relative positions in the world would always present certain limitations. There were none with Faron.

"You are unusually quiet," she said after a long period, which might have been seconds or hours. "Quiet and contemplative."

"Am I not allowed?" he asked, his voice rumbling with a mix of humor and warded-off sleep.

"When it pleases me," she replied, glancing up with mischievous amusement.

"Of course," he countered, rolling his eyes. "Spirits forbid anything happen with motivations other than your pleasure."

Sabine laughed. "My pleasure is quite important. I am always in a better mood when my pleasure receives adequate attention."

"I have noticed," Faron replied, and he playfully moved so he was hovering over her, his long black hair draping around them. "Should I take your conversation topic as a request?"

She laughed then pulled him down for a kiss. "It hasn't even been an hour," she replied against his lips.

"More than enough time," he murmured as he began kissing along her jaw.

Sabine moaned softly as her hand ran up his neck and into his hair. The returned rumble in his throat had her fingers rubbing tiny circles against his scalp. As they fell back into lovemaking, with no concern for anything beyond their bed, minutes and hours ticked by without regard.

Later, they lay on top of the bed linens, breathing heavily and covered in a thin layer of perspiration. Her breasts, sensitive and lightly bruised from his mouth, did nothing to distract her from the cravings she felt low in her stomach. The space between her thighs pulsed from multiple encounters, and she doubted they'd wait long before finding one another again. "I'm starting to think it's not elves. You are just insatiable."

"We can interrogate the next elf we come across if you'd like," Faron replied, laughing lightly.

"You can," Sabine replied, turning her head to grin at him. "I am a duchesse. I'm expected to show more class."

"Oh, of course, Your Grace," Faron teased. He turned on his side and draped an arm around her middle, pulling her close enough he could bury his nose in her caramel hair. His fingers began tracing a teasing path from her sternum, down to her navel, and back up. Sabine laughed, content to enjoy him so close, though she shot him a knowing look.

"You really are an asshole," she said.

"I am," Faron readily admitted against her hair as his hand dipped lower before returning up. "I can only be what

I am, Sabine, but I'd more than suggest you'd be quite disappointed if I changed."

"I would be," she acknowledged. "Your character, your decisiveness, your dedication to what you deem important... All of it draws me to you. If some people read your actions as asshole-ish, that is on them."

"As long as you love it, want it, I don't care what anyone else thinks about me."

"I do, no doubt," she promised. "Though with the reaction you've gotten from some people since we met, it is highly possible your tendencies to not play nicely might leave me a widow."

"I did nothing to earn Tristian's or Grégoire's ire. Both men were just jealous I have something they never will." They both knew Faron did not mean unconditional love. Neither man had cared for such things. Sabine, specifically, with her money, title, influence, and land, would be cherished by such monsters as a much grander prize. "As for your widowhood, I'd not wish for either of us to face such a future," Faron continued. The amusement left his voice, leaving him sounding contemplative and perhaps uncertain. His traveling hand also paused, resting on her stomach. "But I know eventually one of us will be alone... To be honest, I'm not sure how King Aphros has survived without his queen. It's obvious from the little he spoke of her tonight while we played cards that she was his entire world. Same as you are mine."

"His sadness is palpable," Sabine acknowledged. "I cannot imagine what he must think and feel." Nor did she want to. Sabine had lived a lovely, full life before ever laying eyes on Faron. Now that she had him, she didn't want to contemplate an existence without him.

"All we know for sure is he's hurting. He hides it well, but his eyes are so very sad. Even when he's joking with Louis and Eloise." Faron's hand started moving again. "I think his need to protect his people might be the one reason he hasn't stopped and just laid down and joined her." He referenced the way Aphros had spoken about his people the few times the topic had come up after dinner. Eloise had done an admirable job of keeping them from talking business, but questions about the Nereid had come up, and Aphros spoke of his people with love and a deep sense of obligation.

"He's got to be in a terrible place," Sabine agreed. "The loss of his wife is recent, and the Nereid are being targeted by Coralia and possibly Azmarin. I don't know how he keeps pushing through so much pain."

"Obligation, more than likely. A change in leadership could cause more issues and give more ground to his people's murderers," Faron speculated.

"Perhaps. Still, he's so obviously in pain."

"Very much so. As would I be if something were to happen to you." Faron gave her a sad smile and Sabine knew where his mind went.

"I don't plan on anything happening to me for quite a long time," she said, though she knew there was only so much control someone had over their life. She also knew he often thought about how their lives didn't align. "What I do plan on doing is collecting my ring in the morning and promptly finding someone to marry us."

Faron smiled. "Apparently, there are two places where we can find a priestess in town. I'm sure someone will be free to see us wed."

"Good," Sabine declared. "Then we will marry, and we will happily share the next several decades together."

"I will be happy with the time granted us. I will do everything in my power to make sure you never regret marrying me," Faron promised.

"I don't see how I ever could," Sabine replied. "You are who I want to spend every single one of my days with. I know I have fewer than you, but I plan to make the most of them."

Faron lifted the hand tracing Sabine's stomach to run down her cheek. "So do I, even if I know I am destined to spend decades alone after I lose you."

The topic had been brought up enough times for Sabine to know how deeply ingrained the fear remained for her fiancé, but she could do nothing to change the differences between human and elf. "Assuming someone or something doesn't bring your life to an early end, it is absolutely certain elves live longer than humans," Sabine gently acknowledged. "If we both live according to our individual life expectancy, you will outlive me by decades. There is no getting around that. Nor the fact that I will look much older than you very quickly. Those are realities that come with our relationship." She shifted so she could face him rather than let Faron hide his emotions in her hair.

Faron made an unhappy noise, but he nodded, confirming her statement. "There are magics which could link our lives, ensure our lifespans are more aligned, but they are dangerous. I'd never put you in that sort of danger."

"The tales suggest many who undergo the magical processes to link lives often leave injured or die," Sabine agreed. She imagined if she wanted to pursue those magics, Faron would not want her to.

"We could think of it as a last resort measure, then," he said with a weak grin.

Though he joked, Sabine could see the matter weighing on him, though she had to assume he pondered their reality often enough to have considered magical options before now. "What scares you the most?" she asked.

"The idea of living without out for even a moment," Faron replied in a near whisper. "Let alone the possibility of a near century."

No surprises came with the answer, but then, neither did any real answer. "Why do you find it scary?"

"Because I cannot—do not want to picture a world without you in it by my side. I could not tolerate one breath without you, Sabine."

She reached up and cupped his cheek. "You lived in that very world for decades before meeting me, my love. I am certain you could manage it again," she said, trying to comfort him. "Could you not manage again?"

Faron sighed and shook his head as much as he could while lying on his side. "My world before you was bleak, empty, colorless, and devoid of joy. I looked forward to very little, and I existed to get myself to the next day. Life after you will not be worth living."

"By then, I am certain you would find other things to bring you joy," she pointed out. "You did say you wanted children, after all. Surely whatever children we do have would want you around as long as possible."

Faron closed his eyes as if pained. "Our children would be longer-lived being half-elf, but my heart would ache every day. You will take most of my soul with you when you eventually pass. I would be of little use to them."

"Had I any control over these things, I would never let you suffer. That our lifespans are so out of alignment is not ideal. I will grow old and die while you are still young, but there is little we can do about any of that. So we are left with only a few options, and you seem wary of pursuing those."

"This is why I try not to dwell on such thoughts, even if sometimes I can't help it. I can either live our every moment together dreading your loss, thereby losing you long before you are truly gone, or I can live each day with you in the here and now, making the most of the time we are together. I wish to make the most of the years we are granted," Faron said. Though his voice was firm, his eyes held great sorrow and promise.

Sabine remained in his arms, quiet and thoughtful. She hated the sadness she detected in him, knowing she could not change it. "Do you truly wish to magically link our lives?"

"If there was a way that didn't require a great sacrifice or potential harm, yes," he answered honestly.

"Every possible spell I know of could lead to death," she replied. "But if it is something you want, I will pursue it with you once we can return home."

"I would like to at least look, and if there is nothing, then we will have tried."

She nodded. "Then we have a plan."

"Thank you," he whispered once more against her hair.

Chapter Twelve

As it had upon every visit prior, the busy village welcomed Sabine, Aphros, and Eloise with pleasant merchants and wonderful smells of baking bread, fragrant flowers, and the smoky essence of leatherwork and blacksmithing. As discussed, the three had come into town, along with a handful of Louis and Eloise's staff, to spend time with and hand out supplies to the village orphans. Faron had opted to remain behind, though Sabine knew he hadn't been happy with the decision. Faron was, without question, protective over her to the point of obsession, but he respected her enough to know she was not always in need.

Although all three of them ranked highly, each had dressed simply, prepared to experience potential hard work and physical interaction with others. Eloise's gown, a rich burgundy, held no trace of diamond or pearl, and her long hair was pulled back into a simple plait. Sabine had dressed similarly in a shade of green, as usual, though her own braid had been twisted and pinned into a neat bun on the back of her head.

Aphros, on the other hand, had done little to alter his appearance since the day of his arrival. A shirt, overcoat, trousers, and boots, all in shades of browns and blues, had been sufficient for him. Sabine wondered if the decision was based on consistent simplicity of style or if Nereid simply dressed differently.

Word of their visit had reached the village by early morning, and while they didn't exactly receive a parade, merchants stood by carts and near shop windows, bowing and waving as they passed. "Good morning!" Eloise called out to an older woman who swept the doorstep leading into her shop.

The woman beamed and nodded her head respectfully. "Good morning, Your Highness," the woman returned.

"I believe you are quite beloved," Aphros observed as they moved further into the market. Despite the mishap at their shared dinner two nights ago, he gave no sign of lingering resentment or upset. Indeed, his visit to the village had him looking brighter than Sabine expected.

"Perhaps," Eloise replied. "We try our best to do right by our people. It's created quite positive relationships. I'm certain Sabine's people are just as friendly."

"They are friendly," Sabine replied with a soft laugh. "But I have had quite a few interesting conversations, especially with the head of the Weavers' Guild."

"Guild discussions usually are memorable," Aphros quipped as they continued walking.

The orphanage, a building Sabine had not paid much attention to on her last visit, sat perched on a hill just beyond the market square. In truth, Sabine thought it resembled a boarding house, right down to how well it was kept, and she would have continued assuming it was lodging of some kind had Eloise not pointed it out.

"There are about twenty children living there now," Eloise explained. "Only a few infants, thank goodness. I've promised them a delicious lunch and some stories."

They climbed the small hill without much fuss, and Sabine found herself thankful she'd worn sturdier shoes than she might have for walking around the chateau.

Upon reaching the door, they were let inside by a young woman by the name of Jacqueline. Jacqueline's thick black hair had been cut to the shoulders, and she wore two face-framing braids. A practical style for someone who, no doubt, filled her days with chasing children. "The children are so excited to see you," she shared as she closed the door. "The older ones are in the schoolroom, and the younger ones are with Claudine, waking up from naps."

"Wonderful," Eloise said. "We can make sure lunch is set up and ready for them once lessons are done and they are all properly awake."

"That would be perfect," Jacqueline said. "Thank you so much, and we will join you shortly."

As Eloise had been there before, there was no need for a tour of the building. Instead, the princess led Sabine and Aphros past a toy-filled playroom toward the dining room, the chateau staff following behind. A long table with bench seating sat in the middle of the room, and at its center sat a larger vase filled with wildflowers which might very well have been picked that morning.

The table, composed of oak, must have been decades old judging by the sleek, worn surface, but it was clean and in good repair. Counters and open cabinets sat around the space, holding dishes and cutlery for easy access. The dishes appeared to be made of sturdy materials, tin and clay, which were easy to clean and harder to break. A swinging door on the right side of the room led to the kitchen, though they were not in need of that right this minute.

Eloise instructed the staff to aid in laying out the food items, while Sabine and Aphros grabbed plates, cutlery, and cups to sit around the table. As dishes were placed along the middle, Sabine thought the residents of the home might have days' worth of special meals here, though so far, everything within the home suggested they were well cared for.

Chicken, fruit, bread and cheese, along with hand pies and stews made their way to the table. Desserts, of which there were plenty, were temporarily housed on the counter closest to the kitchen door. "I suppose if dessert were well within reach, the children might forgo the rest of the food," Sabine said in amusement.

"Indeed," Eloise agreed. "It has happened before, although I do not think it a great tragedy to indulge in treats now and then."

Eloise, Sabine thought, must be quite the popular patroness.

A rolling, thunderous sound began echoing throughout the house, and Aphros grinned. "I believe the children are coming."

He was right. The door to the dining room swung open, and a swarm of excited children burst inside, many of which immediately swarmed Eloise, hugging her excitedly. "You came!" a young girl of around seven or eight exclaimed. "It's been forever."

"It has," Eloise said with a laugh. "But I brought friends and lots of gifts to make up for it."

Only then did the children seem to notice Sabine and Aphros, and each received their own groups of giggling, happy children. Hugs and promises for a fun day were

exchanged for several long minutes before the adults were able to help the children to their seats.

Jacqueline and an older woman Sabine assumed must be Claudine went around the table, helping younger children spoon portions of each dish on their plates, while Eloise and Sabine spoke with the older children, making sure each had plenty on their plate, plenty to drink, and sufficient forks, spoons, and napkins while they ate. The children chatted with one another and with their adults, laughing and proclaiming how delicious their lunch was. Aphros, who had been helping refill glasses, was invited by a small ginger-haired boy to sit with them. Aphros gave in to the request, and he had a group of children laughing as he told stories about the Nereid.

"The Nereid have a different form on land than they do underwater," he explained to them. "We have more fins, for example, so that we can swim more easily." He ran his fingers along his forearm. "See here? This is where one of the fins appears."

"Oh!" the boy responded gleefully.

"And your skin sparkles!" said a lanky girl with a mass of beautiful curls.

"It does," Aphros agreed. "You can see my scales in the light, even in human form." Again, he ran a finger along his arm, pointing them out. "I guess you've never met a Nereid before?"

The children shook their heads, and Aphros was bombarded with several more questions from them. Those involving his scales, his eyes, and what his castle looked like.

Sabine went to Eloise's side. The princess stood near one of the counters, her hands clasped together in pure joy as she watched the children. "I do believe Aphros may be a new favorite," Sabine said, amused.

"I think so," Eloise agreed. "He is good with children. I should see if he would like to spend some time with Alaoin."

"I think Alaoin would enjoy having someone else to dote on him," Sabine agreed.

"Indeed, he would. Alaoin has never met a stranger," Eloise said, laughing again.

Sabine thought Faron would have enjoyed being here with the children, and if there was time, she would bring him here to meet them. It brought to mind their discussions of children and how absolutely certain she was that her giant elf of a future husband would be the most gentle, doting father.

"Shall we invite Faron next time?" Eloise asked, smiling knowingly.

"I think so," Sabine agreed. "I would be very interested in the children's response to a very tall elf."

As the children finished eating, Eloise, Sabine, and the others gathered empty plates and cups, placing them in a washing basin which was taken by Jacqueline into the kitchen when they were done. The older kids stood from the table, grabbed rags, and ran them along the table and bench seating once the food was put away. Routine, it seemed, had the kids happily working to leave the dining room in much the same way it was found. She heard no complaints and saw no frowns, just happy exchanges while the chores were quickly attended to.

As they worked, Eloise took the time to address the room. "I want to thank you all for inviting us here today. Our lunch has been wonderful, and I have a lovely afternoon planned for all of you. My friends, King Aphros and Duchesse Sabine have never been here before, so let's make sure they have a good time with all of you!" she encouraged.

Sabine laughed as a couple of girls came to take her hands and led her to what they insisted was the library. She could guess how her afternoon would be spent.

Chapter Thirteen

Sabine had been in a wonderful mood when she returned from the village with Eloise and Aphros the prior night. Although she'd been exhausted from playing with children most of the day, her heart had been light, and she'd felt rather accomplished. As Faron had led her back into the village on the more selfish task of picking up her ring, he hoped she would be just as joyful.

Faron stared at the delicate emerald ring as the jeweler carefully slipped it onto Sabine's finger. The intricate silver band, formed into a metallic plait, and the bright green gem surrounded by a clear cluster of tiny sparkling diamonds sat perfectly on her small, delicate hand. Some part of his brain recognized the jeweler asking Sabine about the ring's fit. He saw her gently shake her hand to demonstrate it wouldn't fall off. He was also aware that Sabine may have also called his name. It wasn't that he was ignoring her or anything. Faron just found that he couldn't take his eyes from the ring which stood as proof, even more so than the lock of hair around her wrist, that Sabine was actually going to marry him. This amazing, kind, beautiful woman would be his, and he would be hers.

His dazed smile faltered as a small voice in the back of his mind said the wedding would be a disaster if he froze up from shock. He couldn't respond to moments like this by letting his mind wander, barely present to experience all the special moments they could share. Still, as he blinked and continued looking at the ring, he couldn't help but feel incredibly thankful to have her wear a symbol of their love, their lives, and the time they would have together. Faron knew it was stupid, but everything felt so much more real in that moment.

"Faron?" Sabine asked, drawing him back into the moment. "What do you think?" she said, a little impatient with clearly having repeated herself.

Faron shook his head, but he knew he had a dopey look on his face when he looked up at Sabine with the way her eyes softened. "It's beautiful."

"I think so too," she agreed happily.

"Wonderful," the jeweler said, clapping his hands together. "I am so glad the two of you approve. I know you wanted something delicate, and I thought it would suit her well."

Faron took Sabine's hand in his own and studied the ring. He gently rotated her hand from left to right, but not far enough to hurt her. "Delicate but strong. It's perfect." He looked back up at Sabine as he said so.

"I think so," she replied, practically beaming. "You did quite well."

"Thank you, but it's your beauty that helps it stand out," Faron replied easily, and he meant it. The ring would be a plain bauble on anyone else. Not that he could ever look at anyone else.

"She is quite a beauty," the jeweler interjected, his lips wide in a pleased smile. "If you are both pleased, we can settle up, and you can be on your way. I know your friends will want to see it."

Faron nodded and removed a pouch from his belt and placed it on the counter. "This is the rest of the agreed upon amount with a little more for a job well done."

The jeweler picked up the bag and balanced it in his hand as though weighing it. He nodded his approval, showing the wispy black hair barely covering his shiny head. "It has been a pleasure working with you both. I wish you joy in your marriage."

"Thank you. Have a good day, sir," Faron responded and offered his arm to Sabine to escort her out into the warm sunshine. Despite the mid-morning hour, the square was filled with people. The scent of baking bread filled the air, and a pleasant breeze tempered the bright sunlight. Truly, the day felt perfect. He looked down at Sabine, his heart filled with such deep love for her. "So, should we find a temple now, or did you wish to show off your ring first?"

He was met with raised brows and playfully puckered lips. "I want to marry you," she said simply.

"Then let us find a temple." Faron, thankful for his unusual height, looked around at the market trying to determine their direction. "From what I understand, two separate temples are willing to perform services. One is close to the estate, and the other resides closer to the outskirts." He pointed down the street that would take them back to the estate and then the road that would take them to the other temple. "Pick a direction, and we'll be off."

Surprisingly, Sabine chose the one further from Louis's estate. "I think we'd have fewer interventions from well-wishers," she explained.

"Very true. Though, I am fairly sure we will be coming back to a small party no matter what. I heard Meri asking if she could bake a cake this morning." Faron shook his head, glad their friends were happy for them. He, however, hoped they kept things sedate.

"They are welcome to celebrate. Marriage is a celebratory occasion." Sabine's tone held excitement and yearning. "But I am not terribly concerned about appeasing others today. This is about us."

Faron looked down at Sabine as he guided her down the cobblestone path. "It is about us. But why do you sound wishful? Did you want a large wedding?" He worried if he was robbing her of something grander, something more befitting of a duchesse.

She raised an eyebrow, quietly questioning his reasoning. "If I wanted a large wedding, I would have one. I simply have no desire to worry about pleasing anyone else's desires today beyond our own."

"There was a yearning in your tone, and it made me curious." He shrugged. "I thought it best to check that this was the way you truly wanted to go about getting married."

Sabine stopped and released his arm so she could turn to face him. "I want to marry you with as much expediency as possible. Don't be silly and make me toss you from the estate so soon after becoming my husband."

Faron laughed, unable to help himself. "You would make your poor husband sleep at an inn of questionable repute on the night of your wedding?"

"If he annoyed me enough, absolutely."

"Well then, I shall endeavor to be on my best behavior for the rest of the day." They continued their stroll through the village, pointing out various points of interest.

As they got closer to the temple, Faron realized they'd entered the less prosperous section of town. In Myrefall, the region of Coralia in which he'd been born and raised, the distinction between wealth and poverty existed in striking contrast. One could stroll into the next street, finding tiled roofs turning to straw and thatch. Brick and stone walls into mud and plaster. Clean, well-maintained cobbled streets would give way to packed dirt, littered with waste and garbage.

Here though, it took a moment to fully realize they'd left the more affluent side of town. The buildings kept the same sturdy brick and tiled roofs. The streets, cobblestone in good repair, remained clean and free of unpleasant smells. Only the presence of smaller homes sitting closely together gave away the subtle change. To Faron, it showed how much Louis and Eloise cared for their people and how much time and money they poured into the town directly under their care. He couldn't help but feel even more hopeful than before. "Louis has done a good job taking care of his people," he finally said to Sabine.

She nodded. "There are many reasons why I support him. His treatment of his people remains one of the main ones."

"I can see that now. Not that I doubted you before."

"The unfortunate thing is not every village surrounding an estate like his can afford to keep things so nice. My village, for example, benefits from the fishing industry and lumber. We have wealth not everyone has," Sabine explained.

"Taking care of your people, making sure they have their necessities met if nothing else, is the least a noble should do," Faron said as he looked about. They should be approaching the temple soon from what he'd been told, but so far, he hadn't seen the normally tall, decorated building he was so used to.

Faron slowed as they got closer to where the temple should be, yet nowhere were the tall spires, the stained-glass windows, and the large, solid wooden doors with expertly carved designs he'd expected. Instead stood a modest-sized two-story brick and stone building. It looked just like every other in the area except it had a larger yard, and if one took another look, statues of the Mother were placed carefully in alcoves and around the building. There was also a small cluster of trees with an altar for the Spirit. By those trees sat an older woman with ebony skin and long, white and pink curls, dressed in priestess regalia and surrounded by children as she read to them.

"I guess this is the temple," Faron said, slightly shocked.

"It appears so," Sabine confirmed, her lips turned upward in a smile. "We should let her finish reading."

"We should," he agreed and led Sabine to the other side where it looked like a small garden grew. It took a few minutes for him to realize they could have entered the temple to see if there was another priestess available, causing him to laugh out loud.

"What?" Sabine asked as she studied the ivy creeping along the garden.

"I realized we could have just gone inside to see if there is another person available," Faron explained. He motioned to the nearby doors, which stood open, giving him a peek inside. "Would you like to go in?"

Sabine looked up from the garden and to him. "Of course."

Faron guided Sabine into the temple, and while he knew he shouldn't have been surprised to see the inside was as modest as the outside, he was. It seemed as if the entire temple was set up to help the people and not just a place of worship. There was an area for congregation and the normal large statue of the Mother, her hands raised in subjugation, her face hidden. Scattered around the statue, women in various robes marking their rank within the temple worked. Some sat with visitors while others swept and cleaned. Faron leaned down and whispered, "Which one looks the least busy to you?"

"I think they all look equally busy," Sabine replied. "Do you want me to ask someone for you? You seem awfully indecisive. Not getting cold feet, are you?"

"No! Spirits, no." Faron gave Sabine a warm smile and admitted, "The priestesses in Myrefall were not kind when interrupted, even if they weren't doing anything important. I am happy to get their attention."

"You are a troublemaker," Sabine mused with a playful grin. She proceeded toward the priestess sweeping the floor near a hearth surrounded by candles, grabbing Faron's hand and pulling him along.

Faron happily followed Sabine, eyes on the priestess in case she got upset when Sabine interrupted her cleaning. He'd studied the religion of the Mother back in Coralia, but he didn't worship her. He believed in the Spirits, even if he didn't worship the way he should.

The priestess paused in her cleaning once they both stood in front of her, and up close, he saw she was young and so blonde that her hair was nearly white. "Can I help you?" she asked in a girlish voice.

"We would like to be married. Right now," Faron said kindly.

The younger girl smiled, straightening a bit. "Oh!" she declared, her voice still squeaky. "Of course! Come with me. You can speak with our high priestesses. She likes to oversee marriage rites."

"Thank you. We would love to see her." Faron gave Sabine an amused smile. They followed along behind the young woman, listening as she nervously pointed out the few paintings. They finally stopped at an open door leading into a modestly decorated office.

"Please go inside," the young woman invited. "The head priestess will join you shortly."

"Thank you for escorting us," Faron said. He and Sabine entered the office, and upon spotting the two plush seats in front of the large writing desk, Faron pulled one out and motioned for Sabine to sit.

They waited for only a couple of minutes before the woman from the garden entered the room. Her ebony skin looked even darker in the dimmer light, and silvery curls showed from beneath her head wrap.

Faron stood, a habit drilled into him from childhood, and he barely stopped himself from bowing. "Good day, priestess," he greeted.

"Good day," the woman said as she circled around to her desk chair. She took a seat and folded her hands on the table. "I understand you wish to marry."

"We do," Faron said, looking over at Sabine and giving her a warm smile. "Right away if possible."

"I do not think it will be a problem," the woman replied. "I see you are an elf and human. What rites do you want in the ceremony?"

Faron thought about that, as they hadn't discussed which rites to use. Looking at Sabine, he said, "We did the engagement in the way of the elves. I am happy to go a different direction if you wish."

"I have no preference," Sabine replied. "My parents held many different beliefs. I share the same sentiments."

Faron nodded and stored away the new bit of knowledge he had about Sabine's parents. "We would like the ceremony done in the elvish fashion if you wouldn't mind," Faron said to the priestess. He considered what he knew of marriage rites under the Mother, which admittedly, was very little. He understood the version of the Mother worshiped in Coralia had been corrupted into something ugly, but he'd never sought out information about how Fythias viewed her.

"Certainly," the priestess replied. "We can do that for you."

Faron looked down at Sabine's hand where the ring sat nestled on her perfect finger. "I would like to request to replace the exchanging of tokens with the giving of the rings. Well, ring." He motioned to Sabine's hand.

The priestess glanced down at Sabine's hand and nodded. "It will not take much to change that part," she said, inclining her head. Faron and Sabine both gave thanks and rose when the priestess indicated they should.

They followed her through the temple. Unlike the first trip through, where the younger priestess had pointed out things of note, this trip was done in silence, allowing them to take things in on their own. Faron realized soft music played, echoing throughout the temple, something he had missed the first time.

The priestess smiled, catching Faron's attention. "You hear the chanting," she observed.

"Chanting?" Sabine asked her. "It sounds too melodic for chanting."

"An observation made by many," the priestess replied.

Faron agreed with Sabine. It was very melodic, but if he listened closer, he could make out several voices. "How many people are chanting?" he asked.

"Just over a dozen now," the priestess replied. "Giving thanks to their deity."

Faron blinked. "I would have assumed there were more. I assume different people take up the chant throughout the day?"

"People may come and go as they please. They simply enter the chanting room, and they may join the others who were already present. There is something peaceful about open expressions of joy."

Faron had to agree. The chanting added to the peace and joy of this temple, one that was missing from the temples in Myrefall. He wondered what he'd find if he visited other houses of worship in Fythias. "You know, despite being on friendly terms with several priestesses in the town, I've never gone into the temple by the estate," he admitted to Sabine.

"I've not been in months," Sabine admitted with a chuckle. "The Sirene invite me to their services from time to time, but they do not make use of the temple."

"Where do they worship?" he asked. What he really wanted to know was who, or what, they worshiped, but the question seemed inappropriate at that moment. Maybe he would look for a book when they got back.

"Near the water," Sabine said.

"Of course it is. Maybe I could accompany you sometime?" he inquired.

"If you would like."

"I would," Faron said.

They stepped out into the back courtyard where a beautiful grove of fruit trees stood in neat rows. The priestess led them to a clearing in the middle of the grove where the noise from the surrounding town and those at the temple itself were almost completely left behind.

A gentle breeze blew, rustling the branches of the fruit trees, and a few rounded citrus fruits thudded on the grass below. The priestess looked up, smiling. "A sign of good fortune," she remarked.

Faron closed his eyes and breathed in the scent. It was a good sign. If the Spirits protested their union, they would know. "We picked a good day for this," he shared with Sabine as they faced each other in front of the priestess and joined hands.

"I will need your names to start," the priestess shared. Sabine introduced both of them, and the priestess continued with a warm smile. Raising her hands into the air, she began. "Spirits of the forest, we enter this grove of trees to ask you to witness and rejoice in the union of these two souls, Sabine Vassetre and Faron Istro." She looked at Faron and nodded.

Faron took a breath, knowing now was when he would make his pledge. "I declare my intent to take Sabine Vassetre as my wife until the breath leaves my body and I join our people in the Great Forest. To Sabine I offer my sword to protect her all our days, a ring that she may look upon and know of my love, and a bracelet made of my hair, which I will renew whenever she pleases to remind her that even as we grow old and frail, I will provide for her in all ways. If she'll have me."

The priestess nodded before turning to Sabine. "Please hold up your hand with the ring, present the token of Faron's promise to the Spirits, and declare if you accept."

Sabine released one of Faron's hands then raised her hand with the ring as instructed. "I shall happily have Faron."

"Sabine Vassetre and Faron Istro, the promises you make today are sacred. They are the groundwork from which your marriage will grow and blossom. Always keep one another close to your hearts, especially when you must journey apart. Respect and honor one another, your partnership, your family, and your home. With your hearts true, may you weather any storms. May the Spirits watch over you both and always guide you safely home. Your love is blessed.

May you always be as happy as we are today." The priestess looked at each of them in turn. "You may kiss your spouse."

Faron pulled Sabine forward, kissing her passionately, reverently. Although Faron had proclaimed for months now that he belonged to her, the words had never seemed truer than they did now.

"Congratulations," the priestess said once the kiss came to an end. "I will let you have some time together, but please come and see me before you leave." She turned to go before throwing over her shoulder, "Please remember this is a sacred grove, but not for those particular rites."

Faron looked down at Sabine, a blush crawling up his neck from her parting words. "I had not considered con-summating our marriage here."

"I think everyone would be shocked to hear it," Sabine replied.

"People think I would fuck you in a sacred grove?" Faron asked, blinking in surprise. "There are some places that should be off-limits, few and far between as those are."

"I believe they would be surprised if you didn't think it, even without intent to act," Sabine clarified.

"Oh, I have considered it in other places, such as the garden back at the estate. There are even a few places at Louis's house that might be enjoyable. But here, I had not, especially since there are children around that could stumble upon us."

"Fair enough," Sabine replied. "Well, let us return to Louis's estate. As you remarked, the others will wish to celebrate."

Chapter Fourteen

Faron didn't want to admit it, but he almost dreaded their arrival at Louis's estate. He understood the desires the others had to celebrate and would not rob them of that opportunity, but he truly just wanted time for himself and Sabine. Their time together had been so very rare as of late, and it would become even more scarce once Sargarus made port. Something that would happen any day now.

Shoving those thoughts to the back of his mind where they belonged, Faron continued to enjoy the walk back with Sabine. As they weren't stopping to browse any of the shops, the return journey passed more quickly. He noticed Sabine seemed almost more excited to get back than she had been to get the ring, but he didn't comment on it. Instead, he enjoyed the companionable silence they shared.

Arriving at the estate, he was surprised to note no one was waiting for them. He had felt sure Lisbeth and Avana at least would be there to greet them and congratulate them on their nuptials. "Interesting," he said out loud.

"Isn't it?" Sabine agreed. "But not unwelcome."

"Is it wrong of me to hope they aren't waiting in our rooms for us?" he asked as they continued toward the estate entrance. The doors were opened for them by the guards standing at attention.

"Not at all," Sabine replied as they stepped into the entryway. "We just married. I doubt anyone would expect we'd want to socialize with everyone."

"True," he said. When they arrived at the door to their suite, Faron paused and took a deep breath to ready himself. Once he opened the door, he found an empty room. The fire roared in the hearth, and covered trays sat on the tables, but no one awaited them. It wasn't what he'd been expecting.

"Thank the Spirits," Sabine said as she retrieved a decanter and removed the lid. She poured herself a glass of wine. "I'm not complaining, but I am surprised."

"As am I." Faron walked over to where the covered dishes were, not seeing the note until he was much closer. Leaning down, he picked it up, noting Lisbeth's flowing script. Opening it, he read, "Congratulations on your marriage. Enjoy your wedding night." He scanned it once more. "Everyone signed it."

"Then they know us well," Sabine replied with a pleased smile.

"It would seem so." He put the card down and lifted the first, larger tray. "I wonder what changed their minds. This cake is large enough to feed the seven of us plus the guards we brought." He motioned to the chocolate cake before covering it to check the other dishes.

Sabine's shoulders rose and fell. "Perhaps someone intervened. Perhaps they thought my giant elf husband would require a giant cake."

Faron tilted his head to the side as he considered the things he could do with said cake that involved his wife before deciding those activities might be best saved for home, unless Sabine disagreed. He'd do whatever she asked of him no matter the consequences.

"While I can name several things you and I could do with that cake, let us spare Louis's servants the cleanup." He lifted the tray on the left, revealing two beautifully cooked lobsters. The next plate held palm-sized rolls which had been baked with rich cheese. The third dish held both a crisp green salad as well as steamed vegetables. All in all, they'd been presented with a good meal for the night to help keep their energy up.

Sabine's gaze slid from the food and over to Faron. He saw those vivid green eyes fill with mischief. "Have you asked permission to do anything, Faron?" she asked. "Concerning cake or otherwise?"

"I have not," he admitted with a nod of his head and a gleam in his eye. She usually let him take charge, which made moments like this all the better.

"And why have you not?" she asked.

"Because I was anxious over the idea of our friends being here and then shocked they were not," he said, a sly smile playing on his lips as he approached Sabine, stopping a hair's width from her. "May I have you tonight, wife?"

Sabine tilted her head up so she could meet his gaze. "It depends."

"On what?" he asked as he moved his lips close enough they could feel each other's breaths.

"Specifically, and explicitly, on how you want me."

"Well, for a moment, I had considered what it would be like to eat that cake off of your pristine skin." He paused, watching Sabine's eyes grow wider and her lips part. He could spend hours drinking in her subtle responses to mere

suggestions. "Now, I just wish to worship at your feet in any way you will let me."

"I think I'd like to watch how creatively you can worship," she replied, her voice lower now.

"Would you like to see that now, or should I feed you some lobster? It's been a few hours since you last ate," Faron said, concern lacing his voice. He leaned in even closer, their lips barely touching. "Or we could skip to the worship. Which would you prefer?"

"Oh, I think you and I can worry about eating later."

Faron's grin turned dark before he dropped to his knees before Sabine. And though his height made it so she didn't have to look down too far, it was still enough to leave them simmering for one another. "I am at your command. Tell me to do anything, and I shall."

Sabine reached out, running her fingers through his hair. He felt the tips of her fingers gently graze his scalp, sending pleasure zinging to his toes. "Why should I have to tell you the ways I like to be worshiped, husband?"

"Because I enjoy being under your command," Faron admitted. He had never thought he would enjoy something like this as much as he did, but with Sabine, there was no shame or embarrassment.

"You respond well," Sabine replied. "And eagerly."

Faron nodded, his mind half distracted by the fingers in his hair.

"You know, I think I want my new husband to pick me up, carry me to the bed, and spend hours showing me just how much he adores me."

"As you command," Faron said. He stood and swept Sabine up into his arms before carrying her to their bed at the back of the chamber. Depositing her on the bed, he did not lay down, though he did kiss her lips, unable to help himself. Instead, he sat at the end and placing one hand on her ankle, starting to remove her shoes. He slipped one off and then the second, placing them at the foot of the bed instead of tossing them like he usually did.

Placing his fingers only on her ankle, he slowly trailed them up her stocking-clad leg to where the stocking ended mid-thigh. After pulling the laces free, Faron slowly rolled the stocking down her thigh and calf. Once it was off, he dropped it next to Sabine's slippers before repeating the motion on her right leg.

Now revealed, Faron leaned forward, placing a kiss on the inside of her knee, though he glanced up to meet her gaze. He continued kissing his way up her thigh, nudging up the hem of her dress to reveal more and more of her beautiful legs. He avoided going straight to her core, though he was strongly tempted, and he satisfied himself by kissing and nipping at her upper thighs. She moaned softly, making slight shifts in her relaxed position, and again, that zing of pleasure shot straight through Faron.

Faron continued to nip and kiss Sabine, moving closer to her core before moving away again. He wondered how long he could keep teasing her like this, how long he could tease himself, before giving in to what he truly wanted to do. Each gasp of breath and soft moan only tempted him to go further, and though he knew she liked being teased, he could not help but brush his fingers along the center of that sweet apex.

Hearing Sabine gasp, he brushed against her center again, keeping his touch light and playful. Almost giving her what she wanted but again, not quite. "Do you want something, wife?" he asked.

"Exactly what you're doing," she replied.

"Whatever you wish, my love," he replied as he continued with his teasing touches. It wasn't nearly enough to satisfy his craving for her, but as he watched her increasingly moan, squirm, and pant from his featherlight touches, he could only consent to give her more of what she requested.

He stroked and teased and peppered her with kisses, all the while keeping his dark gaze focused on her. "I think you want more," he judged. "Let me give you more."

"Okay," she breathed out. Sabine now had her head pressed against the bedding beneath her, and one of her hands had curled around the corner of a pillow.

Faron didn't hesitate to give Sabine what she wanted. Bringing his mouth to her core, he traced his tongue along the little bud of tiny nerve endings. She moaned his name in response, leaving him practically aching with his own need. Faron wrapped an arm around her left leg, putting it over his shoulder before bringing his other hand to her entrance and slowly inserting his index and middle finger in.

Another sound of pleasure, higher pitched than before, and Faron knew she was close. He knew his wife so completely now, and he wanted to watch and feel her fall apart.

Faron's eyes never left Sabine's face as she came apart. He watched as her eyes slipped closed, her mouth dropping open in a near silent scream as her climax crashed over her. Faron took pleasure in the way she clenched tightly around the two fingers buried inside her, and for a moment, he considered stopping or pulling away to give Sabine a second to catch her breath. Instead, he twisted his hand slightly, crooked his index and middle fingers, and proceeded to pick up the pace, knowing he was hitting that spot inside of her that would have a second climax quickly following the first. To help this along, Faron pressed the flat of his tongue against her clit, rubbing and rolling.

"Faron," she moaned out, pushing him along his chosen path.

Faron managed a pleased grin even with his tongue occupied. He added a third finger to help make sure Sabine was ready for when they moved past this portion of the night. Her second climax soon arrived without announcement, and she cried out in bliss as she rode the waves of pleasure surging through her.

Knowing Sabine would push him away if it became too much, Faron continued to play with her center, enjoying every noise she made.

"No," she breathed out. "I need more. I need you."

Faron considered continuing on his current path, but the pleading in Sabine's tone, as well as his own need, removed the very thought from his mind. Faron gently removed his fingers before slowly kissing his way up Sabine's body, past the curls at the apex of her thighs, up her stomach, to her breasts, where he stopped long enough to kiss both pert nipples before continuing his way up to her mouth, where he drew her into a deep kiss. She responded beautifully, her kisses passionate and eager, as though tasting herself in his mouth only further encouraged her.

Faron was reluctant to break the kiss, but his need for Sabine only grew more difficult to control as time went on. With an apologetic nip to her bottom lip, now swollen and flushed from their kisses, Faron pulled away. Sitting up, he undid the laces of his trousers and freed his throbbing erection. He then grasped his cock to line it up with her entrance. "Ready?" he asked in a husky tone.

"Please," she practically begged.

"Since you asked so nicely," Faron responded before slowly pressing until he was buried in her to the hilt. He groaned in pleasure and didn't move, just enjoying the feeling of her around him. He found her lips again, kissing her deeply as they just existed, connected to one another. Her arms went around him, pulling him closer as they kissed.

Faron shifted his hips, setting a slow, shallow pace to start. Though he knew their lovemaking would eventually grow rougher, he didn't want to rush or ruin this intimate moment. It didn't escape Faron that every time they kissed, every movement of their bodies coming together, took place between himself and his wife. His beautiful, stunning, extremely clever wife whom he loved with every fiber of his being.

He ran a hand down Sabine's body as he slowly started to pick up the pace, needing more of her taste and feel. He kissed her possessively, groaning his pleasure against her swollen lips. As he reached her hip, he guided her leg around his waist, giving him a new angle. "Wife," he growled out, the word pulsing through him with each deep thrust. Faron buried his head against Sabine's neck, nipping and kissing as he sped up his pace. He was getting close, though he wanted to prolong his time as much as possible.

Sabine's cries of pleasure rang in his ears, even more beautiful than the chanting from the temple. He would do anything to continue satisfying her so thoroughly. "I love you," Faron breathed into Sabine's neck.

"I love you," Sabine replied. She absently ran her fingers through his hair, tugging at the strands.

Faron shuddered against Sabine. His whole body felt electrified by her touch and all the more sensitive as he drew closer to his climax. First, though, he needed her to come again. Using his thumb, he began massaging the little bundle of nerves at the apex of Sabine's thighs, and the way her legs began to tremble told him she'd already been close.

"Come for me," he whispered against her skin.

She nodded, seemingly beyond words, though she shifted her hips a little, seeking more contact with his deft fingers.

Faron thrust several more times before he felt Sabine tighten around him. He didn't try and hold himself back, but instead, let himself follow her into a joined climax. His hips stuttered through the duration of his pleasure and stopped when he was spent.

Coming down, Faron kept his head buried in her neck for a few moments, breathing her in, listening to her deep inhales of breath slowing into soft pants. He smiled to himself, looking forward to years of moments like this with his wife.

Chapter Fifteen

To His Highness, Prince Louis of Fythias,

I hope to find you and your realm in blissful prosperity despite the mourning period I have been informed you and your family currently experience. Prince Grégoire was a visionary and a man who foresaw great things for your country. It is quite the tragedy to learn of his presumed passing. As leaders of our respective countries, we must bravely face the future, as I know it is what Prince Grégoire would have wanted.

Our nations share a long history of mutual respect, admiration, and amicable diplomacy. Though we are separated by the sea, our two countries share many similarities, not the least of which is our mutual need to extend protections for our out-numbered human populace. I trust you will understand why I am compelled to bring such matters to your attention.

Fythias has long been friends with the elves and the Mers. From what I understand, there are those who have fled Coralia as I have adjusted laws and regulations, seeking what some might term "refuge." Fythias, of course, is not the only country to respond to the outpouring, though it differs from many. You will see that it is wise, and necessary, to demonstrate our strategic power within the realms closest to our own.

While I'd not dream of dictating what Fythias must do within their own lands, I do implore you to consider your response to my army's maneuvers across other parts of the world. Maintaining the required equilibrium and hierarchy across the world remains a critical task all leadership must face.

With these concerns in mind, it is prudent we meet to discuss and, hopefully, reaffirm the connections and allegiances your brother so eagerly committed to. It is my sincerest hope that we dispel any misunderstandings about the future. I will travel to your estate in the coming weeks, eager to discuss our futures to mutual satisfaction.

With the highest regard,
King Sargarus of Coralia

News of King Sargarus landing in L'Orilan came late in the week, confirmed both by reports from allies within the city and correspondence from Sargarus himself. Sabine had read the letter numerous times over the past several days, and she detected none of the anger or surprise she'd expected. The Coralian king had arrived on Fythias soil expecting a grand welcome from Prince Grégoire. He'd received nothing more than a request for docking fees from the dock master.

Granted, Sargarus had the luxury of writing after he'd had time to adjust and plan. Sabine actually doubted the king wrote the letter himself. There was something too formal, too intentional to assign the tone to a man who had forged a reputation of rage and irrationality.

"I could always stab him," Avana offered, drawing Sabine's gaze toward the small woman.

"You think you could get past the hundreds of men he brought with him?" Sabine asked, amused.

Avana shrugged as she plucked a tart from the tea tray sitting between them. Her brows furrowed as she examined her selection before tentatively taking a small nibble to see if she liked it. A couple of chews, and Avana took a larger bite. "They wouldn't suspect me to do anything terrible, even if they caught me," she said through a mouthful of tart. She had the grace to shield her mouth with a hand.

"He might very well blame someone here, though," Sabine replied. "If not Louis, then Aphros or even me. And even if they didn't blame you, they very well might kill you on sight," Sabine argued. "I think it best we wait for Sargarus. At least, unless Louis wants to do something different."

"He will, I think," Meri said from her position near the buffet. They'd taken up residence in the sunroom, and though Avana was perfectly happy to sit and indulge in food and drink, Meri's restlessness had kept her on her feet. "Or, at least, I think he will want to be more intentional about a confrontation."

"At least he agreed to a coronation," Lisbeth said cheerily. Her bright ginger hair practically glowed in the lovely sunlight, and her cheeks were red from a morning basking in that sunlight. "That's good news."

Good news, yes, but Sabine felt like she'd had to twist the prince's arm into finally taking action to make himself king. Her time with Eloise had left Sabine with the impression that she was the one who protested a higher role, but Louis had dragged his feet on taking action in declaring himself king. She understood some of the reluctance. Officially, Grégoire was missing, and he was the next in line.

Unofficially, whatever remained of Grégoire existed at the bottom of the ocean.

"I'm pleased he's finally planned something," Sabine replied before sipping from her drink. "Sargarus will never treat him with respect, but others will be more inclined to listen to a king than a prince."

"Thank the Spirits he has you to keep him on track," Meri muttered. Her cheeks reddened when she realized the others had heard her, but she didn't correct herself. "It's true."

"He's young, but I suspect he will be more assertive as he further settles into his position. He knows what he wants to accomplish and how to get there. He just hasn't had a lot of practice as king," Sabine gently reminded.

"You are not yet thirty, Your Grace, and you've been leading for much longer," Meri said with a sigh. She finally approached the table and took a seat. Sabine suspected Meri had decided her leg needed a rest. "I just wonder how long he will rely on you to the point that you must be here, a whole country away from your home and your people. Do you not miss the Vassetre Chateau?"

Sabine nodded as she selected a miniature chocolate cake from the tea tray. Eloise had made sure chocolate was available to Sabine, as it was her favorite. "I miss it deeply, and I have every intention of returning as soon as we can. For now, I'm in service to the person I consider my king. Things won't be so tense forever."

"I'm still willing to go stab Sargarus if that means we go home sooner." Avana spoke up, causing all the women to laugh. "Louis is nice and all," she continued after her giggles subsided, "but our home is better."

"I agree," Lisbeth said decisively. "I miss my garden and the ocean."

"The sea is worthy of being missed," Sabine agreed wistfully. "I think Marcelle grows more and more restive the longer we are away."

"He does," Avana confirmed. "He misses the sea. He said it's not close enough."

"So, really, it is just a matter of time before we all feel compelled to return," Sabine finished.

Avana took a bite of a new tart, clearly having decided she liked them. "Well, if I can't stab anyone, I could escort him home," she said after swallowing a large bite.

"Marcelle doesn't want to go home," Lisbeth interjected before furrowing her brow. "Does he?"

"I think he might in the same way we all do," Sabine replied. She'd known the Sirene long enough to trust he would come to her if he felt some immediate need to flee back east. She wouldn't protest if he did, nor would she be surprised to see Avana follow after him.

"But he will stay and defend our country if needed," Meri surmised. "Just as you will, Your Grace." She poured herself more tea and drank deeply, her brow furrowed in presumed contemplation.

"I think we all feel compelled to do what is right," Sabine said. "Marcelle may not be Nereid, but he knows very little justification would be needed for those who wish to do evil to go after the Sirene. Grégoire made threats about their feathers."

Lisbeth frowned, though she said nothing. She'd heard and witnessed many horrific things since Sabine had taken them to Tristian's estate months ago. Grégoire's threats wouldn't have been anything new. "Have I mentioned I am quite pleased he's disappeared?"

"Not in the last few hours," Avana replied. She paused as she chewed her tart then scowled. "What about Aphros? Is he in danger with Sargarus so close?"

"I would think so," Sabine said. Another complication she'd considered, though Aphros would have some protection from Sargarus thanks to his current residency in Louis's home. "He would be in more danger than Marcelle. Nereid scales are circulating throughout many economies. As far as I know, Sirene feathers are not."

"Then I will escort him if needed," Avana announced. She leaned forward to look at the tea tray and frowned. "We're out of the chocolate ones," she pouted.

"I believe they are also Her Highness's favorites. I can call for more if you would like," Sabine offered. "I'll even go inquire in the kitchen. I am in need of a walk, I think."

"Would you like company?" Lisbeth offered. She put her tea down, ready to stand if Sabine consented.

"You are fine," Sabine insisted. "Enjoy yourselves. I won't be gone for long." The duchesse rose from her seat, crossed the room, then exited through the elaborate door and out into the corridor.

She could hear faint steps and voices from those inside the estate, working and carrying on with their day. She spotted a servant dusting portraits and another nearby mopping the floor. She smiled and greeted them as she passed, earning herself a bow.

As Sabine turned the corner, she saw Louis holding Alaoin's little hand as he guided his son. "Good afternoon, Your Highnesses," she said, grinning down at the little boy. Alaoin giggled, showing off a toothy grin.

"Hello, Sabine," Louis greeted. "I thought you were having tea with your friends this afternoon?"

"I am," Sabine replied. "Avana ran out of the chocolate tarts, and I said I'd ask about more."

"Ah," said Louis. The mention of chocolate had Alaoin looking up eagerly at his father, and Louis laughed when he realized it. "Should we accompany Her Grace?" Louis asked his son, getting an eager nod in return. "That is," he said, looking back to Sabine, "do you mind if we join?"

"Not at all," Sabine insisted. "Chocolate is one of my favorite things. We cannot blame Prince Alaoin for his interest."

"Of course we can't." Louis picked up Alaoin and he fell into step with Sabine as they continued their trek toward the kitchen.

"I have thought about the letters from this morning," he said. "And I think you are right. It is time for me to assume the crown. Officially."

Sabine nodded. She'd expected Louis to come to the conclusion, even with his reluctance. "I think it is the wisest move for you. It legitimizes whatever decisions you need to make going forward. I think even Sargarus would have more respect for a king than a prince. Not to mention, Aphros is here and will support you. He is a king, even if Sargarus doesn't believe so." She glanced at him. "Have you spoken with Eloise on the matter?"

"I have, and she agrees with your assessment." He sighed, stopping just before they stepped into the open corridor leading toward the servant's area. "She does not like it, but I am sure you know that."

"Honestly? I believe you do not as well." Sabine gave the prince a look of deep sympathy. "I am sorry for you, personally, to have to take on this burden. As your subject, I cannot imagine a man more capable of taking on the task."

A reluctant smile formed on Louis's face. "I think you would support anyone with a legitimate claim to the throne who aligned with your beliefs. I am just sorry I am not stronger."

"Your willingness to take on a role you do not want demonstrates your strength," Sabine argued. "And you will not have to face this alone. I would not back you—risking my people and name—if I thought you would fail us."

Louis looked down and let out a slow breath. "Do not let me fail you, Sabine. If there is a choice you think I should make, then I will, even if it contradicts my initial thoughts. I know this role is not one you'd want, but I think you'd be more successful in it."

It wasn't an easy confession to make. Nor was the request, but Sabine appreciated the honesty. She glanced around, making sure no one was listening, something they likely should have done before talking. She just hoped Alaoin didn't repeat anything. "I will serve you however you see fit. However you need me to. You just have to be king, and to be king, we have to get you coronated."

Louis met her gaze and nodded slowly, hopefully understanding her meaning. "Good," he said. "I am glad to hear it." He cleared his throat. "I suppose I need to let my wife begin coronation planning. Should we go retrieve more tarts so I can hasten my discussion with her?"

"I think you should," Sabine replied, and they resumed their walk.

Chapter Sixteen

Sabine had been in her very early twenties the last time she'd attended a coronation. Alain, the elder brother of Grégoire and Louis, had posed a striking figure on the throne. Tall, tan, and in possession of bright blue eyes and wavy chestnut hair, he'd been, in every way, the handsome and youthful king. Having been raised to rule, he possessed confidence born out of experience and knowledge, while maintaining compassion for his people. He'd also embodied an arrogance held by many royals that was, thankfully, tempered by discipline and solicitude.

Then he died.

To this day, no one knew what happened, though whispers of Grégoire's involvement swirled around any social function when Alain was mentioned. Sabine thought it likely the case, but with Grégoire's death came a lack of definitive answers.

Unlike Alain's coronation—attended by hundreds of people in the royal palace, well protected in the north by trees and mountains—this ceremony felt more subdued.

Citizens from the village below, the local aristocracy, and the castle occupants stood on the sides of the large ballroom. Hundreds of candles, some on the floor and others held in elaborate candelabras, glittering on the floor and every flat surface.

Sabine stood close to the dais as the highest-ranking person in attendance other than the immediate royal family. Dressed in fine green silk, she wore her hair loosely, as was custom during what was considered to be a holy ceremony. No jewelry other than her wedding ring and the bracelet of Faron's hair adorned her. Glancing around, she noted others had followed the same customs, including Aphros, who stood opposite the aisle across from her. His own simple clothing, made in red and blue like his scales, still managed to look muted and unadorned.

Faron stood to Sabine's left, positioned just behind her. Dressed in finery beyond his normal choices, with his long dark hair styled to better suit the occasion, he still looked quite handsome. His nervousness over his prominent position beside Sabine showed in the creased forehead and folded hands, but otherwise, no one would be the wiser.

At the front of the room, standing on a dais, stood the beautiful priestess who had married Sabine and Faron. Today, her thick curls hung loosely about her shoulders. Dressed in a muted lilac ceremonial robe and framed in candlelight, the priestess appeared ethereal. The doors across the room opened, and in walked a line of other priestesses, all dressed in shades of dark purple. Sabine saw each woman wore no shoes, and the patter of their bare feet on the tiled floor filled the otherwise quiet room.

As they arrived at the dais, each minor priestess bowed to the head priestess, extending their arms out in a practiced flourish. A shallow nod of acknowledgment from the head priestess, and the minor one would move to the side, allowing for repetition of the process until each of the women stood in their designated spot.

Eloise came through the doors next, dressed in a cream-colored gown lacking any adornment. She, too, walked across the floor barefoot, and when she arrived at the dais, she bowed just as deeply to the priestess. Instead of moving to the side, she took the priestess's hand when she rose and stepped up onto the platform.

"Extinguish the lights," the priestess commanded the room. Soft murmurs of compliance followed, with members of the room crouching and kneeling to do her bidding. The room dimmed along with the flames, leaving observers in near darkness.

Silence fell on the room once again as the final candle was extinguished. Only then did Louis appear in the doorway, illuminated only by dim lights from outside of the great hall. He did not proceed as the others had, waiting for permission. The priestess held up her hand and, with a single bend of her fingers, beckoned him forward.

As with Eloise and the other members of the nobility, Louis had forgone adornments of jewels and finery. His simple white shirt and pale trousers, both made from wool, revealed bare feet and arms. He paused midway up the path as instructed by the priestess's hand motion.

"To your knees, Louis Arsenault," she commanded.

The prince obeyed without hesitation. He waited for the priestess to speak, to give a further command, not complaining of the discomfort that surely followed a prolonged period of knees resting directly on the tile.

"Louis, do you deserve to be king?" the priestess finally asked, her deep voice reverberating around the room.

"No man deserves to be king," Louis replied.

"Louis," the priestess said again, "do you wish to be king?"

"I do not wish to be king," he replied.

Both questions always began the coronation, and Louis answered just as his brother Alain had years ago. Just as his parents might have before him. Whatever amount of sincerity Alain held in his responses left Sabine feeling dubious, but she did not doubt Louis's desires.

"Why should your people allow you to become king?" she asked.

"Because I do not want it or deserve it, but I will serve them with my whole heart, to the best of my ability, for as long as the position is granted to me."

The priestess turned to onlookers and motioned toward Louis. "Is this a king you would want?"

"Yes," Sabine said with the crowd. She glanced at Faron, nodding to show he should join when they were questioned again. He returned a slight nod.

"Is this a king you can trust?" the priestess continued.

"Yes," the crowd returned.

The priestess smiled and looked at Louis once again. "Your people have spoken. You may rise." Louis did so and approached the dais, pausing in front of the priestess once again.

"Your people have accepted you," the priestess continued. "As such, we will adorn you in your royal attire, and you shall take your throne and look out to your people, pledging your life to service. Do you accept?"

"I do," Louis confirmed.

The minor priestesses approached, each donning Louis with an article of clothing, each more elaborate than the next. An embroidered tunic of red and gold. Dark breeches and boots. A jacket and a long cloak. When they were done, he looked more formal and royal than he ever had.

The priestess offered Louis a hand, and he stepped onto the platform before being led to a simple chair sitting in the middle. He sat, and the priestess retrieved an intricate gold crown from Peronelle.

The priestess walked it back to Louis, letting it hover over his head. "May you serve us well," she called out to the room before placing the crown atop his golden hair.

Louis took a deep breath and gave a tremulous smile before rising from his seat. He now reached out to Eloise, whose expression grew pale and anxious. His wife joined him, taking the offered hand and squeezing it tightly.

"My first act as king is to request my people consider my wife as their queen," he said to the group. He smiled down at Eloise, reassuring her with his warm, boyish smile.

"We accept," Sabine replied first, triggering repeated affirmations from the rest of the group. Once again, the priestess stepped forward, adorning Eloise in a fine plum-colored dress accented with pearls and opals. When she was led to the chair, it was Louis who placed the more delicate tiara on her head.

Sabine found herself thankful Eloise was spared having to speak out as Louis had done. Her pained smile more than indicated she'd done as much as she was comfortable doing.

Eloise finally stood and joined Louis at the front of the dais, and both bowed to their people as the priestess spoke again. "We celebrate our new king and queen. May they reign long, peacefully, and happily."

The crowd cheered and clapped, excitement bubbling through the room.

"Finally," Sabine murmured to herself.

The priestesses began a procession down the walkway and out of the great hall. Peronelle stepped in front of the royal couple. "Their Highnesses have invited all of you to a celebratory ball this evening. We shall dine and drink, toasting our new rulers."

Another cheer from the crowd brought about laughter from Louis and Eloise. The new king hopped down from the dais and helped Eloise step down before leading her from the room, leaving the rest of the small crowd to shuffle out as they might.

Faron offered Sabine his arm, pushing through the crowd with ease. "Are all coronations so … informal?" he asked.

"King Alain's was not quite like this," Sabine said, pitching her volume so she could be better heard over the crowd. "But circumstances and temperaments do matter." Louis did not have the desire to rule, nor the arrogance to see himself as superior to those around him. The way he undertook his responsibilities mattered.

"Now what happens?" Faron said as they stepped into the corridor and started back toward their suite. Thankfully, the corridor was cooler than the crowded great hall had been.

"Official announcements will be sent out to the different nobility around the country and our allies," Sabine replied. "And the world will then know." And hopefully, the reality of a reigning monarch would have them all much safer and yield more aid. "Now, come. We have a long evening ahead of us, and I would like to rest before then."

"How long do you think we have?" Faron asked, his tone nonchalant.

"Not long enough for all the devious things concocted by your mind," Sabine replied.

Faron's grin was thoughtful. "I've heard it's fashionable to be late."

Sabine smirked but decided, for now, to avoid addressing his suggestions. "Come along."

Chapter Seventeen

As they stepped into the ballroom, all Faron could think about as he adjusted the red jacket Sabine had bought him was how beautiful it looked. It was decorated for celebration and full of people, delicious food, and plenty to drink. At least he could think about something other than his wife. Since Sabine had emerged from their bedroom in a floor-length radiant teal ballgown, he swore he couldn't breathe or put coherent thoughts together. The dress was fancier than anything he'd seen Sabine wear before. The full skirt was covered in small pearls and green gems, the pattern of which flowed down from the bodice, catching the light when she moved. Her hair, which she wore half up, also had a light sprinkling of pearls. Lisbeth, it seemed, had decided to let most of the caramel sheet hang down in soft curls, almost as if it hadn't been styled at all. The jewelry Sabine wore was also subtle: emerald dew-drop earrings and a single pendant around her throat.

Altogether, it made Sabine look like a goddess amongst mortals, though Faron still felt it was Sabine's own natural beauty that shone through the most. In his mind, she could enter the ballroom in rags and still be the most beautiful person there. Sabine, of course, had found it funny how he'd been struck mute at the sight of her and had been gently teasing him since.

Now though, in the cool lights of the ballroom, with its marble floors, vaulted ceilings, and large glass windows to let in the light of the full moon, she looked even more radiant. "How are you even more stunning? I did not think it possible."

Sabine laughed and looked up to meet Faron's gaze. Her green eyes, filled with mirth and playful mischief, did nothing to deter Faron's assessment. "Why are you so easily distracted tonight?" she asked.

"It's your beauty. It takes my breath away."

"Surely, you'd have adapted by now."

"And yet, here we are." Faron turned his entire body toward Sabine, lifted her hand to his mouth, and laid a kiss on the knuckle. "Spirits willing, I will never adapt to your wit, your intelligence, or your beauty."

"And may you never lose your ability to shamelessly flirt," Sabine replied. She rose on her toes to plant a quick kiss on his mouth, possibly a wise decision given how easily he fell into having his entire focus solely on her.

Faron took advantage, wrapping his arms around Sabine and holding her close so he could prolong the kiss. He only released her because they were in public and he'd never make a spectacle of her. "So, what do we do now?" he asked. He'd attended many celebrations in his life, but never a royal ball.

"You enjoy yourself," Sabine replied. "There is food and drink, and later, dancing. We have a new king, and your wife should not have to tell you how to behave," she teased.

"She might need to, lest I find a dark corner for us to hide in, all night long, away from prying eyes." Faron couldn't help the smile that grew on his face, nor its sharp edges.

"She would remind you every moment of our lives cannot be hidden away in some corner," Sabine replied. She looked up at him, her lips pouted so temptingly. "It would be a physical impossibility."

Faron chuckled. "Not our entire lives, love. Just an hour or two here or there." He looked around the room once more. "Since I am not able to ravish you, would you like a bite to eat instead?"

"Perhaps," Sabine replied. "Are you hungry, or are you avoiding chatting with others?"

Faron would appreciate food, though he wasn't exactly starving. He just didn't know how to fit in with the crowd. Some faces were familiar; you couldn't forget the people who had cleaned and served you over a series of days and weeks. He also spotted members of their own party in the crowd. Avana had a plate of food tucked against her chest as she talked animatedly with Finn, Aphros, and Marcelle. Faron was happy to see Avana enjoying herself. She had been doing well under Sabine's watch, but since Grégoire's death, she seemed lighter, freer and more open.

He was also curious as to what sort of conversation the four could be having. Aphros hadn't quite lost the look of grief which lingered in his eyes, but he laughed and smiled as Avana and the others talked. Perhaps he was enjoying himself.

"Think we'll see Lisbeth and Meri?" he inquired of Sabine as he guided her through the crowd. Even though Louis's household had invited all who attended the coronation, the crowd easily parted for Sabine, with many bowing or nodding in greeting. Her status as duchesse, it seemed, still mattered despite the mix of attendees.

They reached the tables before she answered. "They were invited, as was everyone else. They may or may not choose to come."

"I remember one of Lisbeth's letters saying Meri wasn't one for parties with her injury. I don't recall why, though. Perhaps she has trouble with the dancing." Faron picked up an elegant silver plate for them. "Anything catch your attention?" Faron eyed the crab, already shelled and cut into bite-sized pieces.

"It all looks nice," Sabine replied as her eyes scanned the table. "I think we probably have better seafood back home."

"Ours is fresher," Faron said, though he still grabbed bits of crab. Letting Sabine pick what she wanted, he cast a glance around the ballroom again. His eyes landed on Louis and Eloise, still adorned in royal finery, though Eloise's strained smile couldn't be concealed. "Eloise looks as if she would rather be anywhere else," he observed. His eyes narrowed as he noticed the queen grimace once more at a rather weaselly-looking man who was standing rather too close for comfort.

Sabine nodded, keeping her voice low as she said, "She will be capable in the role, but she has always wished Louis had not been a prince. I imagine the sentiment has grown since he became the apparent king."

Faron nodded. He knew she'd been the daughter of a lower noble, and from what Sabine told him of Eloise, she'd had no plans to move up the ranks, content in her life. "This must have been a great change for her." He watched as Louis stepped in to greet the noble bothering Eloise before skill-fully sending the other man on his way with a smile and a wave. "Louis seems to have fit into the role quite well."

"Leading while maintaining good diplomacy is a skill," Sabine said. "It takes a certain finesse, knowing how to give orders and make demands without the other person becoming offended or worse."

"I think I will leave the diplomacy to you, but I can promise to continue looking menacing in the background," Faron offered as he watched the man who'd been bothering Eloise slink away. There was something about the man he didn't like.

"He's the noble Her Grace threw a teacup at," Meri said as she stepped up beside the couple, Lisbeth at her side. Apparently, they had decided to attend. Meri's short dark brown hair had been arranged in lovely waves, and she'd dressed in a rich coral gown with a handful of floral flourishes.

Lisbeth, dressed in a spring green, looked positively radiant. "I wonder what he's doing here. I thought he was firmly in Grégoire's pocket. Though, I suppose with the elder prince having fled, a lot of people are going to have to play nice with Louis now," she mused softly.

"I believe we will see many emerge to pledge their loyalty to the new king, no matter what they have done in the past," Sabine said.

"I would say we should keep an eye on those we know to be trouble, but we wouldn't want the king's guard to think we are overstepping," Meri said. Her eyes narrowed as she watched the man who'd tried to assault Sabine meet up with two others.

"Overstepping wouldn't be good, but if you gave the guard commander a heads up, I don't see how that would be a problem." Faron looked to Sabine to get her thoughts.

"I think it would be wise to allow our king to make decisions after we have informed him of anything pertinent,"

Sabine said. "We are not at my estate, so it is not up to us to determine how to act."

Meri nodded. "I'll talk to the king's guard commander tomorrow and let him know what we know and offer assistance. If they say no, I will continue to enjoy my time here." Lisbeth gave Meri a proud smile.

"A wonderful plan," Sabine replied. "For now, you should enjoy yourself. The music is lovely, and the food looks equally so."

"We will," Lisbeth said before gently dragging Meri off.

Faron watched them go, ignoring the smile Lisbeth shot his way as he picked up a few more items he felt they both might enjoy before leading Sabine away from the food tables. He held out a small piece of melon for her to try. "Did you know that most of the men in this room can't keep their eyes off you?" he asked softly.

"How would you know since you are included in that observation?" Sabine asked as she accepted the melon.

"I can admire you and watch for threats at the same time. Though, that was a skill I was hard-pressed to acquire."

"Oh?" Sabine asked, playing along. "Why is that?"

"Because you," he held out a piece of crab for Sabine, "are exceedingly distracting."

Again, Sabine accepted the offered food, though she teased and prodded Faron as they ate. Naturally, she knew how to keep his attention without much effort, and Faron could only find himself further ensnared by his wife. Which was why when Louis interrupted them, he nearly bit the new king's head off.

"My apologies," Louis said, keeping his voice low. "There's been new correspondence from Sargarus."

Faron looked down at Sabine at those words, watching as her eyes changed from playful to steely determination, even as her posture remained relaxed to not tip off the other partygoers.

"Something we need to be concerned with?" she asked just as quietly.

Louis nodded. "He plans on coming here. He may already be on his way."

Faron calculated the distance from the capital to Louis's estate. "If he doesn't stop, he should be here midday tomorrow."

"Assuming they ride through the night and are already on the road, it's possible," Louis confirmed.

"He is tenacious enough to do so, even at his age," Faron mused. "So, we have a day, maybe two at best." He pushed down the anxiety and anger that tried to make itself known at the idea of that monster being here with Sabine. With any of the kind and caring people he had surrounded himself with.

Louis nodded, and Sabine stepped forward to place a hand on the king's arm. "Spend the next hour here, celebrating with your people. We shall meet after, including any who you think might be helpful. Your guard captain. Aphros. Any of the nobles you can trust who are in attendance."

"Right," Louis said. "Thank you, Sabine."

Faron watched how easily Sabine took control of the situation and felt the growing anxiety fade into almost nothing. Louis might be king, but Sabine was the one with the knowledge as well as the ability to see them through this with hopefully no casualties. He believed in her even more so than he did the Spirits, as blasphemous as that was.

As Louis walked away, leaving them with their plate of food, Sabine let out a breath. "Eat up," she encouraged. "It is going to be quite a long night."

"I find myself less than hungry now, but for you, I will try." He took a bite of the crab, finding it delightful with the hint of butter and spice he couldn't identify, but it wasn't as fresh as it would have been at home. He offered her a small pastry, and as he did, the music that was playing in the background picked up as Louis and Eloise took the floor in a graceful dance.

They watched the royal couple as they danced across the floor, Eloise happily swirling about the room in Louis's arms. The king, despite his worries, paid nothing and no one beyond his wife the slightest bit of attention. Had his love for his own wife not been so bone-deep, Faron might have found the picture of the royal couple quite aspirational.

As the song came to a close and another one started, Faron placed the mostly empty plate on a nearby table and turned to Sabine. "Would you like to dance?"

"I don't believe I've ever seen you dance before," Sabine replied, surprised delight crossing her face. "But of course."

Right then, Faron decided the embarrassing lessons he'd taken with Finn in secret were more than worth it for the way she lit up. Faron held out his hand. "Then let us dance."

Chapter Eighteen

Aphros sipped from his goblet, a remnant of the ball he, Louis, Sabine, and a couple of others had abandoned early so that they might discuss their options regarding Sargarus. Although Sabine had expected the Nereid to be more concerned, possibly even panicked, he seemed to be neither.

"So Sargarus plans to come to your home," the Nereid began as he pulled out a chair in the king's private office. Like most of the house, the rich colors and fine fabrics made their way into the small space, creating a cozy, welcoming atmosphere. Or it would have had the hour not been so late and the topic of discussion so serious. "What is it you plan on doing?"

Louis leaned against the front of his desk, arms crossed. He'd removed some of the more ceremonial garments since leaving the ball, but his attire suggested he came straight there. "He'll expect a warm welcome and perhaps a continuation of whatever agreements he and my brother arrived at."

"But he will not receive them?" Aphros asked.

"His Majesty rejects the sort of arrangements Prince Grégoire pursued," Guard Captain Brielle spoke up. Her dark hair sat atop her head, pinned into an elegant bun surrounded by crossing braids, and she dazzled in a creamy orange gown that complimented her warm tan skin. No one might guess she led the front-line guards for the Fythian king.

"But does Sargarus know that?" Aphros asked. "Because I suspect he was waiting for a handshake from Grégoire before setting his ships upon my islands and people." He placed his cup on the mantle of the fireplace by where Sabine stood. "He's already going after Mers on the promise of support. The official home of the Nereid hasn't been attacked yet only because he would find himself in great danger and low opinion of many countries if he didn't have Fythian backing."

"He does not," Sabine replied. She'd been given one of the chairs between the desk and the fireplace, likely due to her rank, and she watched the subtle shifts in moonlight through the window as Brielle and Aphros argued. "The problem we're going to encounter from Sargarus is his lack of respect for Louis, regardless of his position. If Sargarus intends to go directly after the Nereid kingdom, lack of permission from Fythias will not be viewed as a deterrent. Not for long, anyway."

Aphros let out a huff of a laugh. "You are right. His hesitation until now has been nothing more than a flimsy nod of respect toward Grégoire. For all we know, something may be happening now."

"We can send troops," Brielle interjected. "They could be near the Nereid islands within a couple of days."

"Coralia could do the same, and they'd likely argue we were coming to attack," Louis said with a sigh. He ran a hand

over his face, his exhaustion only partially obscured thanks to the crackling fire.

"Then what would you like to do?" Faron asked. He'd taken up residence behind Sabine's chair, and his hand rested comfortably on her shoulder. She looked up at him, catching the thin-set mouth and narrowed eyes. Faron doubted his tactical and political abilities, or perhaps was uncertain of them, but he looked right at home in the office with the others.

Louis sighed again and pushed himself from the desk and began pacing. "I think I must meet with him. We are not officially enemies, and as king of Coralia, he has a right to expect certain extensions of courtesy. I could not deny them and hold the high ground."

Brielle scoffed. "We will always hold the high ground when it comes to that monster. Do you not remember the rumors from Dathria?" she asked. "Do you want it to happen here?"

"I've never even heard of Dathria," Faron muttered, so low Sabine thought only she'd heard him.

"I've been told the Anids underwent genocide," Sabine said. "Perhaps a few hundred still exist, scattered throughout the world, having vowed to remain beneath the water for all time." She met Brielle's gaze, her chin held high. "I believe we are aware of the threat Sargarus poses and our position relative to his own, but let us not speak on such atrocities so lightly."

Brielle opened her mouth to argue then closed it, though her jaw still worked furiously for a couple of seconds before she nodded. "Of course, Your Grace."

"Thank you," she said. "Your Majesty," she continued, addressing Louis, "I think the wisest option would be to formally accept Sargarus's desire to meet. We will have the numbers to contend with him immediately should he lash out, though I doubt he will. Not immediately anyway." It was the only reason she would suggest such a meeting. Otherwise, she'd have everyone waiting at the gates of the village to prevent him from coming in.

"And once he is here?" Louis prompted.

"Let him say whatever it is he wishes to say. Let him speak his plans, king to king. That way, you will have a formal proposal in front of you, and you will be able to formally deny him. He may also reveal information we do not already know."

"What of the Mers who are here?" Louis asked. He looked to Aphros, though he was hardly the only one within the chateau.

"Give them the opportunity to retreat if they would like," Sabine replied. "Or provide them safety while Sargarus is near. I will not claim Sargarus will avoid attacking people under your care while he is here, but he would be less likely to do so until after you've spoken."

Louis nodded and turned to Aphros. "Would you like to be present at the meeting, or should you be hidden away?"

"Given what I know he's done, personally and through proxy, to other Mers, I think it best I lay low in the village for his duration. I'd also suggest the same for Marcelle, the guard in Her Grace's travel party."

"I will talk with him," Sabine said. Marcelle was, by all accounts, a reasonable person, but his dislike of Sargarus and all he stood for could tempt an otherwise rational Sirene into something less rational. "If he chooses to be present when Sargarus arrives, it will be because he chooses to do so."

Aphros picked up his cup from the mantle and examined the content. "Might I suggest that, regardless of who chooses to stay, Sargarus not be given much opportunity to openly roam the chateau? He should be escorted in, monitored, and escorted out when the time comes. You will demonstrate your lack of trust in him, and perhaps a bit of disrespect, all while making sure people are protected." He tipped his cup in Faron's direction. "The man doesn't just dislike Mers, as I'm sure Faron can tell you."

Sabine heard Faron's intake of breath and felt the slight flexing of fingers on her shoulders before her husband spoke. "Indeed. No elf, no Mer, dwarf, or magic user is safe while Sargarus breathes. That is why Fythias is home to so many from Coralia." He chose his words carefully, just managing to keep the growl of anger from showing, but his unhappiness and trauma were still present, compelling Sabine to reach up and place her hand on top of his in silent support.

"I see," Louis said gravely. "Then that is what we will do. Sargarus will have numerous escorts while he is here so that those who are most vulnerable will come to no harm." He took a breath and focused on Sabine again. "I know he does not like women, but I also know you are accustomed to dealing with men with those particular biases."

Sabine gave a short laugh. "There is nothing he could say to me I could not handle. He might be upset when I do not respond as he wishes, but it cannot be helped."

"She's going to be present for discussions?" Brielle asked, eyebrows raised in surprise. "Is it wise to have her there? No offense meant, Your Grace," she added quickly when Louis raised one of his own.

"Sabine is the third-highest ranking person in the country," Louis explained. "And she is my acting political advisor. Unless she greatly objects, she will be there and will be invited to speak to Sargarus."

"I have no objections," Sabine replied. "Though given the manner in which he will be received, I think we should limit the people directly in the meeting to ourselves. It lessens the number of people in his line of potential attack."

"It also shows that we do not take him or his threats very seriously," Aphros added. "All the subtle signs of disrespect will add up for him, but not one will be enough to suggest Fythias started any conflict."

"Then I think we are in agreement," Louis said. He came to a pause in his pacing and crossed his arms. "Let's all of us try to get some sleep, and we can reconvene come morning when we have more updated information on his whereabouts."

Brielle nodded and excused herself from the room, perhaps to inform the other guards of tentative plans.

Aphros placed his now empty cup back on the mantle. "I think the uncertainty works in our favor," he mused to the three remaining people.

"Let us hope so," Louis said. "I hate to think of what might happen."

"We can predict nothing with certainty," Sabine reassured him as Faron helped her from her seat. "But we all have those we care for, and we will do our best." She offered the king a reassuring smile. "Now, might I suggest you take your own advice and try to sleep? Morning comes soon, and with it, the promise of Sargarus growing closer."

Louis nodded his consent, and the remaining four left the office, each going their separate ways to their assigned rooms once they were in the corridors.

"You know, you are also meant to be outside of whatever meeting space Louis decides on?" Sabine asked quietly as they moved through the dark, near silent chateau. Faron had not protested during the discussion, but Sabine had no doubt of his feelings.

"I'd prefer not to be, no matter how dangerous everyone thinks it might be," Faron replied.

"I know, and I knew as much when we were talking about it," Sabine replied. "But Aphros had a point, and Louis agreed."

"Louis himself could not keep me away if I thought you'd permit it," Faron swore, but he sighed as he placed a hand on the small of her back. "But if you think it is for the best, I will remain outside of the room. He can glower all he likes about the elf in his presence."

"As long as you do nothing foolish, I will not object," Sabine replied in compromise. And if he did, well, she'd likely never forgive him.

Chapter Nineteen

Sargarus arrived two days after the coronation ball, though he brought with him far less flourish than Sabine had expected. Sargarus and his men had taken residence at a local inn closest to the city gate on the night of their arrival. No reports of destruction or rowdiness reached the estate, and nearly a whole morning had passed before someone arrived at Louis's home, bearing a letter from Sargarus announcing intention to meet the next day.

"What is he playing at?" Avana had demanded as they sat around Sabine and Faron's suite discussing the strange moves.

"He wants to come across as reasonable if I had to guess," Sabine replied. "He's not treating this as an invasion."

"He doesn't have enough people for an invasion," Meri quipped from her seat next to Avana. Both had chosen the sofa, though Avana seemed much more relaxed.

"Not unless you count the reported numbers to the north," Finn interjected. He'd set himself up at the desk, poised to take notes as needed.

"They'd have to cross the mountains to get into the country," Meri countered. "It's not as easy as it seems."

"They'd manage if they had orders," Finn replied.

Both made good points in Sabine's estimation, and while she had no doubt Coralian soldiers were waiting for a signal to take on the mountains—an easier feat this time of year than when it grew colder—she felt as though Sargarus was attempting a more peaceful route first. It was the wisest approach given Louis had not yet indicated his position beyond a brief returned correspondence confirming Sargarus would be welcome.

The following morning, Sargarus arrived with a small troop of men, each atop beautiful, strong horses. Peronelle and a selection of house staff had been tasked with bringing Sargarus into the palace, supplying him with food and wine. Louis, a man in a position of equal rank, had not been expected to greet Sargarus upon arrival, and as such, he had chosen to forget the niceties.

Sabine now sat back in her chair, listening intently to the deliberate footsteps echoing from the other side of the door of the large meeting room. Her fingers gripped the edges of the chair arms, but no other sign indicated nervousness or concern.

The room, decorated only with a long oak table and draperies at the one window that sat across the room from a large fireplace, offering a secure, quiet location for discussions. Sabine had no idea how open Sargarus would be to talking, but even in her pessimism, she wanted to reassure Louis.

Without turning her head, she glanced in the king's direction, noting the creased brow and firm set of his lips. Louis's nervousness showed in other ways. His hands fidgeted and his leg bounced up and down in a rhythmic pattern. She could also hear his breathing, louder and a touch heavier than usual. Sabine felt compelled to lean over and place her hand on top of his.

"You are our king," she said, her words just above a whisper. "You have the support of all of us. He is a weak, old man who needs to subjugate others to feel important. Powerful."

Louis smiled weakly but nodded just as a rapid succession of knocks sounded on the door. Peronelle entered, her face grim. "Your Majesty, King Sargarus of Coralia waits."

"Let him in," Louis replied after receiving a reaffirming nod from Sabine.

Peronelle bowed and then exited without a word. The next time she knocked, she entered the space without waiting for an answer. "Your Majesty," Peronelle said, inclining her head to Louis. "Your Grace," she added, repeating the motion with Sabine. "Your guest."

She stepped aside, allowing the Coralian king to enter. Though nothing on Sabine's face gave away her thoughts, she had to admit the king looked nothing like she'd expected. Atop his head sat a thick, wavy mane of red-gold hair, though his temples had grayed, indicating the rest would soon follow. In the right humidity, his hair might well have curled, though she thought curls were unlikely to make him appear friendlier, more good-natured.

A lean, muscular build, a beaklike nose, small, intense, red-rimmed gray eyes, and small lips the same shade as his patchy red face gave him the tired, irritable demeanor of someone used to the sidelines. Of course, Sargarus had been on the throne for nearly fifteen years, but Sabine supposed some people never got over feeling ignored.

Despite his less-than-intimidating appearance, he moved with the agility of someone much younger than his fifty or so years suggested. Confident and condescending, Sargarus did nothing to greet Louis and Sabine. He didn't even bother with the façade of keeping a hand near his sword hilt. Those steely eyes took in Sabine with a sneer, and Louis fared no better. "This is nearly insulting," he said, forgoing greetings.

"What is?" Louis asked. No longer wearing the signs of intimidation or nerves, the Fythian king took on the appearance of offense Sargarus claimed.

The Coralian king gestured to them. "You give no welcome to a king of my stature. The presence of whom I assume is your whore. The general lack of hospitality. Is Fythias so poor as to do no better, or is it too uncivilized?"

"You will not speak of the Duchesse Vassetre in such an insulting manner," Louis warned, his voice stern and inflexible.

Sargarus's eyes widened as he turned to look at Sabine. "Ah. You are the one who refused to come pay respects to my daughter. I thought surely you'd be more," he paused as his eyes ran down Sabine, "impressive."

"I thought the same of you," Sabine replied. "I guess we're both disappointed."

Sargarus stared at her for several long moments before he gave a derisive laugh. "You want to muzzle her before she further embarrasses herself?"

"I think you'll want to show Her Grace some respect," Louis replied. "Men who do otherwise no longer breathe. Her husband takes great offense on her behalf. As does her king."

"Oh. You style yourself as a king," Sargarus replied. "Really? It was my understanding you weren't yet crowned. And what of your brother, Grégoire? Does he not have more rights than you? Is he not older?"

"My brother ran off from his responsibilities the first chance he got," Louis said with a shrug. "He has shirked his duties. The rest of us still have to move forward. As I am the next in line, the throne is mine. And I have been coronated. I am king."

"You are a boy," Sargarus scoffed. He approached the two, stopping when he was merely an arm's length away, but he gazed upon them both with contempt and mockery. "You're a boy playing at king while a woman sits beside you, whispering in your ear to do all the little things she requests. No one will take you seriously. No one will feel you are a threat. You're better off allowing me to ravage and conquer as I like, and you can sit on your throne and feel special, as long as you don't interfere."

Sabine laughed in disbelief. "Tell me, what do you plan to do with this daughter you have? The one you think I should have visited."

"She will be raised to know her place, and when the time comes, I will marry her off to any hand which suits my needs. I can only hope your possession of a husband means either your husband or king would have made sure you know yours."

Sabine scowled now. Although this was not the first time she'd witnessed others spout stupid opinions about women, the overtness of Sargarus's claim astounded her. Those in Fythias who agreed with the sentiment often prettied up their terrible views. Even Tristian and Grégoire expressed the view with careful language. "I think you will be lucky, should you accomplish your goal of subservience."

"And I think you would be happier if you were limited to your natural place," Sargarus countered. Again, he turned his attention to Louis. "Now, do you want to have an actual conversation, or must we be subjected to the emotional outbursts from this woman?"

"We can talk," Louis replied. He motioned to one of the chairs at the table. "However, please keep in mind I will not tolerate any more disrespect shown to Her Grace. She is the one who thought there might be something gained from meeting with you. I hope there is."

Sargarus rolled his eyes, but he said nothing as he dragged his chosen chair across the floor, the scratchy squeals echoing painfully. He threw himself into the seat with a loud *thump* and leaned back with his arms crossed. To Sabine, the whole act reminded her of a child throwing a tantrum, though she doubted Alaoin ever got away with such spoiled behavior.

"I'm listening," Sargarus drawled, ignoring a servant who approached the table to pour him a drink. He snatched the silver goblet up before the young man had a chance to back away, and some of the contents of the pitcher sloshed onto his shirt.

The young man mumbled an apology, and Louis kindly dismissed him to change before his attention went back to Sargarus. "I suppose I should start by asking what your plan is now that you've arrived in Fythias."

"I should think possible invasion is obvious," Sargarus replied without looking up from his cup. "Your response determines what happens to you. I cannot personally oversee the whole of the continent, nor do I want to."

"Then what do you want?" Louis asked, meeting Sabine's gaze before looking back.

"Regular taxation, inclusion on trade profits, military support, and access to your Mers," Sargarus listed. He held up a finger with each item, though none of them were given much attention or emphasis.

Sabine's jaw clenched all the same. The man might not see a difference between taxation and exploitation, and probably genocide of Mers, but she did. Judging by Louis's pale face, he thought the same. "We are allied with the Nereid and the Sirene, you know," she said.

"Then drop them," Sargarus replied. "You have more than enough military strength to end them if you wanted. I don't think it would prove too difficult, and if you did need help, well, that would be a benefit of falling in line. I'd be more than happy to send a military unit to aid."

Louis laughed and stood from his seat then walked over to the discarded pitcher. "You want us to turn on two of Fythias's longest-standing relationships, knowing you plan to maim every single Mer you can get your greedy hands on, and pay you through taxes and trade. And in response, you might send us help if ever we are attacked. Do I have it right?"

"You have it right," Sargarus replied with a sly grin. "Of course, some would think being under the protection of Coralia would be worth the price. We are powerful, and we have money. The connection could give you the same." He placed his now empty cup on the table with a loud *clang*. "Of course, you have the right to turn me down. In which case, I will act accordingly. My people would be here in weeks, and I would take great joy in taking everything you possess." He smiled demonically. "You understand, if I am forced to act, you and your whole family would feel my wrath."

Sabine didn't realize Louis threw the wine pitcher until it ricocheted off the wall, sending dark red liquid everywhere as the container bounced across the floor. Sabine was only surprised the heavy thing hadn't been used to bash in Sargarus's skull.

"I ought to kill you where you sit, you smug son of a bitch," Louis growled. "I humored a meeting with you. With an aging, impotent old man who is hemorrhaging money to the point of allying with nobles from another country. Do you think Fythias is scared of Coralia? Of you?"

"Louis—" Sabine interjected, only to be ignored.

"We protect our own here," Louis continued. "Mers, elves, humans, and whoever else is in need. I will not let you ruin what so many have fought hard to build." He pointed to Sabine. "She is the custodian of the Sirene lands. She'd strike you dead before you got near those beaches. I suggest you rethink your plans."

Sargarus raised an eyebrow. If he was insulted or amused, he showed neither. He rose to his feet with more elegance than he'd shown upon sitting. "And to think, I accused the woman of emotional outbursts." He tilted his head as he studied the spilled wine. "I plan on leaving the village come morning. If you come to your senses before then, I will show mercy. If not..." He shrugged as his words trailed off, then he walked from the room without warning, leaving Sabine and Louis to their thoughts.

"I suppose Aphros was correct in sitting this meeting out," Sabine said since Louis still seemed beyond words. She left her seat and approached him, resting a hand on his shoulder. "We are not going to let Sargarus accomplish even one of those threats," she promised, hoping to calm him down.

"We won't," he admitted after a few calming breaths. "The idea he would go after my family—" He shook his head. "I let that asshole get to me."

"No one can blame you," Sabine assured him. "Go take some time with your family, and we'll meet back up with Aphros in a few hours to discuss strategy."

Louis nodded, thankfully sounding more like himself. "What would I do without you, Sabine?"

"I imagine you'd take Sargarus out with a wine pitcher," she suggested.

"It wouldn't have been the worst idea I ever had," the future king admitted before sighing. "Go spend time with Faron. I'll see you soon."

"Of course."

Chapter Twenty

Faron ignored the eyes on him as he paced back and forth in the small garden nearest to the meeting room where Louis and Sabine had chosen to meet Sargarus. He had wanted to be there, to help keep Sabine safe should the worst happen. Since it had been determined that a human retinue would be best to greet and monitor the Coralian king, Faron had been relegated to wait. He might have argued his point had his wife not been tired, irritated, and less than amused with his protestations. So, he'd instead announced his intentions to wait out of sight in the nearby gardens.

Thankfully, his wait was not an isolated one. Lisbeth sent judgmental looks his way as he paced, probably because he was damaging the grass. Meri, also present, did not hold his pacing against him and instead focused on a thick book which was perched in her lap. Marcelle talked about joining them but had changed his mind last minute, as had Avana. Finn was sitting on a bench a ways away but still within earshot. Meri had implied it was to keep an eye on Faron in case something did come up, but he was fairly sure she'd been joking. The surprise guest had come in the form of King Aphros, who was also within earshot while keeping a bit of distance between them.

"Everything is going to be fine," Meri said, not looking up from her book. "Sargarus did not bring enough men to be a problem, and if there is an issue, there are enough guards around to handle him. Also, Sabine is armed." Here, her gaze did lift to meet his, and Faron had to concede the point that out of three attacks, he had only been needed for one of them. If Sargarus was a problem, Sabine would be fine. That didn't mean he didn't wish he was there, however smart it was for him not to be.

"If you're that worried, I can go check on things," Lisbeth offered, only to wave a hand in dismissal at his raised eyebrow. "I wouldn't go into the room or anything, just go check in with the guards closest to the doors or one of the maids who are likely to be hanging about. You know how maids and footmen gossip. If one of them hasn't spent the last hour dusting the same vase, I'll eat my own plants." That said, Lisbeth rose from the bench before Faron could protest and walked away.

"She's nervous and needs something to do. She'll stay out of sight of the door and more than likely inquire from the lurking helpers if they need assistance," said Meri.

"You said that as if you aren't just as anxious," Faron pointed out.

"I am on edge, just not as much as the two of you." Meri put her book down. "It's different for myself and some of the others. You and Lisbeth lived under his rule, experienced horrors we here in Fythias have only heard about. For you, it's real. For a lot of people in Fythias, while we know and understand what's happening, those horrors are still not our reality. So yes, I am worried. I am scared for Her Grace and all of Fythias. It's just not the same fear I had for Grégoire."

Faron thought over Meri's words as Aphros moved closer to them.

"I can see where you're coming from, if only because I'm often taken aback by how different things are in Fythias. Tristian's lands notwithstanding," Faron admitted as he thought back to the atrocities Tristian and his guards had committed against his own people.

Meri gave a very unladylike snort. "You came here expecting rampant homelessness and poverty?" At Faron's nod, the amused expression on Meri's face fell to be replaced with a more thoughtful one. "I think Lisbeth was the same way when she first arrived as well. We barely glanced at each other her first year at the chateau. Well, I barely glanced at her."

"She wrote as much in her letters to me," Faron said.

"One day, I would like to see those letters."

Faron gave her a look and was about to tell her he would let Sabine see them before Meri when he heard rushed footsteps headed their way. Faron spun in the direction the steps were coming from and had barely taken a step forward when Lisbeth burst into view. "I think the meeting is about to end. I was talking to a maid when there was a loud crash from inside the meeting room. There was no shouting, so I assume everything is as alright as possible but..." She gave a helpless shrug.

Faron felt his anxiety skyrocket. Deciding to go check for himself, Faron started forward, only for someone to grab his upper arm in a surprisingly strong grip. He looked back, assuming it was Meri, only to be surprised that it was Finn who had stopped him.

"You need to wait," Finn said as he released Faron's arm. "A crash could be anything."

Faron let out a harsh breath. "You're right. We would know if there was something truly wrong."

"You are right to worry, though." Aphros spoke up from his chosen spot. "Although I doubt Sargarus would be allowed any chance of harming Sabine or King Louis, do not doubt his willingness to cause harm."

"That man always seems willing to cause harm or sow enough discord that others will do it for him," Faron agreed.

Lisbeth, who was now being held by Meri, nodded as well.

"It is surprisingly easy to convince others to act abominably. It is how otherwise decent men have been convinced to maim Mers for scales," Aphros said. He might have continued, but the entrance doors to the chateau crashed open, and out stormed Sargarus, followed by a handful of his people. Thankfully, the non-humans and magical amongst them remained concealed in the side garden.

"He seems angry," Finn observed.

"Extremely so. Do we want to assume it was Sabine or Louis that set him off?" Faron thought about that for a moment. "No, a combination of both sounds right."

"Either way, I will go in and see," Aphros said, departing without another word.

Faron looked to Finn. "I know I should follow, but it's best I wait."

"Perhaps," Finn agreed. "Though, if you want to go in, I see no reason not to. You are now married to Her Grace."

"True," Faron said and started for the doors the monster had just exited. He wanted; *needed* to make sure Sabine was alright, even though he was sure she was. Sargarus would always make him less than rational, knowing what he was capable of.

He hurried into the chateau through the same way Sargarus had just exited, but he was only halfway to the meeting room when Sabine stepped out, Aphros by her side. Faron took her in from head to toe and was pleased to see not a hair out of place.

"In a rush to see me?" Sabine teased.

"Yes," Faron said, his voice sounding breathless with relief. "We were told there was a crash from the meeting room."

"Louis threw a pitcher," Sabine said, lowering her voice. "It's a shame it wasn't at Sargarus's head."

"Indeed," Aphros agreed. "And since your king stormed from the room before I could ask questions, perhaps I could tempt you both into having a drink while Sabine provides a summary of the meeting."

Faron looked to Sabine before answering. "I am alright with that."

"I think it would be fine," Sabine agreed.

Aphros nodded and folded his hands behind his back. "I understand Faron does not drink. I know of a place which can offer some privacy and an assortment of drinks which should suffice."

"Thank you," Faron said, surprised by Aphros's observational skills. Not a lot of people noticed he avoided alcohol, and not during such a short period of acquaintance.

"No problem," the Nereid said, offering the couple a smile. "Would you like to leave now, or do you need a moment to recuperate after your meeting, Sabine?"

"I think it would serve us well to leave now."

Faron held out his arm to Sabine, pleased as always with the easy, perfect way Sabine's hand rested on his forearm. Then, they set off, following Aphros away from the chateau and into town.

Chapter Twenty-One

Faron reluctantly walked through the hallways of Louis's estate, his steps dragging in a way they almost never do. It had been highly suggested by Meri that he stop by one of the less familiar libraries as soon as he could. She wouldn't say anything else about it, but the hints of a practical work-room for research purposes, and her devious smile, had worried him an awful lot.

As he considered the reason for Meri's secrecy, Faron began to worry that he might have been summoned for another hands-on lesson in politics with one of Louis's advisors. Earlier in the week, he'd run into one of the advisors while in the main library, one of the books Sabine had suggested open in his lap. This somehow led to an hour-long lecture that had been very informative, and yet extremely boring at the same time. They'd reviewed the nobility of Fythias during the discussion, including the establishment of titles, how new nobles were chosen, and the associated responsibilities at each level. Some he'd determined on his own as he'd watched Sabine work. Other pieces of information had surprised him.

At the end of the lecture, Faron tried to be gracious, thanking the advisor for their expertise and time commitment. The appreciation had earned him a second round of lectures, although he thought there must have been some miscommunication since the new advisor spent a handful of hours explaining the intricacies of Fythian water systems. Faron could now recite how many different waterways had been constructed, the usefulness of each, and the cost of maintaining them. He doubted he would ever need the knowledge.

Worse still were the dancing lessons with Finn. These had been going on for much longer than either of the history, economic, and political discussions he'd participated in or witnessed. The hours of hard work had more than paid off the night of the ball. Sabine's surprised delight had been worth the more militaristic training style Finn had taken toward teaching him to dance. It had been effective but very, very difficult, especially since Finn accepted no errors.

Reaching the library, Faron paused, bracing himself for what he might find, only to open the doors and find no one waiting for him. Confused, Faron cautiously stepped into the library. It was smaller than the one on the other side of the chateau, warmly lit, with a few comfortable-looking chairs scattered here and there. What this one had that the other didn't was large open spaces with a desk or two near each other.

Similar setups were spread out across the room, some with people busy at the desks. One diligently worked on what looked to be potions, and another played with smooth stones, though what he was doing, Faron did not know.

As he drew closer to the far side, familiar muttering caught his attention. Intrigued as to why Avana would be there, Faron, finally realizing Meri hadn't sent him here for himself, headed in her direction. Moving around one of the bookcases, Faron found the small half-elf leaning over one of the work tables. Several books lay open on the table in front of her, and next to those were several plant clippings and what looked like berries. On her other side sat several glass vials and a small well-used cauldron on a porcelain base. Faron would bet good money there was a lit candle or some other heat source inside of it. A used pestle and mortar lay abandoned on the corner of the table, and the formidable olive-green residue confirmed Avana was up to no good.

Deciding not to interrupt yet, Faron leaned against the bookshelf and watched as Avana worked. She moved with an easy and practiced grace around the table, confident in what she was doing and rarely checking the books. Though when she did, Faron noted she knew exactly which book to reference and what chapter she needed. He counted her referencing the books' table of contents twice throughout. Had she spent time here before without him knowing, or had she used these same books elsewhere? He could think of no other explanations.

He watched as Avana ground up one of the plants, adding it and some water to the small cauldron before she mixed the ingredients together. That done, she picked up two of the purple berries, squishing them over the cauldron and letting the juice drip down into it. At first, he thought maybe she was working on a potion, but as she sniffed the cauldron before reaching over to grab a container full of beetles he'd somehow missed earlier, Faron came to the conclusion she was making something much different.

Opening the container, she grabbed a pair of tongs from next to the cauldron, picked up a large beetle, and dropped it inside the dark pot. She watched for a moment before clapping in delight. Using the tongs once more, Avana pulled the very dead beetle out, and Faron knew this theory was correct. Avana was making poisons.

Faron waited as she poured the contents of the cauldron into an empty vial, placed the cauldron back on the porcelain basin, and stoppered the vial of poison. Only then did he speak, pitching his voice so the others in the room wouldn't hear him.

"So, who are we poisoning?"

The momentary pause to Avana's otherwise smooth motions told Faron she'd been so wrapped up in her work, the assassin hadn't realized he was there. "No one at the moment, but enough people have attacked Her Grace recently that I thought maybe these might come in handy."

Faron couldn't disagree with that sentiment. Poisoning Grégoire and Tristian was a nice thought, though he was sure Sabine would be against such things. Then again, there had been a certain pleasure in beheading Tristian. "Does Sabine know you're planning on poisoning her enemies?" he asked jokingly.

"Of course not, but I think Her Grace will be appreciative after she agrees to make me her spymaster."

Now Faron's eyebrows did go up. "Since when did she need a spymaster?"

"She's always needed one. She just didn't know it." Avana gave Faron her full attention, her expression growing serious. "I'm not saying that having a spymaster could have prevented what happened with Tristian and Grégoire, but we could have had more warning about how Tristian was treating his village, what all we would find at his estate, and exactly how much contact Grégoire had with Coralia. You know, things like that. Because that's a spymaster's job, to collect information, and if that information sometimes makes it necessary for someone to disappear, well..." Avana shrugged.

Faron wanted to be concerned over how nonchalant she was about murder, but considering she'd spent the majority of her life being trained to kill people, he knew she did not take it lightly. He also didn't think she was wrong. At least, not about identifying a useful role for the Vassetre household. They needed someone who could secretly gather information when needed, someone who would not hesitate to act. Faron just wasn't sure how Sabine would feel about it. She wasn't one to shrink from violence and hard decisions, but she also didn't seek opportunities for brutality.

Deciding to change the subject, he said, "You seem to be rather skilled in this area." He motioned to everything on the table.

"For some reason, poison-making comes easy to me." She held up a vial. "It's fascinating how everything comes together to form such a simple, harmless-looking liquid. And yet, if you were to ingest even half of this, you'd be sick for a week. An entire vial and you'd be dead in a day." She gave a contented sigh. "I want to try my hand at potions too, but for some reason, they're just not as interesting to me as poisons. Oh well." She shrugged as though she'd confessed to not being able to bake as well as she would have liked.

"Well, we could use healing potions and salves as much, if not more, than poisons," Faron pointed out. "If you're serious about seeking out the position of spymaster within the estate, I'd devote some time to those as well."

"I know, which is why I'm trying to make those as well. However..." She reached to the far side of the desk and held up a sickly green potion and a container with a dead beetle.

"This was my last attempt." The flat look she gave Faron, as well as the potion and bug, made him reconsider having her make potions for the group. At least right now.

"Practice makes perfect?" he said as a joke, knowing it was the wrong thing to say almost right away.

"I will put this in your tea," she threatened, causing Faron to hold his hands up in surrender.

"Okay. I'm sorry," he said. "Though if you're serious about learning potions, salves, and antidotes, there are people around who can help you."

"I will ask," Avana decided. "And in the meantime, I'm going to continue practicing."

"Well, you're doing great work," Faron assured her. "And I'll let you get back to it."

"Thanks," she said brightly. She blinked and her brows narrowed. "Maybe don't mention this to Her Grace just yet."

"I promise nothing," he informed her as he turned to go, laughing at her muttering.

"You're one of those married couples who don't keep shit from each other. I forgot about that."

Faron shook his head and headed for the doors to the library, wondering if maybe he could steal his wife away for some time together.

Chapter
Twenty-Two

Hi Bine,

I write hoping to assure you things are going as well as possible within your estate. Fishing remains prosperous. Crops are growing well and promise plentiful yields. More people arrive almost daily from Coralia and Azmarin. We have worked diligently to provide immediate relief to new arrivals in the forms of shelter, food, and any needed medical attention. Long-term, we seek to help establish those capable of work with appropriate opportunities to join established businesses as employees and apprentices. The arrangements work well, and we receive positive reports from the Guilds and your new citizens.

I know you wish to be here, to be personally involved in the efforts, but rest assured we are acting decisively and thoroughly in your name. You know I would never do anything to bring shame or harm to your reputation, and I hope you will be proud upon your return. Should you need anything, let me know. I shall always endeavor to make you happy.

Yours,
Thaumas

Faron chuckled to himself as he entered his shared suite with Sabine, still amused by Avana's efforts and declaration of intentions to become spymaster. He hadn't missed her gradual adoption of "Her Grace" rather than using Sabine's name. Perhaps she thought designating work for herself meant having to take on a more formal relationship with Sabine. He would leave that to them to figure out.

"What's so funny?" Sabine called out from her position in the office area of their suite. He stepped forward, finding her at the desk, a quill sitting in her perfectly poised hand. She looked radiant, as always. Her long silky hair hung in loose, gentle waves around her shoulders. She wore a pale, shimmering green day dress, and a casual glance toward her feet showed she wore her favorite pair of warm, comfortable slippers. He loved when she found moments to relax. She so rarely had them, even if the choice was self-imposed.

"Avana wants to be your spymaster," Faron shared. He walked around the desk, leaned over to kiss Sabine, then leaned against the desk so he could look at her.

"Ah," she said, her green eyes sparkling with amusement. "We've not had a spymaster since Onfroi retired."

"Was he not the captain of your guard?" Faron asked.

"He did both, and he was quite skilled. It was why you arrived without a replacement for our guard captain, and the troop discipline had grown a little lax." She put the quill down and sat back in her chair, looking up at him. "So, are you in support of Avana's goal?"

Faron had to consider the question. He thought Avana had the capability, but she was young and impulsive, and those traits could present problems. "Perhaps, with some time and guidance, she could be quite useful in the role."

Sabine nodded. "Then, you should work with Marcelle in determining what the path to spymaster should look like for her. I think more training, some maturing, and some formation of what her job would entail would be needed, at minimum."

Faron nodded. Sabine's short list made sense, and he had no doubt he and Marcelle would come up with something more comprehensive once they had the opportunity. He knew Avana would respond well, especially since complying would get her exactly what she wanted.

"What brought up her desire to be a spymaster?" Sabine asked, cutting through his reflections.

"Oh, Meri had me go to one of the libraries earlier. Avana was practicing poison-mixing," he explained.

Sabine's brows raised. "Poison?" she repeated. "Why poison?"

"Taking the whole conversation into account, I think she is interested in improving her potion-making. She just has more talent with the more dangerous types."

"I imagine she was exposed to poison-making when she was with Grégoire," Sabine suggested, and Faron suddenly realized this was likely the case and he should have realized before. "But if she can mix poisons, she should be able to learn potions. I know some people who might be able to instruct her once we return home."

"I believe we have a plan, love," Faron replied. He leaned down to kiss her again, unable to help himself. "I will chat with her about your approval once Marcelle and I have time to plan. In truth, I don't think she wanted me to say anything yet."

Sabine nodded. "That sounds like Avana. She likes to keep things to herself until just the right time. We won't let her know that I know. Not yet."

"Of course," Faron easily agreed. He saw no reason to argue against Sabine's request, and he thought Avana would appreciate it. He moved a bit closer, looking down at the parchment on her desk. "Are you working, or are you writing for pleasure?" he asked.

"I'm returning a letter from Thaumas," she replied. "He reports more refugees coming into the village, but that is not shocking. There are more than enough homes and resources for them. When we go back, we may need to look at what's available for allocation and make necessary adjustments."

"We can," Faron said with a nod. "I have no doubt you'll do what you can. You always do." He loved her for it, and he knew he would spend their remaining time together, however many years that turned out to be, supporting her efforts. "Since you're working, I can leave you alone."

She smirked as she tucked a strand of hair behind her ear, revealing a shiny gray pearl stud. "Do you think you're that distracting, my love?" she asked.

"Oh, I think I am quite skilled at distracting you when the mood strikes," he replied.

"True," Sabine conceded. "Though I think I often serve to distract you from everything, including reason."

"You often do it on purpose," Faron added, grinning wickedly at her. "You wait for me to look at you, then suddenly, you play with your hair, lightly tugging on the ends." He reached out and took some of her hair in hand, demonstrating the accusation. "Or your lips form the most delectable pout when you are just out of reach." He leaned in and ghosted his lips across her own. "Or the way you press your fingertips against your collarbone when you talk about yourself."

"I think you like when I emphasize the bite marks you leave on me," Sabine replied, her voice a little deeper now. "And isn't it funny how you always seem to leave at least one right around my collarbone?"

"Very funny," Faron agreed as he pulled Sabine to her feet so that he could kiss her, deeply and possessively. He'd never dream of telling Sabine what to do, to restrict herself from anything, but he needed her to know, without question, that she belonged to him just as thoroughly as he belonged to her.

His hands rested on her hips, thumbs caressing across the bone through her skirt. Such a simple touch made his skin sizzle, and he craved to pull the layers up, to reveal her legs and give him access to her delectable center. He abandoned her lips when he needed to breathe again, his mouth trailing along the line of her jaw and down her throat as his hands moved to her backside. "Why do you taste so delicious?" he asked just before flicking his tongue across the dip between her neck and shoulder.

She groaned softly in response at first, prompting Faron to repeat the action. Anything that brought her pleasure, anything that made her want him more, he would give. "Mark me up," she replied.

Faron nearly growled at the command, and he happily complied, biting into her shoulder and sucking on her perfect, smooth skin. When he pulled away to examine his work, only the faintest of teeth prints remained, forming a perimeter of what promised to be a beautiful love bite. "Where else?" he asked before he started kissing the other side of her neck.

"Lower," she replied.

"Of course," he said. Faron nudged her back a few inches and had her turn around so he could begin undressing her. His actions came slowly and deliberately, inching fabric down her shoulders and hips, all the while pressing kisses as more and more of her skin was revealed.

When her perfect breasts were free of her gown, Faron turned her back around, taking in the pale orbs which fit so perfectly in his hands, before lowering his mouth over one of the rosy nipples. She gasped in pleasure as he swirled his tongue around the little bud while he gently kneaded the other breast with his hands. He let his teeth teasingly graze her nipple before trailing his lips across the soft flesh. Again, he sucked on her soft skin, leaving another mark on the upper part of her breast.

"For any more, I will need to move you elsewhere," he said before he straightened and kissed her lips. Faron didn't wait for a response before carrying her further into the suite and laying her on the bed. He wasted little time in kicking off his boots before joining her, again starting with her lips before kissing his way down. Faron took his time exploring her, leaving more marks along her torso and stomach as his hands caressed her thighs and warm center. Eventually, he covered her thighs in the same markings before finally burying his head between her legs.

Bringing her to climax the first several times took little effort, though Faron used every skill he possessed, along with intimate knowledge of what she liked, to make sure she screamed and moaned his name time and again. Really, no other sound would ever sound more beautiful to his ears

Later, after multiple rounds in just as many positions, both laid naked on top of the covers as their breathing slowly returned to normal. Faron let out a content sigh and turned his head to take in Sabine. The bruises she'd wanted had already grown darker, and he looked upon them with pride. "You're going to be quite sore for a few days," he observed.

"You should see your back," Sabine returned with a breathy laugh.

Faron conceded the point, but really, he never could complain about his wife's nails dragging across his skin as she writhed in pleasure. "If I cannot handle it, I will order a balm to soothe away the pain," he assured her. "And I will get you some, regardless. I doubt all of your new marks will be concealed by your dresses."

"Likely not," Sabine agreed. "But it is not as though others have not seen them before. You like my neck in particular."

She was right. Faron's mouth had left bruises along her throat from time to time, and the marks had been, without question, results from their frequent and vigorous lovemaking. "You are all the more beautiful when people know you are mine," he replied.

"Yours without question," she agreed.

Faron watched an easy smile form on her lips, and he turned so he was on his side and could pull her closer. "As I am yours," he reminded her, his nose pressed in her hair.

"The priestess did make it official."

"And yet, I was still yours even before then." He always would be.

They hadn't given much time to further discussions of spells which could link their lives, not since shortly after learning of what had happened to Aphros's wife, but every now and then, in the quiet aftermath of their lovemaking, the thought arose in Faron's mind. He wanted to pursue it, and as soon as possible, because life without Sabine would be no life at all.

He decided, for now, he would focus on the present, because how could he not when someone so beautiful was next to him? When they returned home—and they would one day—they could move forward with their plans. "You should get some rest," Faron suggested. "I know we have a formal dinner tonight with Louis, Eloise, and Aphros. Those dinners always run late."

Sabine didn't argue. Instead, she turned so she was facing him and snuggled closer against his body. "Sometimes, I feel as though all I ever do is fuck, get fucked, and sleep so I can recover," she joked.

"No questions about that," Faron replied. He relinquished his hold on Sabine long enough to reach down for the blankets, pulling them over their entwined bodies. "I'd say at least half of your time is spent on those activities. It's really not enough if you ask me, though."

"Oh, shut up," Sabine replied as Faron's arm went back around her.

"Only for now," Faron said. "And only because you do need sleep."

Chapter Twenty-Three

A week passed before Sargarus reached out again. Sabine suspected he'd make some new attempt given that his party had remained beyond the city gates. They'd made no additional work for Fythias and caused no trouble, so Louis had not felt compelled to send someone to clear out the Coralian soldiers. Their lingering presence only confirmed there was more to come, which caused more meetings so they could plan for any situation which might arise, as well as reach out to their allies for assistance should the worst happen.

The lack of action had also caused Eloise to enforce a rule that stated Sabine and Louis had to take at least one meal with their loved ones, though she often stole Louis away for dinner with Alaoin and herself in the evenings as well. Sabine had appreciated the effort, because it was nice to have quiet moments that were just her and Faron. She hadn't gotten nearly enough of them lately.

When the messenger arrived during a group breakfast one morning late into the week, Sabine was more than annoyed but said nothing as Louis accepted the parchment.

She exchanged a glance with Faron, seated to her left, before sipping from her glass. Sabine decided it was wise to remain neutral, even cool, for now. Sargarus might not be here, but his servant, no doubt, would report back any detail he deemed important.

Faron gave a nod of recognition but said nothing. She was, once again, grateful that she could count on him to defer to her in moments like this. Faron was always happy to recognize when he should defer to her.

Thankfully, Aphros had chosen to dine in his quarters that morning. Sabine preferred to keep him out of the gaze of Coralians as much as possible. Though he was strong and willing to stand up in the face of those who wished him and his people harm, Sabine knew repeated exposure would weigh on him. Aphros had far too much on his shoulders already.

"What do you want?" Louis asked him, bored annoyance at the disruption in his voice. "I have his letter. There is no further need for you."

"I have been instructed to remain for your official response," the messenger said, his voice proud and haughty. Louis hadn't had the opportunity to break the seal of the letter, yet here was a mere messenger behaving quite arrogantly for all to witness.

Fortunately, Sargarus's minion didn't move any closer to the king, nor did he speak disrespectfully, but his solidly planted feet and clasped hands resting behind his back more than demonstrated he had no plans of leaving. Sabine studied the man. His pale complexion underlaid with a rosy base, lanky build, pale gray eyes, and red-gold curls reminded her of Sargarus. He might have been a relative or an illegitimate son, but it mattered very little to Sabine.

"You may not be from Fythias, but it would serve you well to behave as though you are," Eloise warned him, earning herself the smallest of nods from the messenger. Perhaps he was intelligent enough to avoid insulting Louis's wife.

Louis glanced across the small dining table at Sabine, meeting her gaze with a great amount of skepticism before turning his attention back to the letter. His brows furrowed and an angry countenance settled on his boyish features, the same anger she'd seen in the day Sargarus had arrived himself.

"What does your master hope to accomplish?" Louis asked, looking back to the messenger. "Surely, he cannot have expected me to change my mind."

"His majesty does not discuss his plans with me," the messenger replied. "He handed me a letter and instructed me to stay until I have a response. So that is what I will do. I would suggest compliance on your part. It would yield the best results."

"Bold of you to assume you'll get any sort of response," Sabine replied, ignoring the small giggle from Eloise, who sat on Louis's right. Eloise smirked while Sabine simply looked at the man.

"I do not believe I addressed you," the messenger replied without looking back at Sabine. Clearly, he planned to tolerate Queen Eloise and ignore her. It was hardly the most insulting thing to have happened to her.

"And I do not believe you have any say about whether you are permitted to remain in my home," Louis countered. "Especially when you talk to my advisor with such impertinence. You will address everyone in my home with the utmost respect for whatever time I allow you to remain. There will be consequences otherwise." He finally ran his finger along the seal, breaking it open so he could read it. It took the king very little time to read it, and he scoffed before handing it over to Sabine.

Chapter Twenty-Three

Louis, King of Fythias,

I grow weary of your insolence. I have attempted to show you my merciful nature, to demonstrate a willingness to work for the betterment of your kingdom in exchange for helpful and willing obedience. I find I can no longer tolerate your defiance. This is your final warning.

I appreciate the position you find yourself in. I worked with your brother and his followers before you came to power, and I understand you have different views and goals than he. However, a change in leadership does not negate agreements and treaties, both of which I have regarding Fythias's cooperation.

Instead of yielding as expected, you have ignored our agreement, my authority, and most egregiously, you have tested my considerable patience. You are young, naive, and foolish enough to surround yourself with women, elves, and Mer, and this foolishness blinds you to the truth of my power and what that power could mean for you.

I implore you to respond appropriately. To accept that my rule is absolute, and my word law. If you continue to refuse, I will ensure that you and yours will come to learn of my wrath most intimately.

Consider this your final warning. I look forward to receiving your acquiescence.

Sargarus, King of Coralia and
High Ruler of the Unclaimed Islands

Sabine rolled her eyes and handed the letter back to Louis. "He's the most ridiculous man I've ever encountered, and I've met many ridiculous men. It makes me think he wishes to compensate for certain shortcomings."

Her words displeased the messenger. "When His Majesty, King Sargarus, has conquered these lands, people like you will no longer be allowed to wag their tongue so dismissively. You should beg me to not reveal your impertinence."

Both Louis and Faron began to retort, but Sabine held her hand up to silence them. Both listened, and she leaned forward, resting her arms on the table as she met the messenger's gaze. "Speak to me again, and I will have my husband hold you down so I can cut out your tongue and hang it on the wall like a trophy."

The messenger sneered and rolled his eyes in disbelief. "Just wait until I report you to the king. He'll make sure you learn your place."

"Faron," Sabine replied without hesitation, and her husband stood, no doubt to do exactly what she had threatened. Faron would, forever, completely keep her heart. He showed no hesitation, nor regret, in carrying out whatever she needed or wanted.

The messenger paled as he took in Faron's size. "You cannot!" he declared, shuffling backward as though it would prevent Faron from grabbing him. "Tell your elf to stand down," he demanded of Louis.

"I believe Her Grace warned you of what would happen if you insisted on speaking to her," Louis replied without intervention. "Why should she not follow through?"

Whatever the messenger expected, it was not for Louis to sign off on something so cruel. His eyes widened in horror as Faron approached him, grabbing him forcefully

by the scruff of his neck. He forced the messenger to face Sabine, pushing him toward the table.

"Do you wish to proceed, love?" Faron asked without any hint of hesitation. "I think you'd be kinder than I."

Sabine made to nod before she looked at Louis. "Your Majesty, this man came to address you. I think I should consult your wisdom before acting."

Louis snorted. "I should let you rip his tongue from his mouth given how disrespectful he has been." His harsh gaze went to the messenger. "I think it's important for visitors to understand how valued Her Grace is, not only in my court but throughout the country. Insulting her is really one of the most foolish things a person could do."

He picked up his glass and drank deeply then set it aside. He then picked up a roll from his plate and bit into it. Only once he swallowed did he continue. "If Her Grace is amenable, I think I would like to send you back to Sargarus with a verbal response of, 'No.' Are you amenable, Sabine?"

"As it is your wish, absolutely," she easily agreed. "But if we ever cross paths again, I should like your blessing to take care of him in whatever way seems appropriate."

"Of course," Louis acknowledged. "You are being too kind to go along with me on this." He took another bite of his roll. "If you insisted, I'd have gone along with you." He finished his roll before he nodded to Faron. "You can see him out. I've nothing else to say to him."

"I'll be back," Faron replied, giving a respectful nod to Louis before he physically began escorting the messenger from the dining hall. The man tripped over his feet, falling hard onto the ground. When he rose, Sabine noted a split lip, though this did not deter Faron from seeing him from the room.

"And here I was waiting for a show," Eloise remarked when she, Louis, and Sabine were left alone.

Sabine laughed. "I'm tired of being spoken to like a dog because I am in possession of a vagina." Perhaps the response was rude, but Sabine didn't care. She'd been stalked, assaulted, and berated again and again, and she was done.

"I don't blame you," Eloise replied. "And I'd have backed you had you decided to relieve the man of his tongue."

Faron returned a few minutes later, looking relaxed despite having to play escort. "He's off the grounds," Faron reported as he resumed his seat. "But I wouldn't be surprised if Sargarus responds violently within the day."

"He'll respond. And soon," Louis said. "He was likely going to, regardless. At best, I'd be a reluctant follower if I went along with his plans, and one he couldn't trust. He'd have disposed of me as soon as he'd deemed it prudent."

Sabine nodded. "Indeed, and he'd have made you trim what close support you had at hand. We were always going to end up here. Thankfully, we know he will have to wait for more support to arrive, and that buys us time." Louis had been wise enough to begin reaching out to others throughout the kingdom, and both Nereid and Sirene forces had increased within the estate and the wider village. With luck, they'd have support before Sargarus did.

"Before you two disappear into an office with Aphros to plan, finish eating," Eloise encouraged. "I know you'll get overly involved in planning, and next thing you know, it will be midnight and not one of you will have had a bite to eat since morning."

Louis smiled and leaned over to kiss his wife's cheek. "As you wish, my dear. I'd dare not do anything to anger you."

"You are a wise man," Eloise said with a laugh, then she motioned for the group to continue with their meal.

To the most honorable and esteemed members of Fythias,

I write you, humbled by our time of need. King Sargarus of Coralia has issued threats and ultimatums which put Fythias and its people in peril. He wishes for Fythias to go the way of Coralia. To torment and kill those who are not human. To force our tradespeople, our farmers, and our fishers into poverty and starvation. In exchange, he promises Coralian protection, a promise which would yield nothing for Fythias.

Our rejection of this offer leaves the looming threat of war, a response, I am certain, Sargarus will soon declare. A battalion of Coralian soldiers wait at the norther borders, slowed only by the mountain range. Sargarus holds an echelon of soldiers in L'Orilan, and another in a camp outside of the Maison de L'Harmonie city gates. The rest of his army, spread throughout Azmarin and other distant countries, could be here within weeks if called.

I call upon you, my loyal protectors of our realm, to gather at Maison de L'Harmonie with your guards and standing military units, where we will secure our walls and strategize to ensure the ongoing independence and strength of the kingdom. Without your strength, courage, and wisdom, we surely could not succeed.

I await your swift arrival at the Maison de L'Harmonie. You and yours will be gladly hosted, fed, and well cared for throughout the duration of your visit. I thank you for your enthusiastic response, and I will see you soon.

Yours,
Louis Alaoin Arsenault, King of Pythias

Chapter Twenty-Four

In the weeks following the last message from Sargarus, Faron replayed the forcible dismissal of the messenger in his mind again and again. Walking the man from the chateau had been brief and without much struggle. It had presented a clear message that any alliance Grégoire had attempted to broker with Sargarus before he vanished was now null and void under Louis's reign as king. He liked the decisiveness of the request to throw him out. The absolute certainty of the line Louis had drawn, but Faron was still dissatisfied.

Since the dismissal, reports of the activities in Sargarus's camp had changed. The king of Coralia planned on leaving, though he took his time with the preparations, as if to give Louis time to rethink his stance. Even now, remnants of the camp remained, with a dozen or so soldiers taking their time in vacating the space. He'd hoped they'd be gone before Fythias's nobility descended upon the chateau, but that was not to be.

Numerous people, all with names and titles he barely remembered, now occupied the estate, leaving very little room for more visitors or chances for privacy. Faron had expected, and accepted, that particular problem. And the nobility did take up room. Though most were perfectly amiable, inviting, and even amusing to speak with, so many of them lounged about, needing every single member of their staff to linger nearby in case any inconvenience arose. Leisurely meals with Aphros, who Faron quite liked, Eloise, Louis, and Sabine had given way to overcrowded tables filled with people talking over one another. Thankfully, Sabine had consented to private meals with him in their suite at least once a day.

There were other things, things he couldn't quite get his head around no matter how much he tried. The emptying of Sargarus's camp had led some to behave as though a victory had already been won, and those guilty of the misguided belief openly called for celebrations of Louis's first victory as king. No one bothered to correct the foolishness or call them out for carelessness when they still faced so much danger.

Faron had also heard rumors of a ball, which only served to further irritate him. According to Sabine, the nobility coming together as they hadn't in years, with their soldiers and staff, had created a need for levity and brightness, no matter the cause. This was why they dressed as they did, ate sumptuous formal suppers in the evening, and on occasion, danced when a musician or two who could be talked into playing.

As much as it frustrated him, Faron wished he could be as optimistic as some of the nobles. It would be pleasant, drifting through life, thinking they could get out of a conflict with Sargarus without a fight. He was just smart enough and experienced enough to know that even the smallest of conflicts with Coralia would result in death, and the conflict which would come would not be small.

Leaning against the window frame in the sitting area of their suite, Faron looked out past Louis's well-maintained estate, past the surrounding protective walls which encircled the whole city, and toward the space where remnants of Sargarus's camp still stood. He prayed to the Spirits that his worries of war were over, that the others who held more positive views of the future were right. He doubted the Spirits would listen; they knew he wasn't stupid enough not to realize Sargarus would try and come at them again.

Faron knew he shouldn't be focusing on his worries, not when Sabine would soon join him. They'd have the rest of the afternoon and evening to spend focusing on one another. He just couldn't get his mind in that space. Why would Sargarus pack up and leave after his demands were refused? Why didn't he strike back? It seemed too simple an ending for a madman who should have struck out when rebuked. Especially by Sabine, someone Sargarus thought so far below him that he didn't even wish for her to speak in his presence.

Knowing that trail of thought would just lead to more anger, Faron pushed off against the window frame and headed to the main door to see if he could catch Sabine on her way here, maybe convince her to take a walk with him. Anything to help keep his mind off their current situation. He was reaching for the handle when the door opened suddenly, and he was face-to-face with the person he'd been planning on looking for. "Well, hello there," he said, smiling down at his wife.

"Hello," Sabine said, returning his smile. "Where were you off to?"

"I was about to come find you," he admitted as he studied her face. She appeared a little tired, though not beyond what someone might expect after a long day of work.

"As though I would not seek you out the moment I was free?" she asked in a teasing tone.

"I know, but I thought I might see if you wanted to go for a walk through the garden or something similar, and the easiest way to do that was to go to you," Faron explained, chuckling. She was right, of course, and no doubt, she would see through whatever attempt he made at trying to avoid his fears. Thankfully, she seemed happy enough to go along with his whims that afternoon.

"If you would like to go for a walk, then we should," Sabine replied. "Eloise and Peronelle are busy settling the latest round of Louis's visitors in their rooms, so I doubt we will encounter many seeking prolonged discussions or entertainment."

Faron's face twisted in displeasure at the idea of running into anyone else while on their walk. Maybe he hadn't thought this idea through as well as he should have. Oh well. "Good, I just want to spend time with you. Not with others. Not right now." He'd already been through rounds of introductions as Sabine's husband. And when it was time to meet even more people, he would comply and wear a pleasant smile the whole time. Right now, though, he wanted it to be just them.

"Then let it just be us together this evening. We won't worry or think about anyone or anything else for the rest of the day."

"That is the trouble, though," Faron admitted. "I thought a walk might help since I cannot seem to keep my mind off what could still go wrong. Being in your presence does help." He held out his arm to Sabine, and when she placed her smaller, more delicate arm in his, Faron started toward the nearest garden exit.

"It's natural to worry, though," Sabine said as they walked. When they reached the corridor, she'd dropped the volume of her voice, presumably so others wouldn't overhear them. "Another three groups are scheduled to arrive in the coming days, and I don't think any of us will be surprised to see Coralia and Sargarus pop up again."

"That's what I'm concerned about. It seems too easy that he's just leaving." Faron sighed. "I just feel as if I'm dwelling on it too much. Who knows."

"If it helps, I do not believe anyone thinks he's actually gone or that he doesn't plan to retaliate as soon as possible." She motioned around the corridor as they passed a couple of different groups. "None of these people would be here if anyone truly believed Sargarus was no longer a threat."

"And yet, people are already saying Louis has been victorious over him and we're having a ball for some reason." Faron couldn't keep the incredulous tone from his voice. "I know a part of the sillier behaviors I'm seeing is because people want to believe Sargarus's threat is over and need that hope. No one wants a war and what comes with it. Well, except maybe Sargarus. I'm just struggling with all of this," he admitted.

Sabine nodded as her expression grew thoughtful. "Then let me try to soothe your worries," she said gently. "Firstly, Louis has been victorious over Sargarus thus far, as he has refused to give into unreasonable demands. Additionally, people have a natural inclination to exaggerate the depth of that victory. That does not suggest that Sargarus is no longer a threat, nor do most think so. Counting early wins, no matter how feeble, isn't a sign of any other belief. If you wish to spend your time dwelling on the strange tendencies of human nature, I cannot stop you, but your time would be better spent on other things."

She smiled and patted his forearm. "Secondly, no one is throwing a ball, and I would be among the first to hear of it if one were to happen. Louis and Eloise are hosting many nobles and their parties in their home. They are obligated to feed and entertain them, and an open dinner is easiest given the numbers. Were this really a ball, there would be fine clothing and music and all manner of planned events."

Given Sabine's response, Faron realized he had laid out his concerns in such a way that it made him look like quite the idiot. He took a breath and tried to offer a more coherent response. "Sorry," he started off. "I know how I must sound with my complaints. I know others are worried about Sargarus as well. I just don't quite grasp the reactions I'm seeing, not the politics of it all. You, Louis, and Eloise have been raised in the intricacies of court life, and it continues to elude and baffle me." He ran a hand through his hair. "I'm starting to understand why Eloise doesn't enjoy court life. It's so very confusing." He held up his hands in faux defeat. "Though, I know, with your instructions and help, I'll adapt as time goes on, I just wish I understood it all better now."

"You forget you've only been in the middle of court life for a handful of months. You are learning, and you will continue to," Sabine replied. "You're doing well."

"I don't always feel like I am, but I know I'll get to a point where I feel differently."

"You will, and I will be there to make sure you continue to learn and adapt," Sabine assured him. "For now, do what you need to do to relax and enjoy your time."

"Well, I'm with you. That makes everything much more enjoyable," he said, his tone brooking no argument.

"You are indeed," Sabine replied. "And so far, we've strolled along chateau corridors, enjoying one another's company. Did you still want to try our luck outside?"

"I would, yes. We're less likely to run into others while out there." Faron paused and couldn't help but to lean down and whisper into Sabine's ear. "Less likely to get caught if we decided to do more than walk, as well."

"Oh?" Sabine replied with a mischievous grin. "Would you like to do more than walk?"

"With you? Always."

Sabine brought their walk to a pause and pulled him down by the shirt for a deep kiss. When it broke, she did not release him. "Let's go walk before my attention is demanded by someone else."

Chapter Twenty-Five

Your Majesty,

We've received information from city scouts who have detected movement back toward the estate. It may be nothing, but with fears and rumors of Sargarus running amok, we will put out feelers to see what we can find.

Brielle

"Thank you," Sabine said as she took the offered glass from one of the palace servants. She smiled, appreciating the inviting dark red shade of wine swirling around the chalice. The influx of visitors, all there to aid in the threat posed by Sargarus and the few Coralian allies, led the new king and queen to host a casual dinner gathering, which in Faron's defense, might very well have been called a ball. The mood was celebratory, both because of their newly ordained king and queen and because Sargarus showed no signs of returning. Tables laden with food and drink sat around the edges of the room, and servants mingled throughout the crowd, refreshing glasses and collecting used plates.

Sabine wasn't exactly in the mood for a large party. The threat of Coralian invasion lingered despite the slowly emptying Coralian camp just beyond the city walls, and with it, concern for those she cared for. Faron, giant elf though he was, couldn't defend himself against dozens or hundreds. Avana, at her petite height, couldn't either. Meri and Lisbeth would be at even greater disadvantage.

Fortunately, Louis and his guards would have time to know of a larger army approaching. All of the men Sargarus brought with him from Coralia wouldn't be enough to overtake the country or even the estate until the soldiers in southern Azmarin crossed the border. Sabine suspected they never would.

"This is almost better than the coronation ball," Lisbeth shared from her right. She'd forgone the wine for now but had a glass filled with an orange-colored punch. Beside her, Meri held a small plate of finger foods: small tarts and fruits, all of which looked delicious, though Sabine suspected her old friend could do better. Both women were dressed in the same clothes they'd worn to the coronation ball, though Sabine had offered to buy them something new for the evening dinner.

"We are not of your station, Your Grace," Meri had insisted. "No one will expect us to own multiple gowns for such lavish parties." Sabine had honored their wishes, though she'd still purchased gold earrings for each woman, hoping they would see the small tokens as proof of her appreciation and love.

"Why do you think so?" Sabine asked her, pleased almost all of her party had been invited to participate.

"I don't know," Lisbeth replied with a delicate shrug. "The atmosphere feels less urgent, I think. We aren't celebrating because the king was forced to hurry into the position."

"It makes a real difference," Meri agreed. "Though, the influx of more nobility undercuts the sentiment for me. Things feel even more worrisome than before. Like we're just waiting for something to happen."

Sabine nodded. "I would have to agree." The question as to what would happen lingered, unanswerable until the strike occurred.

And it would come. Sargarus had vacated the village after the confrontation with Louis, but he and his people made camp a few miles out. The entirety of his group, a few hundred total, created little real threat, but numbers weren't the only way to cause harm.

Avana sauntered over, having spent several long minutes conversing with Louis. She enjoyed his presence to the point that Sabine might have asked her if she would prefer to stay with Louis when the time to return home finally arrived if she hadn't been positive Avana would find the question insulting. "People are strange," she announced.

"How so?" Lisbeth asked, the corners of her mouth twitching in amusement.

"We're eating dinner and everyone is dressed up like it's some special occasion." Avana motioned randomly toward a newly married marquess from the southern region. Her hair, a silky ginger hue which reminded Sabine of Lisbeth, had been pinned up and dotted with pearl-tipped pins. Her husband, a handsome older man with a fluffy mahogany beard, wore similar pearls at the collar of his velvety jacket.

"You bring a group of nobility together, they are going to show off," Sabine replied.

"You're not," Avana pointed out.

Sabine's hair, half pulled up so that her caramel strands brushed her shoulders, was dressed more simply. "True, but I was occupied with other matters before coming down."

Avana rolled her violet eyes. "You're always occupied with Faron. He's not that impressive."

"You'd be surprised," Sabine managed to say through a chuckle. Meri and Lisbeth joined in the laughter.

Aphros walked over. His dark hair hung loosely around his shoulders, and he had abandoned his normally casual attire for once. That evening, he was dressed in a deep red for the occasion. The Nereid seemed to favor the colors of his scales. "Good evening, ladies," he greeted with a nod of his head.

"Good evening, Aphros," Sabine replied with a smile. "Have you been enjoying yourself?" She took a sip of her wine and glanced down at the sweeter-than-expected liquid before turning her gaze back to the Nereid king.

"I have," he confirmed. "I had the pleasure of finally meeting Comte Dion. He facilitates the fishing trade between Fythias and my kingdom." Aphros gestured toward a young, lanky man with hair the color of corn silk, bright blue eyes, and lashes so fair, he appeared to have none.

"He can't be more than fifteen," Meri observed dryly.

"Oh, he's twenty or so," Aphros replied with a chuckle. "Took over for his father a couple of years back. He's far more organized and has a head for numbers."

"I doubt I would," Sabine replied. "My mother used to manage estate finances because my father would get terribly confused by the numbers. Thankfully, I inherited her business sense."

"And you allow Finn to assist," Avana interjected. She looked at Lisbeth's drink with interest and excused herself to get some.

"Your friend is amusing," Aphros said. "No inhibition when she speaks. It's refreshing."

"Indeed. One never has to wonder what she thinks." So far, Avana's openness had been a good thing, though Sabine believed she would one day need to call the young half-elf to task.

She smiled as she spotted Faron walking toward the group. A head above the rest of the crowd, he easily parted the scattered guests and found his place beside Sabine, who he leaned down to kiss. "Hello, wife."

"Hello, husband," she returned. "Everything okay?"

"I'm not sure. Brielle's security unit reported movement from Sargarus's camp, but they didn't see any attempt to reenter the city. It was decided to reinforce the guarding of the estate out of an abundance of caution. Marcelle went to inform our own guards, just in case we need them on standby. I spoke to Finn on my way in. Our whole group is up to date now."

"I see," Sabine replied, her brow furrowing in concern. "Should we talk to Louis about clearing out the banquet hall?" She considered going over to the king herself, but Sabine did not want to appear as though she ran to give orders to the king, no matter what else happened.

"Brielle and Peronelle were going to consult with His Majesty. If he thinks it appropriate, I'm sure he'll have everyone evacuate," Faron reassured her.

"We're all safer in the chateau, especially if he's not moving in on the city," Aphros said. "But I will be happy to listen in. See what Louis thinks. With other important people in attendance, he'll surely want to act decisively."

"Thank you, Aphros. Let us know if there's anything we can do," Sabine said. Aphros nodded and walked away from

the group, his scales glinting brilliantly as he passed beneath one of the chandeliers.

"Try to relax, Your Grace," Lisbeth said with a happy smile. "There's not anything to do about Sargarus right now."

"Not unless he makes for the estate," Faron corrected. He put an arm around Sabine and drew her closer against him. "At least, not officially."

Sabine let out a short chortle. If something terrible befell Sargarus, he would deserve it, but she was aware of how any action taken against him would look and how careful such a thing would require them to be.

"Just imagine what an assassin could do to that black-hearted tyrant," Meri said, her voice strangely cheerful despite a discussion of death.

"If I hear any of you sent Avana to assassinate a foreign king, I will be quite put out," Sabine warned.

"We'll not tell you, then," Faron joked, then he leaned down to kiss her once more.

This kiss broke apart seconds later at the sound of heavy glass hitting the floor, followed by the thud of a body dropping. Sabine looked around, trying to see what was happening, only for a scream to draw her attention toward Eloise, Aphros, and Louis, who was on the ground, turning a nasty shade of purple as white foam poured from his mouth.

"He's been poisoned!" Aphros yelled out at the same time Eloise screamed.

Horror crept onto Sabine's face as more people around them dropped to the floor, convulsing and clutching at their throats and chests, a similar foam issuing from their mouths and noses. More shouts of, "Poison!" filled the room, and more cups of a dark red liquid spilled to the ground, reminding the duchesse of blood.

Sabine looked at the goblet she still held in her hand, green eyes growing wide as she realized the drink in her hand had been responsible. The glass remained mostly full, but Sabine recalled sipping from it at least once. Possibly twice. The violence and abrupt appearance of the deaths around them told Sabine a couple of shallow sips would prove more than strong enough to end her. She looked up at Faron. "I've had some."

Faron's brows knitted in confusion before dread flooded his face. He removed the goblet from her hand and sniffed it, as though demanding it to promise him she'd not con-sumed enough to be affected.

"By the Spirits!" Meri proclaimed. "Tell me you didn't drink," she practically begged, though they'd watched her do as much.

Lisbeth took the goblet from Faron's hand, sniffing at it as well, though she surprisingly remained calmed. "Someone get Finn," she said, only to be interrupted by Avana, who'd apparently rushed over from where Louis now lay.

"She's had some," Avana announced as she plucked the goblet away from them and began examining the content.

"Maybe two sips," Sabine replied, thinking through the evening while managing to keep her panic at bay. She knew, without question, the first symptoms would soon come, and likely would be followed by death given the increased shouting and confusion. She was going to die unless an antidote was identified and available, but she was not going to spend what could be her last moments screaming and wailing in terror.

Meri pressed her lips together. "Okay. Two sips should buy us time," she said, her voice steady and reassuring even if her eyes conveyed just how worried she was. "We will figure this out. You will be fine."

Finn joined the group next, his face pale with worry. "One of the servants has been asked to find the crate the wine came in," he announced. "Aphros sent them."

"How do they not know where the wine came from?" demanded Meri, grasping her short hair in frustration.

While they bickered, Faron pulled Sabine to him. "You will be fine," he said, repeating Meri's words. Like Meri, his calm tone suggested a lack of worry, but Sabine knew better. Worry lines popped up between his brows, and the set of his jaw grew tense.

She did not blame him. Already, Sabine felt the faintest stirrings of something very wrong. No pain or nausea. Not even dizziness. Just a feeling of not quite being present. She looked up at Faron, voice and expression calmer than she felt. "You are going to be okay," she said.

"As will you," Faron insisted, desperation growing more and more in his gaze.

"Don't taste it!" Meri shouted over the screams and panic, drawing Sabine's gaze.

Avana scrunched her face up in defiance. "I'm not stupid!" she insisted.

"There's no taste," Sabine supplied impatiently. "Or none I could detect. It was sweeter than expected, but that doesn't mean anything."

"More than humans are dying from drinking it," Finn pointed out. "If there was a taste to detect, an elf or Mer would have noticed it."

Sabine opened her mouth to respond, but she paused as the room began to blur. She closed her eyes, trying to make them refocus.

"No," Faron commanded. "Open your eyes." In a much softer voice, he added, "Focus on me."

Sabine nodded and opened her eyes, looking up at Faron once more. Although he was mostly in focus, she couldn't ignore the encroaching fuzzy edges of her view. She reached up and cupped his cheek. "It's okay," she told him gently.

In her periphery, she noticed Finn dashing from the group, only to return a second later with an empty cup, while Avana dug through a kit she kept on her person when traveling. A bit of the poisoned wine was added to the clean cup by Meri, and Avana, after uncorking a vial, poured a dark oozing liquid into the cup. Lisbeth took the cup, hands glowing green, perhaps looking for a possible plant-based poison.

When nothing happened, Avana yanked the cup away from her. "I'm going to mix a few substances in with the wine to see if we can identify the poison."

Sabine nodded, the intensity of the poison's effect slowly oozing its way through her. The blurry vision grew more intense, accompanied by a lightheaded dizziness. She wrapped her arms around Faron, both because her own worry was seeping through and because she increasingly needed the physical support.

"Hey, focus on me," Faron repeated. He leaned down to kiss her, a mere brush of his lips against her own at first, and then became something more primal, more terrified.

"Oh! Oh! It's glowing purple," Avana exclaimed.

"With a green tint," Meri supplemented, her voice tremulous. "It's Rodan berries. Fuck."

"Why 'fuck'? Rodan berries have an easy antidote," Avana asked.

"They aren't in season. There will be no blooms," Meri exclaimed.

"I can fix that," Lisbeth interjected. "I can make it grow."

"I think I saw some of the dead plants near the gardens," Finn said, looking relieved. The group sprinted from the room, their footsteps almost drowned out by the surrounding cries and screams.

"Did you hear that? They've figured out how to save you," Faron whispered. His arms went around her, helping Sabine stay up as long as possible. He must have sensed how much the poison was affecting her. He kissed the top of her head, his hold tightening. "You're going to be okay," he said. "You have to be. We just got married."

"We did," Sabine quietly confirmed. Concentration grew more difficult as her head spun, but she was going to hold on to whatever time she had left. It didn't seem possible that the others would be able to find an antidote in time.

"And we still have so much to share and experience together. A honeymoon. Children. Whatever you want," Faron said, his tone coaxing as though he could keep her alive long enough. As her legs gave out, Faron helped her to the ground. "All we have to do is survive this moment, and we can have all of those things, Sabine." His voice remained steady as he spoke, but his eyes had grown glassy with unshed tears. "All you have to do is just stay with me."

She gave him a sad smile. "I don't think I'm going to, my love, and I think you agree."

"You are. You must," he told her as he touched his forehead to hers. "Fight, Sabine. Please fight."

She was, as much as she could, and they both knew it. "I have always loved the way you say my name."

"You have a beautiful name."

She cupped his cheek again, their closeness seemingly some of their last. "I love you, Faron," she whispered.

"As I love you," he replied desperately. "Do not leave me, Sabine. You cannot." His voice was rough as he issued the command, tears falling down his cheeks.

"I do not want to," she promised him weakly. She looked upon him, barely able to keep him in focus despite their closeness. Her eyes fell shut, too heavy to continue fighting it, her breath increasingly hard to draw.

"Sabine," she heard him say, the anguish in his voice palpable despite how far away it seemed. "Sabine!"

Chapter Twenty-Six

Faron closed his eyes, hands shaking and holding his breath as he pressed his ear against Sabine's chest and listened to the slowing beats of Sabine's heart. For a long moment, he didn't believe it, could not believe it. She could not be dying. He lifted his head to look at her face, almost able to pretend she was asleep. The tears made their way down his cheeks as the color slowly leeching from her skin ruined his ability to pretend.

Faron's next emotion caused him to bite back a scream, to force himself not to give in to his grief as her body grew lifeless in his arms. He did nothing to staunch his tears, nor did he relinquish his hold on Sabine. Despair radiated through him, and he could think of nothing beyond the pain.

His eyes drifted to a discarded goblet sitting on one of the tables, half full of the poisoned wine. He could join Sabine if he drank it. A life without the woman he held was no life at all, and a quick few sips would ensure a quick end. The sound around him faded to nothing, his resolve hardening. He would join Sabine in death rather than live without her.

A pair of hands settled on his shoulders as another tried to remove Sabine from his grasp, drawing Faron from his dark thoughts. He lashed out, almost striking Meri without realizing it.

"Let go, Faron. Let go," she said urgently.

"We think we have a cure," Lisbeth added from his other side.

Even though he thought it likely too late, Faron gently transferred Sabine, his entire world, over to Meri. In a daze of grief, he watched Meri tip Sabine's head back and pour an aqua-colored liquid into her mouth. Avana rubbed her throat to make sure it went down. Finn stood over the group, protecting them from interference from others, while Lisbeth rubbed Faron's back, murmuring nonsensical words and prayers.

As the potion disappeared, Meri lowered Sabine's body onto the ground, hands checking for breath or a pulse. Worry reappeared as she checked and rechecked. "Come on, Sabine. You're stronger than this."

Several more desperate seconds passed without breath returning to Sabine's lungs or her heart resuming a beat. The remnants of hope abandoned Faron, and he cursed himself for allowing the possibilities of revival to penetrate his resolve. He started to stand, intent on grabbing one of the wine glasses, just as the most silent and shallow breath passed through Sabine's lips.

"Did you hear that?!" Avana cried.

Faron had. He'd heard the most beautiful sound imaginable, and he sank back to his knees, gathering her up in his arms once again. "Come on, Sabine," he whispered. She obeyed, drawing in another stronger breath. He did not care about his streaming tears as he watched color return to her cheeks. "Thank you, Spirits. Thank you," he whispered as he rocked back and forth.

Behind him, Lisbeth took a deep, shuddering breath. Still focused on Sabine, he heard Meri begin shouting to those still standing around to check for any signs of life. Maybe they could save a few more people with the antidote ready. Maybe they could save Louis.

Lisbeth stood as she and Finn began to circulate the ballroom, looking for any who could be saved. Avana, still on her knees, tears streaming down her face, just continued to watch Sabine. Faron finally took in the cries of the few remaining nobles for whom the antidote had come too late.

Faron knew he should offer to help, but he couldn't leave Sabine, not now, not ever. "Open your eyes, my love, please," he quietly begged, ignoring the sound of running and panicked voices headed toward the ballroom. He prayed to the Spirits it was just news of the poisoned wine spreading and not some other horrific news. He wasn't sure the few survivors who were left could handle any more.

He looked up as the doors to the hall burst open. Brielle, Marcelle, and Peronelle appeared, ashen faced and worried. "What is it?" Aphros demanded, still kneeling beside Louis's still body. Hushed whispers circulated the hall, silencing the last of the desperate cries.

"Sargarus and his troops are marching toward the chateau," Brielle replied quickly. "We've word he's demanding the surrender of the kingdom."

"So, send out the guards," Aphros directed over Eloise's initial wave of loud sobs.

"Most of them are dead," Brielle retorted. "The barracks were gifted wine, which many of my people drank before Sargarus started toward us. Our soldiers are dead."

Meri dropped the bowl she had been using to mix the antidote. "No, no. They can't all be dead," she said frantically.

"About a third didn't partake in the wine," Brielle replied.

Lisbeth ran to Meri's side, fear on the redhead's face.

"It's okay," Meri said, pulling herself together for her wife's sake.

"We need a count of the remaining soldiers," Aphros interjected, stepping away from Louis's body and Eloise, who'd practically collapsed on top of him, loudly wailing her grief. "And talk to anyone who brought soldiers with them. I have a few dozen at my disposal."

The living guests who had people to spare shouted out their numbers, offering to volunteer, and had Faron paid attention to anything outside of Sabine, he might have regained a little hope as numbers slowly crawled up.

"We have soldiers, too," Finn spoke up for the Vassetre party.

"I've already promised our help," Marcelle spoke up. He crossed over to where Faron knelt with Sabine. "We're going to need your help. You worked with our guards. You can get the others in line long enough to face this."

Faron wanted to argue, to insist he could not leave Sabine's side. Not while she was still so sick. What if the worst should happen while he was gone? How could he ever forgive himself? "I can't," he said.

"You have to," Finn insisted. "You cannot help Her Grace any more than you already have, and if you do nothing, she might be in even more danger."

"I will make sure she is well guarded," Peronelle spoke up, hurrying over to the group. Usually poised and professional, the steward's worry lines and frizzy hair emphasized how much danger they were in.

Faron nodded without thinking. If he gave himself time to debate, time to reconsider, he knew he would reject the request. Cradling Sabine close, he stood, feeling his heart skip a beat at how close he had come to losing her. She remained unconscious even now. "Where's the safest place to take her? And what about the survivors?" he asked the steward.

Peronelle motioned for Faron to follow. He stepped around and over bodies as he carried Sabine out of the great hall and into the corridor. She hurried Faron toward a wing he'd never been down, one he understood to house the royal suites and family rooms. Sabine would be safest there, so he didn't object. They soon arrived at a large ornate door, which Peronelle quickly unlocked and threw open. It revealed a small library, lined with wall-hugging shelves and filled with a sofa and desk. "Put her there," Peronelle directed, pointing at the plum-colored sofa. "We'll have someone stay with her. The other survivors can stay in the attached rooms. Everyone should fit."

Faron nodded. "Find Finn, make sure he knows to come here, and I will make sure the guards have someone to help lead." He moved to the sofa, setting Sabine down and kneeling next to her. "Love, open your eyes, please," he begged. She was in no state to defend herself should someone get through, but he wished she was well enough to rise and flee if the need arose. Finn would do the utmost to protect her, no doubt, but most would not give their life for another.

He listened carefully, noting her breathing sounded stronger. Faron ran his fingers along her cheek, smiling in relief as she responded. "Sabine. Sabine," Faron said, a catch in his voice. "I'm right here. You're going to be alright."

Behind him, Faron heard the door open and Lisbeth and Avana entered. After a brief, hushed discussion with Peronelle, the two women began issuing orders to the servants and non-poisoned nobles who were carrying the other survivors into the surrounding rooms. He paid them no mind as he watched Sabine's eyes slowly open.

Dazed confusion crossed her expression before her beautiful green eyes settled on his face. "What's happened?" she asked in a weak, quiet voice.

"The wine was poisoned with Rodan berries. Lisbeth identified the poison, and Meri was able to make an antidote," he explained as he stroked her face. "You almost died," he said brokenly.

She reached up and cupped his cheek as she took in his words. "It's okay, my love."

Faron took a shuddering breath and rested his head on her chest. "I know. I know." He looked up and kissed her softly, his heart swelling with renewed hope. With Sabine awake and talking, as whispered and exhausted as her words were, perhaps they could get through the next several minutes.

"Most of Louis's soldiers died," he said, deciding to quickly cover what was happening. "And Sargarus is on his way. The surviving guests have volunteered their guards to help ward him off, our own included. I have been asked to lead, but I swear I won't step foot away from you if you demand it."

"If they need you, you should go," Sabine replied. She closed her eyes for a long few seconds and opened them again, blinking several times as if to wake herself. "I will be here, waiting for you."

"Are you sure?" Faron asked. He'd never leave her side again if he could help it. She nodded, and he grasped both of her hands in his, placing kisses on each. "Okay. Whatever you wish, my love."

Finn entered the room, hurrying over to the sofa. "Brielle and the others are waiting for you," he shared. "And I am here to watch her and oversee the survivors."

Another kiss to Sabine's lips, and Faron rose. "I will be back," he promised Sabine. To Finn, he gave a dark look. "Whatever happens, do not let any more harm come to her. Whatever you have to do, protect her."

"I swear on my life," Finn said, placing a hand against his chest.

"Good," Faron grunted. He took a breath, cast another long glance at his wife, and strode from the room, back toward the great hall where he could join Brielle and the others.

Chapter Twenty-Seven

Faron stepped into the great hall, his expression schooled into serious reflection. He was uncertain how focused he could be on the task at hand, especially with Sabine so pale and weak. He doubted he would ever be able to scrub the image of her, moments from death, from his mind. He couldn't focus on that now. No, he needed to do what he could to protect the people in the chateau and, by extension, throughout the country.

A grave-faced Marcelle approached, his inky eyes studying Faron with wariness. "How is Her Grace?" he asked as Faron watched a stocky servant help an elderly man from the room. Most of the ill survivors had been removed from the space. He also saw Louis's body had been moved, and no sign of Eloise remained.

"She was awake when I left," Faron replied. "But weak. Who knows how long it will take her to fully recover." If she ever did.

No. He was not going to think like that right now. She was alive, coherent, and awake. She would be fine.

"She's a strong woman," Marcelle said, putting a comforting hand on his shoulder. Faron didn't voice it, but he was thankful for the support. "Shall we meet with the others?"

"Yes," Faron agreed.

They stepped forward, pausing in front of Aphros and Brielle, both of whom had been quietly chatting. Aphros, who always seemed a little distant to Faron, kept a calm demeanor, especially compared to the more determined anxiety of Brielle.

"Good," Aphros said, nodding toward Marcelle and Faron. "You're here."

"We are," Faron confirmed. "What are we looking at?" He didn't know their numbers, but the numerous dead bodies now occupying the chateau left him doubtful of good chances.

"In total, we have about a hundred people with any battle training," Brielle summarized, her arms crossed. "Though we don't have firm numbers, Sargarus has more."

"That doesn't necessarily mean anything," Aphros said. "And I doubt we can avoid any direct conflict." He sighed and ran a hand through his hair. "They will be here within the hour, which gives us the opportunity to get in position. Maybe even head them off."

"We could also try to flee, but with the number of sick people we have, I doubt we'd have much of a chance," Brielle said.

"No, and we'd only open up the survivors to another threat of death," Aphros said. "We'd just be looking at more loss."

"If Sargarus is demanding surrender, he'd take pleasure in hunting down anyone who escaped. He's a sadistic madman." Faron could only imagine what evils the Coralian king planned for the survivors. "We are going to have to fight, and whatever happens, it cannot look anything like a victory for him."

"Agreed," Aphros said. "So let us figure out positioning."

The four quickly divided their numbers along the most beneficial points along the perimeter of the estate. They were fortunate of the bottleneck in coming onto the grounds, which would surely slow down encroachment from Sargarus's soldiers. With any luck, good aim combined with the narrow entrance would give them enough leverage to quickly end a skirmish. "Let's go talk to our fighters," Aphros suggested.

Meri returned to the great hall before they could file out, her expression resolved, determined.

"Did something happen?" Faron asked, feeling his stomach lurch. "Is Sabine okay?"

"Her Grace is as well as can be expected," Meri replied. "I came to help with the fight."

Marcelle spoke up before Faron could. "You're a good fighter. You always have been, but Meri, how do you propose to fight with your injury?"

"I can stand and shoot an arrow," Meri deadpanned. "I am not useless, and you will need all the hands you can get."

"We don't have time to argue," Aphros interjected, cutting off Marcelle, who tried to argue back. "If Meri wants to fight, we will have a place for her. Now, come." Though he'd objected before, Marcelle gave no further complaints as the group of five left the great hall.

The makeshift group of soldiers had been directed to gather in the foyer of the main building. They wore different colors, representing their different estates and allegiances, but none of them protested when Brielle, Aphros, Marcelle, Meri, and Faron took position in front of them.

Aphros addressed the group first, sharing the information they knew as well as what they suspected. "We will likely be outnumbered, but we aren't sure of actual numbers. We are in a better strategic position, which we plan to use to our benefit. We have a number of survivors, and those who did not drink the poisoned wine, counting on us to keep them safe. We cannot afford to let them down."

Murmurs of agreement sounded from the soldiers, cutting through the somber mood. Aphros nodded his approval and motioned to Faron. Faron took a step forward, looking over their numbers, hoping they would be enough. Without preamble, he began explaining formations and plans. The process of explaining plans and providing details aided Faron in moving forward, in focusing on something other than his wife, though her near-dead form lingered in the periphery of his mind, haunting him when the opportunity to made itself known.

When he finished, his gaze swept the group once more. "Any questions?" Again, a rumble of responses sounded, and a nervous energy filled the room. They were as prepared as could be.

"Then disperse, grab your weapons, and take your post," Brielle ordered, and the room slowly emptied.

"I don't know if we'll win," Marcelle said as they filed from the room. "But we are about to put up one hell of a fight."

"We have no choice but to win," Meri replied. "The country is counting on it."

"Sabine is counting on it," Faron replied.

The sun continued to sink in the sky, the shadow of evening creeping with each passing second. Evening battles always presented more problems than those under daylight. Faron circled the watchtower, peering out toward the grounds. Sargarus, atop the same horse he'd used upon visiting before, rode in front of his soldiers. Though he was too far away for Faron to see his expression, the straight posture and manner in which he held his chin aloft told Faron the old king already counted his victory against Fythias.

"He's got more people than we anticipated," Meri said as she took up position next to him. If her leg pained her, she showed no sign of it.

"I know," Faron replied. "Perhaps double what we've got. I don't know where they came from. Did he have that many upon docking in L'Orilan?"

Meri shook her head. "My guess is some passed over the mountains weeks or months ago and have been lying in wait." She looked up at him, her chocolate eyes studious. "Do you think our chances have diminished?"

"We didn't have great chances to begin with. Even with the replenished numbers, most of these people have never fought as a solid unit. I doubt more people on Sargarus's side is going to make more of a difference."

"You could take Her Grace and flee, you know," Meri said after several long seconds passed between them. She scoffed as he looked at her, confused. "Do not deny where your mind is at, and do not deny what you would do if you thought we'd lose. You'd be down in the library again, grabbing her and running for your lives."

"As though you would not when it came to Lisbeth?" Faron asked, not bothering to deny her accusation.

"Lisbeth could run on her own if needed." She patted her hip and smiled wryly. "There is no running for me. But I would do what I needed to protect the people I loved. For you, there is no love greater than your wife. None would judge you for acting selfishly, especially when she's one of the very few people in this country who has any right to lead."

Faron went silent, knowing Meri was right. If it came down to it, there was nothing he wouldn't do or give to protect her, even if it meant turning his back on the whole of Fythias. He could deal with Sabine's wrath later. "If the situation turns grim, I will do what I must," he confirmed.

"I thought so," Meri replied with a nod. "There is another option. One I think might save many lives."

"Oh?" Faron asked, his brow raised.

"I can unleash my powers," Meri said, shaking one of her arms so her enchanted golden bracelet, the one that held her powers back, was revealed from beneath her sleeve. Faron had seen it a million times since coming to work for Sabine, and because of the familiarity, he no longer thought about it. At least until now.

"No, you can't," Faron argued immediately. There was a reason Meri kept her ice powers carefully restrained. "You could die."

"I could die fighting without using my powers," Meri said with a shrug. "This way, I have some control over what happens."

"And what about Lisbeth?" he demanded, feeling outraged. "You'd just leave her alone?"

"I return to my prior point. I've no guarantee I walk away from this. Nor do you, for that matter. This is an option that ensures at least one of those things. Besides, we don't know for a fact that using my powers would kill me."

Faron wasn't going to argue. He wouldn't have time or ability to stop her should Meri choose to follow through, and he thought she had the right to make decisions for herself regardless of what others might think.

By the time Sargarus and his troops surrounded the outside of the estate, night had fallen. Lanterns surrounding the chateau illuminated those along the perimeter, casting

Sargarus with a demonic glow. Behind him stood at least two hundred men, clad in armor and brandishing weapons.

Faron clenched his jaw and reminded himself, time and again, to breathe through his nose. To keep himself calm. He did not like so many swords pointing in Sabine's direction.

"Your troops seem light," Sargarus called out, mocking laughter lacing his tone. "You can surrender now and save the remainder of the living."

"Does this look like surrender?" Aphros called out from his position below.

Sargarus laughed, a deep, booming sound despite his age. "It looks like the desperate last pleas of a dying kingdom." He looked around, the movement exaggerated and mocking. "And where is your king?" he called out. "He must have enjoyed the wine."

"Fuck this," Meri growled, and she dropped the bow and arrow she'd been holding. Rolling up her sleeves, her bracelets came into view, and she removed them without thought. Her palms took on a blue tint and ice formed on her fingertips. Meri winced, and Faron realized even this she had little control over.

"Are you sure?" Faron asked. No one else seemed to have noticed what she was doing, though he paid no heed to the back-and-forth between Aphros and Sargarus.

"No, but I'm not willing to risk more." Meri raised her hands, flexing her finger a couple of times. A shimmering coating covered her fingertips, and Faron realized it was ice.

"You can stop," Faron reminded her as he watched the ice crawl up her fingers, soon reaching her knuckles.

Meri shot him an annoyed look but otherwise ignored him. Pointing her palms toward the soldiers below, streams of ice shot from her hands in large, sharp shards, impaling

several of the front-line soldiers. They fell, and Meri focused on the next group.

For a moment, Faron had hope; hope that whatever that magical arrow had done to corrupt her powers had worn off. That Meri could control her ice and would live through this. That hope was shattered when Meri gave a shout of pain as the ice started to spread further up her fingers then her hands. Her body began to softly pulse blue, and the ice that was so finely controlled before started to spread faster, the spikes shooting up at random, sometimes hitting a soldier, sometimes doing nothing more than causing chaos and confusion in the ranks of the men. And worse, they were getting bigger.

The door leading to the top of the tower slammed open, revealing Lisbeth, eyes wide and gingery hair tousled. Her cheeks were flushed with patchy red. She must have seen what Meri was doing and hurried across the chateau.

"Meri!" Lisbeth screamed as she hurried closer. "Meri!" Her shouts were nearly drowned out by the high-pitched formation and soaring of ice toward the soldiers below. Somehow though, Meri heard Lisbeth.

Meri turned her head, unable to rotate the rest of her body as her legs were now frozen to below her knees. "Lisbeth, no. Baby, no. You can't be here," Meri screamed, tears streaming down her face as the blue light grew brighter and brighter.

Lisbeth didn't retreat. She shook her head stubbornly. "No, I'm not leaving you. I'm not letting you do this alone! You promised we'd be together forever," Lisbeth shouted as she wrapped her arms around Meri, her plant magic forming a green glow, beautifully contrasting against Meri's blue. Together, the two lights grew brighter and brighter until Faron could hardly stand to look at it.

Some innate part of him suddenly realized what was about to happen. He retreated back toward the door leading from the tower, shouting for everyone nearby to get down. Still, even tucked behind a half wall, he couldn't help but to peek out. Faron could just make out the two women thanks to Lisbeth's green glow. Lisbeth clung to Meri, who couldn't move to return her wife's embrace, most of her body frozen now.

"Till the end, Meri. I love you," Lisbeth called out. Her light pulsed and small vines crawled up her body.

"And I you, Lisbeth," Meri said through choked sobs before her light grew too overwhelming and her magic exploded out of her.

Chapter Twenty-Eight

The explosion gave way to an unnatural silence, though Faron's ears rang with the echoes of gore and death. He clutched the wall as he rose to his full height, certain he was about to see more horror. Lisbeth and Meri, he thought, might somehow be splattered across the tower wall, and he braced himself, hating he would be among the first to witness such a thing.

As he looked around, peering through a chilly mist, he found no sign of human death. Not where he was, anyway. Instead, sitting in the middle of the tower walkway, a large, dark brown, gnarled knot of tangle limbs and vines sat, sifting slightly in the light breeze.

"What..." Faron began, stepping forward cautiously, his hand extended. He shook his head and let his hand drop just before his fingertips brushed the massive plant. Instead, he approached the edge of the tower wall and looked down. Coralian soldiers, some impaled with large shards of ice and others frozen, were scattered along the bottleneck entrance.

He did not see Sargarus amongst the dead, but that did not necessarily mean anything.

Brielle, who was below and carefully looking through the remaining numbers, spotted Faron, and she raised an arm to catch his attention. "No sign of the king!"

"Fuck," Faron cursed. It would be their luck that the snake had managed to escape the widespread destruction Meri's powers had caused. He knew there was still a chance the monster hadn't been found yet, but Faron didn't think so.

"Do we have enough people to send a search party?" Aphros called from his position.

Faron wanted to say no. He wanted to position the people they still had left at strategic places around the chateau in order to keep Sabine and everyone still living safe. But as he glanced once more at what was left of his best friend and her wife, he knew he had to do better, to think this through. "We can put together a small one, yes."

"I'm on it," Brielle called out, and she began the task of walking the perimeter of their various formations, pointing at their own soldiers here and there.

Faron nodded even though he knew she couldn't see it, his mind already moving to the next task. Though honestly, he wasn't completely sure what that should be other than taking stock of who survived and how to handle the large number of bodies they had to contend with. As Sabine's husband, he had a feeling a lot of people would look to him for guidance and answers, something he wasn't sure he could give. Maybe if he stayed close to Aphros and those Louis had been closest to, they would get through this without the situation getting worse.

"We should have the soldiers not in the search party take up defensive positions around the estate. That way, they can at least warn us if any other problems arise. I'm going to go see how Sabine, Eloise, and the others are doing," Faron called out.

"We'll let you know if anything arises," Aphros called back.

"Thank you," Faron shouted, taking one last look at the tree that was all that remained of Lisbeth and Meri. He pushed aside the empty spot in his chest Lisbeth had claimed for her own and started down the tower steps. He would mourn them later, when everyone was safe.

After reaching the bottom steps, he hurried into the estate proper, all but sprinting toward the library. Even when he arrived, he pushed past the servants keeping watch and made his way to Finn and Sabine. "How is everything?" he asked.

"Her Grace is asleep," Finn began. "And survivors are being attended to." He stepped closer to Faron. "You know this, of course, but there was nothing to be done about Louis. We are, once again, without a ruler."

Faron muttered a curse under his breath. Louis has been one of the first people to go down under the poison's effects, but a small part of him had been hoping the Spirits would grant them a miracle. If not for the kingdom, then for Eloise and Alaoin, but it was not to be. "Eloise can act as regent until Alaoin is an adult, correct?" he asked, his mind racing through the information in the books Sabine had brought him. He hated that Eloise couldn't just rule as queen.

"Theoretically, should she wish to," Finn said with a shrug. "Louis was only king for a short time."

And Eloise would not wish to rule. They all knew that. It wasn't that she couldn't, but she was ill-suited to the role. No, Faron had a feeling he knew exactly who would end up regent, and it made him unreasonably angry. Taking a few deep breaths to calm himself, Faron told Finn, "Sadly, I have more bad news."

"What news?" Finn asked, issuing a deep sigh.

Faron decided to give Finn just the facts. "There were more soldiers than we'd anticipated. Meri unleashed her magic on them, and it overtook her. While that was happening, Lisbeth appeared and grabbed Meri. I don't know what she was trying to do, but there is now a tree instead of our friends." He sighed sadly, keeping himself together through his grief. "We also cannot find Sargarus amongst the dead."

Finn blinked several times, as if unsure of what to do. He pressed his thumb and forefinger against the bridge of his nose, thinking. "A tree?" he finally repeated.

Faron nodded, giving an abortive shrug. He'd expected their dead bodies, not the twisted tree they'd left behind. "Yes," he finally said.

"I'm going to look," Avana said. Somehow, he'd not noticed she'd been there.

Faron realized how tired he was. How much all of this, especially almost losing Sabine, had taken out of him. All Faron wanted to do was gather Sabine into his arms and take her to bed, but there was still too much to do before he could rest. Moving Sabine wasn't a good idea right then. "Is there anything that needs my attention in here right now?"

Finn shook his head. "Eloise has retreated to the safety of her rooms. Marcelle and the others were on the lines. Apparently, we've lost Meri and Lisbeth..." He looked around. "Choose a task."

Faron assumed Alaoin was with Eloise and they were under guard, so seeing to them wasn't important. Sabine was asleep, and as much as he wished to stay with her, it was better not to. He needed to have things somewhat in order when she awoke. So back outside it was. "I'll head back out," he informed Finn. "Send someone for me when she wakes up, please."

"I will," Finn promised. "No doubt she'll be wanting you."

"Thank you, Finn," Faron replied and headed back outside. He'd been hoping to spend at least a few minutes with Sabine. Instead, he would contend himself with the fact that she was still amongst the living when so many others weren't.

As he reached the main door, another thought occurred to him, and he stopped one of the soldiers who was entering the chateau. "I need a count of how many people and soldiers are still alive after the attack," he told the young woman, barely an adult really, who nodded and ran off to complete her task.

Heading toward the main gate, he spotted Aphros and hurried over to him. "Tell me we've word that Sargarus was caught up in Meri's attack, please."

The Nereid shook his head, his golden eyes grim. "It is looking like he and a handful of soldiers escaped, though he lost most of those he brought here. It is of some consolation."

"Some. However, a loss like this due to magic causes me some worry. It may only make his hatred of it worse." Faron shook his head before looking around. "What needs to be done?" he asked.

"The enemy's dead need to be cleared from the grounds and dealt with," Aphros said. "There is a group working on this now. They will be buried in as respectful a manner as possible."

Faron held back his opinion of exactly what should be done with the bodies of those willing to work for Sargarus. Differences in policy, in political discourse would always have its place, but support for genocide would not. "Good," he said instead. "I have a soldier collecting the number of those still amongst the living. Eloise has retreated to her room to mourn, and Sabine is asleep."

Aphros nodded then paused to speak with a passing Nereid soldier. Once the brief conversation passed, he looked back to Faron. "Given everything, none of the news surprises me." He pointed back up to the tower where the contorted mass of branches and vines sat. "Avana went up."

Faron nodded. He didn't want to be anywhere near that tree, but there were many things he didn't want to do right now. "I'll go check on her," he told Aphros, getting a nod in response before the man turned back to one of his own.

Steeling himself, Faron slowly made his way to where Avana was. He wasn't sure what he was expecting when he reached her, but her sitting cross legged on the ground in front of the plant, a small smile on her face, was not it.

Avana looked up at him for a moment, and he saw the sheen of unfallen tears in her eyes before she looked back at the tree. "It's beautiful. A perfect memorial for them," she said, her voice tinted with sadness and exhaustion.

He wanted to argue. The twisted, ugly thing that stood where once Meri and Lisbeth had could never be beautiful, but looking at the tree, he had to admit it was a fitting memorial for them. "I think Lisbeth might have liked it," he conceded after studying it for some time. She would have appreciated the various components better than he could, and she'd have made it thrive. Already, its dry leaves and vines showed signs of cracking. Of breaking down.

Watching the vines and leaves crack, Faron found himself sad that what was left of Lisbeth and Meri would be lucky to last the week if not the next several hours. Not having anything else to do at the moment, and wanting to be there for Avana, Faron sat down next to her, letting her rest her head on his shoulder.

They sat in silence for a while before Avana whispered, "I don't want them to be gone. They were my first friends, and I don't want them to be gone."

"I don't either," Faron responded before deciding to try and lighten the mood, something he was not good at. "I thought Sabine was your first friend?"

"No," came Avana's simple answer. "I didn't trust her enough for that. I kept waiting for her to ask for something. For the room, the food, the clothes. It took a while for me to really trust her."

Faron knew he should have picked a different topic. "I'm glad you're friends now," he replied.

He was thinking of another topic when a loud *crack* pulled his attention from Avana to the tree. Running down the middle, a large fissure grew.

Avana let out a small whine and stood before moving to the tree. "I was hoping it would last longer." She stopped short when the vines suddenly withered away, falling almost as ash to the ground.

Faron reached out and pulled Avana away as the fissure grew, and with a sound as loud as thunder on a stormy night, the tree split in two. The two covered their eyes as bark and dust were tossed into the air by the tree breaking. Dust and debris littered the air, clouding their gazes. As it began to settle, Faron blinked and found himself running forward with Avana in tow, desperate to reach the two bodies that lay on the ground where the tree had once been.

Faron gathered Lisbeth in his arms while Avana went for Meri. Lisbeth's skin was freezing cold, yet she was covered with a thin sheen of sweat, her lips tinged with blue. He placed two fingers on her neck, slightly below her jaw, finding a weak but steady pulse. "She's alive," he told Avana, who quickly checked Meri and found a pulse as well.

Getting a better grip on Lisbeth, Faron stood. He knew Avana wouldn't be able to carry Meri; her shorter stature would make it too difficult. He glanced over the wall and called someone up to help. Several soldiers hurried into the tower and up the stairs. The first who arrived, a woman named Anais with short, spiky, blue-black hair, immediately hurried to Avana and Meri. "Get her and follow me," Faron directed.

Faron kept an eye on Anais as she carefully gathered up Meri before he led them, quickly but safely, back to the estate. Faron wasn't sure where to go, but the library seemed like the best place. Despite the urgency, he motioned for Avana to go in first and see if Sabine was still asleep or if any healers had been called in from the village. He'd expected her to come back with answers quickly, not dragging Finn behind her when she did so.

"See, no longer a tree," she said, motioning to Lisbeth and Meri.

"I see that," Finn replied, his eyes wide and his face pale. "Get them to one of the side rooms," he told Anais and Faron.

Faron nodded, and they quickly moved them. Finding a set of comfortable looking lounge chairs, Faron set Lisbeth down and motioned for Anais to do the same with Meri in a nearby chair. "The tree broke apart and they were inside," he explained to Finn as he checked Meri's pulse, finding it the same as Lisbeth's: steady but weak. "Has anyone gone to get a healer?"

"How do you expect a healer to get through outside?" Finn asked Faron, practiced patience in his voice. "All we have are those inside the chateau right now."

"One could hope," Faron replied easily. "I have no idea how to help them. They are both extremely warm, so they may have a fever."

"I'll have someone down here look at them," Finn promised. "Once some of the bodies are cleared out from the front of the estate, I'm sure someone will get the healers."

Faron nodded, looking down at Meri and Lisbeth, watching their chests rise and fall softly. "Well, I know what I need to do, then." Faron gave a decisive nod and headed out to help clear a path to the estate.

Chapter Twenty-Nine

The days following the poisoning and attempted attack on the Maison de L'Harmonie were somber, although that was to be expected. Louis was dead, a victim of the poison which had so savagely struck down two-thirds of his guests. Eloise, in mourning, had locked herself in the royal suite with Alaoin, leaving the country and the immediate estate without leadership.

Sabine still felt too weak to do much of anything beyond sitting, and even the struggle of rising from bed to wash and eat took far more effort than she liked. Though she'd never liked hovering, she'd tolerated it from Faron, Meri, and Lisbeth with more good humor than she normally allowed. She estimated another week would pass before she was well enough to travel home, and only then would it happen if the future of the country had been determined to her satisfaction.

She sat in front of the fireplace, her caramel hair pulled back in a loose ponytail, dressed in a warm robe over her night things. She'd not felt up to dressing just yet, despite

Lisbeth's earlier protests, and she was enjoying the warmth of the fire while she ate and observed the grounds below. A gardener trimmed hedges, and distantly, a group of young soldiers trained. The world continued forward as though the village, and country, had suffered no great loss.

Sabine sipped from her tea as a knock sounded at her door, a quick repetition of announcement she'd associated with members of Louis's household, and Sabine did not hesitate to invite them in.

Peronelle appeared, bearing a tray of pastries and a fresh pot of tea Sabine had not requested but wouldn't object to. Louis's cook was an excellent baker. "Good morning, Your Grace," she said as she approached. The tray went down on the table with the tiniest of clings before Peronelle straightened.

"Good morning," Sabine greeted. "How is Her Majesty faring today?"

Peronelle's mouth pressed together in a grim line. "I am afraid she suffers greatly from grief. The loss of His Majesty was too much to bear."

Sabine nodded. If she lost Faron, she did not think she'd desire to continue breathing, but Eloise held more responsibility than Sabine. She had a son who would be king and a country in need of leadership. She wished the queen had more time to wallow in grief, more time to take care of herself, but the luxury would not be afforded to her.

"Would Her Majesty be open to speaking with me?" Sabine asked, deciding to take action. "I cannot end her pain, but I would like to offer some comfort if I might."

"I shall ask her," Peronelle promised. She smiled sadly. "Speaking frankly, Your Grace, I wonder of her ability to serve as regent to Prince Alaoin. He will need someone strong by his side. Someone who will work in the country's, and his, best interest until he is of age to serve."

"If I am permitted to see her, I will discuss the future as best I can. Her Majesty is not unreasonable, and she will want to protect Alaoin as best as she can."

"Certainly," Peronelle agreed. "I shall let you know of her answer once I have it."

Sabine thanked the steward and smiled as she opened the door to leave, passing Faron on the way out.

"Did you enjoy your walk?" Sabine asked once he was back in the suite and the door was shut.

"Yes, and yet, no," Faron admitted as he moved to her side, leaning down to gently lay a kiss upon her lips. "There are still too many reminders of what could have been."

"And yet, so many more moments of people pressing forward," Sabine replied. "Lisbeth and Meri stopped by this morning," she shared, hoping to lighten his mood. "You would never know the two of them recently found themselves encased in a magical tree."

Faron laughed, though not as brightly as he might have weeks before. "I am glad to hear it. They were having morning tea with Avana and Aphros when I returned from my walk."

"Good. I know Aphros has been swamped. I'm glad he's taking a few moments for himself here and there."

"As am I," Faron said. "He's assured me he and the Nereids will remain in Fythias until you are better and we have more definitive plans for the future."

"Well, I am looking to figure out what the plans for the future will be. I have requested to speak with Eloise," she shared. "I fear if I do not, someone will move to take power before much longer."

"You are not wrong. Thankfully, I don't think Sargarus factors into that." He paused to break off a piece of one of the pastries, holding it up for Sabine to eat if she wished. "Avana has apparently been sneaking around, listening for anyone who may cause a problem, and it seems Lisbeth teamed up with one of Eloise's head maids to mobilize the servants to do the same." Thankfully, Meri and Lisbeth had risen from their near fatality after a couple of day's rest without need for more medical intervention. "I'm hoping between them, we will have advanced warnings if needed." Sabine accepted the piece of pastry, pausing Faron's train of thought. "I'm interested in what you want to talk to Eloise about. Are you going to motivate her to stand as regent with your backing?"

"I do not think she is capable," Sabine replied with a sigh. "She hasn't ever been, and the loss of Louis has rendered her even less so. I might have to step up."

The look Faron gave Sabine was full of compassion. "This wasn't a role you wanted to step into, but you're right. As wonderful as Eloise is, she's not fit to rule." He sat next to Sabine and took her hands. "I will be here to help however I can."

"I know," Sabine said. "Of all the things and people I can count on, you never present doubt. Still, this is not a life I would choose if there were another option, and it will change things for everyone."

"It will, but it will change things for you most of all. You are the one who will bear the weight of ruling and preparing Alaoin to rule when he is of age," Faron said.

"I am aware, my love," Sabine replied. "I am aware."

"How are you feeling, both physically and with all this?" Faron waved a hand as if to encompass the situation with Eloise. "If you are overwhelmed or weak, we can always put off discussions."

She shook her head, knowing delay was not an option. "I feel like I swallowed and nearly died from poison days ago," Sabine quipped. "And despite that, I get to talk a grieving widow into handing over power so no one takes advantage of her son."

Faron laughed at himself. "Okay, you're right. Stupid question."

"Not really. You were checking in on your wife, which is one of your many, many responsibilities," Sabine replied. She leaned over and kissed him. "And when I am better, I will be sure you see to all of the others."

Faron laughed softly and nodded in agreement. "I fully intend to see to all of my responsibilities. Thoroughly," he added in emphasis. "Now, do you want me to come with you when you see the queen?"

"I do not know if she will even consent to see me, but if she does and she allows you to be present, then I would like it."

"I'm happy to be there for you. Whatever you need, my love."

Sabine easily recognized his sincerity, and she was more than happy to accept his assurances and promises without fail. Having those in moments when she knew her life would be so different than anticipated provided her with a calm which covered resignation.

They finished sharing the meal, focusing on lighter topics given her physical state, though a knock at the door, another rapid succession of taps, drew her attention.

"That will be Peronelle," Sabine said before calling out to allow her in.

"My apologies for the interruption, Your Grace," she said. "Her Majesty has consented to see you."

Faron stood and gave Sabine a warm, encouraging smile. Holding out a hand to help her up, Faron said, "Let us go."

Sabine stood, keeping ahold of Faron. Though she didn't ever mind the contact, she needed the physical support for anything beyond a casual walk. "Thank you, Peronelle," Sabine said before they left the suite.

As they proceeded toward Eloise's quarters, Faron leaned down and whispered, "Do you need me to carry you? We could pretend I'm being overbearing if so. You can even act offended."

"Everyone knows what happened to me," Sabine replied. "And I am fine for now. I make no promises for the immediate future."

"True, and at this point, they also know I'm terribly protective of you." He shrugged. "The offer is open, even when you're feeling better."

They soon arrived in Eloise's quarters, a pair of chateau guards ushering them through. One of the guards knocked, using the same rapid short beats Peronelle had used. "Her Grace, Duchesse Vassetre, and her husband are here to see you, Your Majesty," the guard announced once he opened the door.

"Thank you for announcing them," Eloise said from deeper in the room, though her voice seemed to be getting closer. "Please come in. Help yourselves to refreshments. I will be right there."

Sabine found a seat in one of the plush chairs, not bothering with refreshments. She hadn't been especially hungry while eating her own breakfast, and she'd only finished that a few minutes before.

"She's not eating much from the looks of things," Faron quietly observed while they still had a moment alone.

"She did just lose her husband," Sabine pointed out just as quietly.

"True," Faron admitted. "I wish she had more time to mourn him."

A noise from the back room echoed in the open parlor just before Eloise came into view. Her ashen face and puffy red-rimmed eyes were hardly concealed by the tremulous smile she gave in greeting.

Sabine rose to her feet and bowed, though Eloise quickly motioned for her to sit again. "You are still not well," the queen chastised.

"Indeed, I am not," Sabine agreed. "But you are still my queen, and you deserve the respect all the same."

Eloise let out a small huff, but she hid it well before she joined them by sitting on the sofa across from Sabine. The queen seemed unsure what to do with herself at first, placing her hands in her lap for a moment before moving to pour tea. "How are you feeling?" she asked.

"Bluntly?" Sabine asked. "Not well. I am quite tired and weak, still, though I've been told I am faring well enough."

Eloise's weak smile faded completely, and she leaned forward in her seat. "I am so sorry for what happened. That you are still with us is a miracle and the work of the Spirits, surely. I am glad you are getting better."

"I think the worst of it has passed," Sabine said, pushing beyond her current state. "Tell me, how are you holding up? And Alaoin, of course."

"I... I am doing as well as possible, all things considered," Eloise said, though she wouldn't look at Sabine. "Alaoin keeps asking for Louis. He—" She drew in a long breath. "He doesn't understand that his father isn't..." Eloise cut herself off, a hand rising to her mouth as if covering a sob.

Sabine sat silently, allowing Eloise a moment to pull herself together. She couldn't imagine the pain, though Faron had come close only days before.

It took a few minutes before the queen was finally able to make eye contact with Sabine again, even sparing Faron an apologetic glance. "It's been hard," she said, her voice raspy.

"I can only imagine," Sabine replied sympathetically. "Louis was a wonderful man, and I know he loved you."

"He was my whole world, and now, other than Alaoin, it's gone. And I'm left with just him and this Spirits forsaken kingdom," Eloise said.

Sabine nodded. She debated sitting more and allowing the queen a place to vent and grieve, but the opening was there. "Alaoin won't be ready to assume the throne for years yet. Have you considered who might act as regent until then? I know you've expressed little desire for it yourself."

Eloise shook her head. "I assumed the role would fall to me," she said. "The reports I've been given make it sound like we lost half of the nobility. Possibly more. You're the only one I would trust enough, and I know this isn't something you wish for."

"I do not, but I know it would be less of a burden on me than it would be on you," Sabine replied. "And I would happily relieve you of the task if you wish it."

Eloise's eyes widened and she opened her mouth to reply but then closed it and cleared her throat. "I am touched by your offer, but I will have to take time to consider if it is right for me to do such a thing. Though we both know you are much better suited."

"Of course. You would need time to consider your options. We are talking about your son's future and the future of the country." Sabine felt as though Eloise would arrive at the expected conclusion, but the queen had the right to form whatever opinion she liked on her own time.

"I'm so glad you understand," Eloise said as she picked up her now cold tea and took a drink before grimacing at the taste. "It has been strongly suggested that I will need to resume my duties until a regent is selected. I have no idea where to start, though. I've had reports and such delivered here since the incident, but other than a funeral for Louis..." She stopped again, looking away from Sabine and Faron. "I suppose I should announce a time of mourning, not just for Louis but for all those lost."

"You will," Sabine agreed. "And from there, you will need to determine how to reallocate the titles of those who we've lost. Their estates and the people living on them, working the land, fishing, and hunting, and the craftspeople all need leadership."

Eloise looked down at the teacup in her hands and then back up at Sabine. "Will you help me?" she asked, her voice soft and quiet.

Sabine nodded. "Of course." There would be a list of those nobles who had been present, and records of those who'd perished. Determining the titles to replace would be easy enough, but picking those who would be capable of filling the roles might be more difficult.

"Thank you," Eloise said, gratitude and relief in her voice. Though Sabine knew the other woman had requested time to consider her offer, Sabine would soon become regent. Hopefully, sooner rather than later.

Chapter Thirty

Duchesse Sabine,

I was pleased to hear from you so soon after we parted. I know your travel back to the Vassetre estate was a long one, and probably much rougher than anticipated given your ongoing recovery. I pray you continue to heal and, upon our next meeting, you will be in better spirits and health.

I arrived home only a week ago. Thankfully, the Nereid Kingdom has suffered no more attacks since I left them. Rumors from our scouts suggests this will not be the case for long, but we do as we must to survive. I can confirm for you that Sargarus has been spotted back in Quenall, the capitol of Coralia, so it seems we now know he escaped during the ice blast.

Finding your friendship in the middle of such terrible circumstances was a blessing for us all, I think, and I know we have much work to do to aid in improving the world. I shall make a trip to your home as soon as I am able, and we can continue discussions of treaties and formalizing our alliance.

I wish you and your husband joy as you finally have the opportunity to celebrate your union.

All the best,
Aphros

Sabine covered her mouth with her hand, concealing a yawn as she caught up on her work. Being on the brink of war did nothing to stifle the flow of correspondence, nor the work needed to manage her estate properly. They'd returned home a week ago, and she felt she'd hardly made a dent in her designated to-do pile. Aphros had written, and given the nature of the letter, she suspected she would receive correspondence at least once a week from him going forward. She found she was looking forward to it.

She took a bite of pastry which had been delivered with her morning tea before selecting another letter. As she chewed, she broke the seal and quickly scanned the page, smiling more broadly as she took in each line. She laughed softly as she tossed a letter onto the desk then occupied her hands with her ceramic teacup.

"Something funny, Your Grace?" Finn asked from his seat on the other side of her desk. He, too, had tea in front of him, though unlike Sabine, who'd positioned herself closer to the fire than usual and was wrapped in a thick shawl, Finn's contented comfort showed in his relaxed posture. He balanced

a ledger on his lap, and he sipped at his tea as he casually reviewed numbers.

"Your mother has written to ask why you have not visited Glaucus," she explained, nodding in the letter's direction. "Read it if you like."

"I have!" Finn declared as he grabbed the letter. Sabine grinned as her steward rolled his eyes and wadded the parchment into a ball before tossing it in the fire.

"You may need to go more often, or she'll be up here complaining in person," Sabine pointed out. She picked up the next letter, this one newly arrived, and found Eloise's neat handwriting on the front. Sabine broke the red wax seal and unfolded the letter.

"I see him plenty," Finn insisted, distracting her. "And you're still on the mend, so it is not as though I can pop off anytime I get a spare moment."

Finn was right, of course. Although Sabine had recovered well in the weeks since being poisoned, she found she grew tired more easily and more quickly. The local healer Faron insisted on coming to check on her each week continued remarking on her expected progress, and she had no complaints as long as she continued to improve.

"I think the estate would be fine if you wanted to get away a bit. Glaucus would be quite happy, I am sure." Sabine put the letter from Eloise down and slouched a bit in her chair. She could read it later, as Sabine knew the former queen and the toddler king were tucked safely away near the northern mountains. Sabine, who now acted as regent, could spare her time to check in later. "In fact, I insist you do make time."

"As you command," Finn replied, one corner of his mouth pointed up. "You'll be the one explaining to Faron."

"Explaining what, exactly?" Faron asked as he let himself into the office. Although he'd been on the grounds with the guards earlier in the day, he'd since washed and redressed, so he did not hesitate in coming around the desk to kiss Sabine before taking a seat.

"Finn's mother is tired of waiting for her son to marry," Sabine shared. She straightened in her seat and poured Faron some tea as she spoke. "So, I have insisted he dedicate some of his time to attend to his relationship."

"Ah," Faron said, then he thanked Sabine for the tea. "About time. We need things to celebrate."

"I think there has been much to celebrate," Finn replied. "Her Grace is well. We've aided in preventing a Coralian invasion. Meri and Lisbeth will return from their holiday soon. We have a new spymaster..." He paused and finished the tea in his cup. "Oh, and Avana convinced Marcelle to go into the village with her on his next day off."

"All reasons to celebrate," Faron agreed. "And you even ranked the reasons similarly to how I would."

"I feel as though you would approve of any arrangement that listed Her Grace as first," Finn joked. He lifted himself out of his chair. "I will get on with my day since Faron is clearly here to see you."

"Go see Glaucus," Sabine encouraged. "Seriously. If you want to continue having something meaningful with him, it's worth seeing if that letter comes from him or your mother."

"I will tend to it. I promise," Finn replied. He gave Sabine a shallow bow and inclined his head to Faron before exiting, closing the door behind him.

"He ran away quickly," Faron noted after sipping from his tea. "You'd think he didn't trust us to behave."

"We rarely do when we're together," Sabine pointed out. "You cannot blame anyone else living under our roof for reminding us to be courteous." She picked up Eloise's letter again and began reading.

Dearest Sabine,

Alaoin and I have settled in nicely. The estate at Domaine de la Foret is comfortable and well-furnished. The fireplaces are numerous, and I find myself completely understanding why you favor them, and heavy blankets, as much as you do. I do believe I was made for a warmer climate.

I am holding up as well as can be expected. I shall always miss Louis. His warmth. His goodness. The way he loved without hesitation or restriction. I cannot even begin to express what his loss means to me. I know your Faron knows the fear of that sort of loss, and perhaps he is more eloquent in such explanations than I can be. Hold onto him and love him well.

In times of uncertainty, we must all press on, knowing others rely on our guidance. I know we have much to plan for Fythias's future. I recognize you never wanted to rule, which is now your burden as regent, but my trust in you, your wisdom, goodness, and grace shall never falter. I shall never forget, or underestimate, your dedication and unshakable commitment to our kingdom and people. I shall always remember what a friend you've been to our family, even when you did not have to be. You might have chosen so much else for yourself and your people, and you've consistently stepped up to do the right thing.

Yours,
Eloise

"Eloise is well," she shared when she finished reading. "Though I doubt she will even get over the loss of Louis."

"I do not doubt it," Faron said. He set his teacup on the desk, a crisp *click* of porcelain meeting wood, before he rose to his feet and circled around the desk. He took residence behind her chair, letting his hands rest on her shoulders, which he began kneading. "They were deeply in love, even if she was so unhappy in her position as queen."

"I don't think many derive a lot of pleasure from royal titles, even with the advantages. Louis and Eloise didn't want the responsibility, which is likely why I got along with them so well. Even King Sargarus, with all of his confidence and power, suffers from constant fear."

"He should be afraid," Faron growled. "One of his own people will take him out if his proclaimed enemies do not."

"Let us hope for such a bright future," Sabine replied. She allowed herself to focus on the feel of his hands kneading her shoulders. Strong, decisive hands that knew her intimately. She had years of this to look forward to. "You are distracting," she shared.

"I am," Faron agreed. "It is not my fault, however."

"How is it not?" Sabine asked, tilting her head up to look at him.

"You are the one who tempts me. I can't keep my hands from you," Faron argued, his voice dipping into a lower pitch. Even so, he kept his touch light and appropriate for eyes outside of the office. He'd worried over her condition since having been poisoned, and though she'd recovered for the most part, her current health condition left him cautious.

"I like tempting you, my love," Sabine teased. "I intend to spend the rest of my years making sure I occupy a majority of your thoughts." Those years, she knew, would eventually be linked up once they pursued the spell Faron had mentioned weeks ago. They just had to wait until she was in better health.

"You will not have to work very hard to accomplish it," Faron replied. He leaned down far enough to kiss her cheek and then her lips when she turned to face him. "Though, I admit, other things are occupying my mind some of the time."

Sabine's expression softened, and her hand went to her abdomen, still flat despite the promise of new life before the year was out. In truth, they'd shared the information with no one outside of the local midwife, and she only knew because Faron had wanted confirmation.

"Just remember, I will kick you off of the estate if you become overbearing," she said.

"I've never once set out to be so," Faron argued. "But I will keep my tendency in mind and avoid irritating you as much as possible." He grinned and straightened up. "Besides, Meri and Lisbeth will likely annoy you more than I ever could."

"True," Sabine agreed. "But they are not here, and we have some time before telling them. Let me enjoy my peace." Even when they returned, Sabine suspected Meri would be occupied with getting accustomed to always walking with her cane. Though she'd survived the ice magic she'd unleashed, she'd forever suffer from hip and leg pain, and she'd never be able to remove her protective bracelets again.

Faron moved so he could lean against her desk, facing her, just as handsome as he'd ever been. Sabine didn't think she'd ever quite get used to the fact that they were married and that he loved her so ferociously. "I will singlehandedly ensure your peace if required," Faron said.

"I know," Sabine replied. "Right now, though, I find myself thinking of something else." She raised her eyebrow, bringing a knowing look to Faron's face.

He offered his hand, which she accepted, and he pulled her to her feet. "By all means, let's satisfy whatever thoughts you might have."

Sabine led him from her office to enjoy some alone time. There wouldn't be much of that going forward. Duchesse. Regent. Future Mother. Wife. All titles she now bore, and each would demand her time. For now, though, she would embrace "lover."

"You're not going to Quenall, Joss," Rion said, rubbing at his gingery beard. He sat in a far corner of the room, legs stretched out in front of him. He'd shed his armor, though the pile of metal remained within reach. "They'd kill you before you step foot in the city."

Collette looked over at her former lover, her expression void of humor or sarcasm. "Either I am your queen, in which case I shall do what I want, or I am not your queen, and you cannot stop me anyway. I am going to Quenall, and I do not need permission."

Whyldon stood, his blue eyes concerned, and he approached Collette as though to reason with her. "Why Quenall?" he asked. "To go after Riken? There are better plans to draw him out." He too looked washed, and his gray-streaked brown hair, though dirty from battle, was pulled back.

"I don't give two shits about Riken," Collette replied to her father. "Not right now, anyway." She would eventually punish the man for his role in killing her husband.

"Then you don't need to go to Quenall," Rion argued.

"I'm going to Quenall so I can bring him back," she said simply. Silence followed her explanation. She knew the others in the tent probably thought she'd finally lost her mind, but she didn't care.

Thomas gave her a look: sympathy, cynicism, and pity rolled into one. "No one can bring a person back from the dead. Not truly."

"I can," she replied.

Book Club Questions

1. Louis, Eloise, and Sabine all dislike the idea of ruling. What are their motivations, and how similar or different do you find them?

2. Faron often questions decisions and actions made concerning Sargarus and the threat he poses to Fythias. Do you think this is because Faron truly doesn't understand politics and court dynamics or because Faron would take different actions altogether?

3. Faron and Sabine trust one another implicitly, as has been demonstrated throughout the series. Why, then, do you think it took three books before they finally put the blue rope to use?

4. Had she not handed the regency over to Sabine, could Eloise have learned to be a good ruler, or would she always hate the position?

5. Did Louis overreact to the way Sargarus treated Sabine? Could he have handled the situation more calmly, or did Sargarus's behavior warrant a volatile response?

6. Lisbeth tries to manage her stress by controlling everything around her. In response, she is chastised by Finn and Faron. Were they fair in their assessment? Why or why not?

7. What is your assessment of Sargarus? Does he come across as a legitimate threat, or is he an old man reaching for validation?

8. Did Meri need to use her ice powers toward the Coralian army, or could the poison survivors win without her intervention?

9. Should Avana and Marcelle pursue a romantic relationship, or are they better as friends?

10. Faron often speaks as though others are lacking when they don't conform to his expectations. For example, Sabine's lack of guard captain when he first arrives and his judgment of the nobles at Louis's estate. Why do you think he comes across so harshly during these times?

Author Bios

Kate Jenkins enjoys writing fantasy, sci-fi, and romance as much as she enjoys reading them. She lives in a small town in Idaho with her autistic teen who is her whole world, her parents, and between them, four dogs and six cats. When not hanging with her son, she loves gaming, especially first-person shooters and asymmetrical horror games she can play with friends. She's a K-pop enthusiast and harbors a secret love of K-dramas and Anime, much to her mother's displeasure, as she's slowly being sucked into them with her. Her favorite tropes are currently enemies-to-loves, only-one-bed, coffee-shops, time-travel-fixes-it, and soul-mates/soul-identifying-marks. She is hopeful one day she can talk her co-author into writing these with her.

Morgan Moreau's literary interests span across various genres, showcasing a love for the realms of fantasy, historical fiction, crime and mystery, as well as contemporary stories. She is an enthusiastic lover of *The Little Mermaid*, as is evident in her vivid red hair, mermaid tattoos, and growing Ariel collection. Morgan also holds a deep affection for pirates, especially those who "wear fine things well," though those in possession of jars of dirt will always hold a place in her heart. She lives in Alabama with her dog, Scarlett, and she looks forward to adopting more puppies in the future. Her current passions include higher education, animal rights, and watching the 1995 *Pride & Prejudice* at least once a month. In addition to her current literary loves, Morgan is a fan of mermaids, vampires, pirates, and superheroes, and she hopes to incorporate this into future works.